SERPENTUS

Other Fiction by A.J. Calvin

THE RELICS OF WAR

The Moon's Eye

The Talisman of Delucha

War of the Nameless

The Ballad of Alchemy and Steel

Serpentus

THE CAEIN LEGACY

Exile

Guardian

Harbinger

Legend

HUNTED

WRAITH AND THE REVOLUTION

PRAISE FOR SERPENTUS

"Whether you are already a fan of the Relics of War trilogy, or a newbie like me, this one is well written and well done."

– *FanFiAddict*

"With strong action scenes, a multitude of unique races and cultures, good character building, and a sprinkle of romance…This is a must-read."

– *Exploring All Genres Blog*

"Serpentus is a…brilliant example of fantasy world-building. I genuinely love *everything* about this book."

– *Baskerville Book Reviews*

"A fun read, plenty of action and intriguing, growing, characters."

– *Greg Schroeder, author*

"This book spares no feelings in that depiction. You'll likely get your stomach churned at least once and your emotions will be raked across the coals so to speak. But that's what makes it so effective."

– *Cat Bowser, author of The Second Star series*

SERPENTUS

A RELICS OF WAR NOVEL

A.J. CALVIN

This is a work of fiction. All of the characters and events portrayed within this book are fictitious, and any resemblance to living people or real events is purely coincidental.

SERPENTUS
A Relics of War Novel

ISBN 979-8-9883193-7-5

Absolutely no portion of this book, including its artwork, was generated using artificial intelligence.
Human authored registration # 8039889,
https://authorsguild.org/human

Cover illustration and design by Jamie Noble
(www.thenobleartist.com)

Map illustration by Dewi Hargreaves (www.dewihargreaves.com)

HUMAN AUTHORED

To Joshua —

I brought her back one last time just for you.

AUTHOR'S NOTE

The idea for Serpentus came to me several months after I finished writing the final version of War of the Nameless. It was one of those ideas that, once lodged in my brain, I couldn't ignore. I needed to write this story. It would not leave me alone.

While it is related to my Relics of War series, Serpentus can be read as a standalone novel. If you've read the series, you'll encounter a few familiar characters along the way, including a couple fan favorites. Serpentus differs from the trilogy in that it's written in first-person, from a single character's perspective—and this character is one seen only briefly in the final chapters of the trilogy.

Serpentus is a dark story. There are themes of imprisonment, forced servitude, and body horror that may not be suitable for some readers. And since I decided to write this in first-person, even knowing what it would entail, it was one of the hardest and most emotionally-draining books I've ever written. It was a relief when it was done.

But as with so many of my stories, this one has an undercurrent of hope, even when events are at their darkest and most terrible for the characters involved. For that reason, I hesitate to categorize this as "grimdark fantasy," though there are certain passages that would fit well within that genre.

If you've read The Relics of War, I hope you enjoy this additional story. And if you haven't read the series, welcome to a world of magic and meddling gods, as told through the eyes of Owen Greenwaters, knight of Balotica.

Thank you,
A.J. Calvin

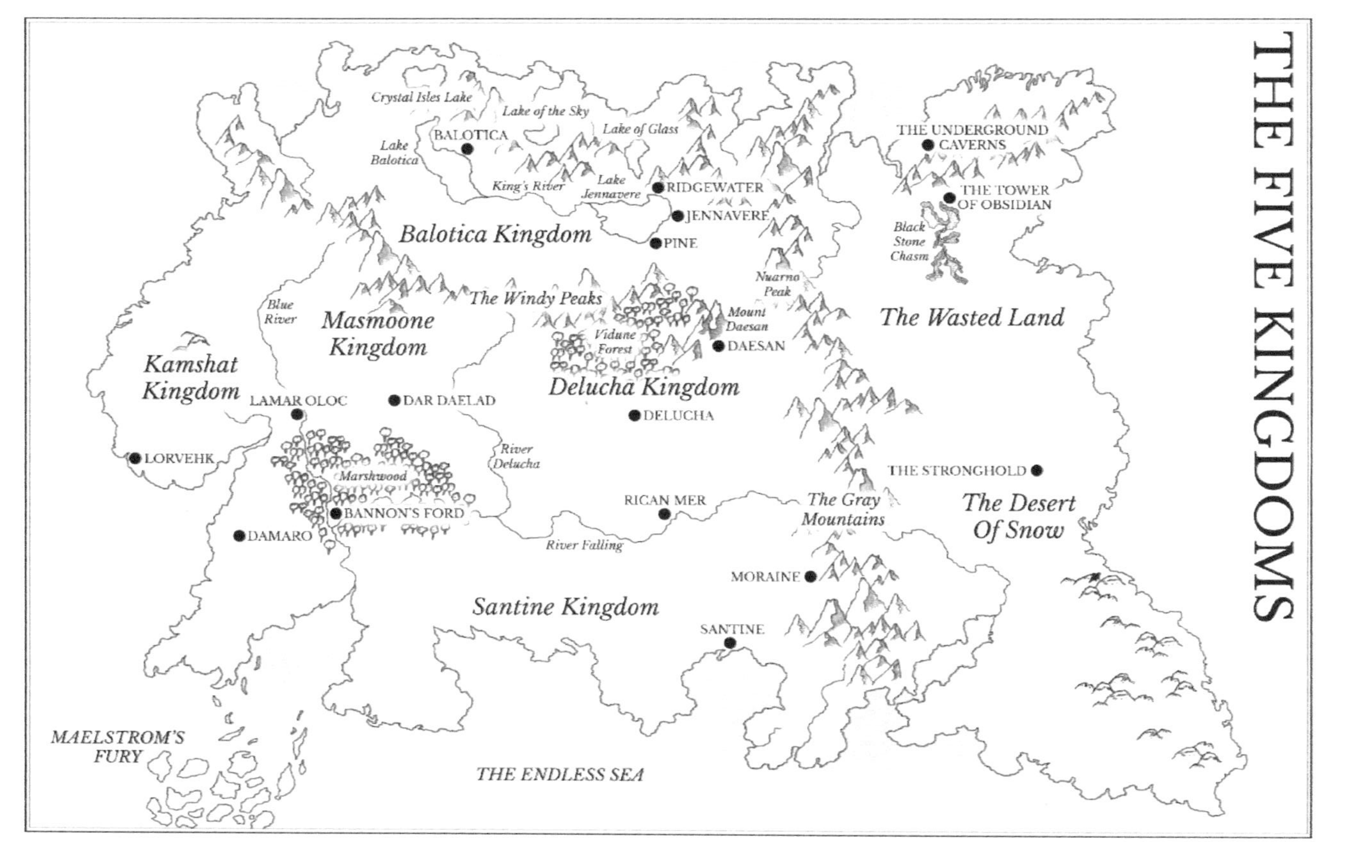
THE FIVE KINGDOMS
Crystal Isles Lake
Lake of the Sky
Lake of Glass
BALOTICA
Lake Balotica
King's River
Lake Jennavere
RIDGEWATER
JENNAVERE
PINE
Balotica Kingdom
THE UNDERGROUND CAVERNS
THE TOWER OF OBSIDIAN
Black Stone Chasm
Nuarno Peak
The Windy Peaks
Blue River
Masmoone Kingdom
Mount Daesan
Vidune Forest
DAESAN
The Wasted Land
Kamshat Kingdom
Delucha Kingdom
LAMAR OLOC
DAR DAELAD
DELUCHA
LORVEHK
River Delucha
Marshwood
THE STRONGHOLD
RICAN MER
The Gray Mountains
The Desert Of Snow
BANNON'S FORD
DAMARO
River Falling
MORAINE
Santine Kingdom
SANTINE
MAELSTROM'S FURY
THE ENDLESS SEA

1

MYTHS AND MONSTERS

There is nothing worse than being forced to remain indoors for a prolonged period of time. I was restless, pacing, frantic to leave the confines of my makeshift office—yet the storm persisted. It was as if Maelstrom had chosen this moment to smite Stone Hill for some perceived slight, the looming threat from the east be damned.

I glowered through the nearest window, its panes blurred by the relentless onslaught of rain. The storm's timing was nothing short of rotten luck. My orders had been to travel to Stone Hill, then assist the city guard as they bolstered defenses. With the storm unleashing the gods' fury on our heads, we'd been forced to postpone our work. Fucking gods, it was maddening.

Other knights had been sent to the nearby cities—Jennavere, Pine, Ridgewater—with the same directive from our king. He'd provided few details, but believed the rumors of an army from the Wasted Land held merit.

For weeks, there had been whispers of the Shadow Council's return, and if the perceived threat to our borders was real, I was certain they were behind it. It didn't bode well for us—I'd been dispatched alone, without a wizard. How were we to defend against corrupted mages without our own brand of magic? It was yet another point of frustration, one that I could do nothing to remedy.

The door to my borrowed quarters in the guard's barracks banged open, interrupting my latest circuit of the room. I spun around as a blast of cool air whipped through the space, scattering the papers I'd left on the writing table and causing the candles to flicker in their sconces. A bedraggled woman scurried inside, her cloak dripping water across the scuffed floor. She struggled with the door for a moment before she wrangled it closed and mercifully cut us off from the storm.

"Apologies, Ser." She saluted, then turned to hang her sopping cloak on a peg beside the door.

"Ira, isn't it?" I asked, though I wasn't certain that was her name. Since I'd arrived two days ago, I'd been introduced to a third of the city—and recalling names wasn't something I excelled in.

"It's *Ina*, Ser." She fidgeted nervously and remained near the door.

I swallowed an exasperated sigh and gestured to the empty chair near the writing table. It was always the same in the border cities. Few knights were dispatched this far east, and the residents were never comfortable in our presence. And perhaps Ina was more prone to nerves than most; she was young, likely less than twenty by my estimation.

"Please, sit." I paused to collect the paperwork the wind had scattered, then sat across from her. "Why have you come?"

"A runner arrived at the guard post," she replied, pulling a rumpled and water-logged message from within a pocket. She slid it across the table, her eyes wide. "It's from Jennavere, Ser. Something's happened."

I lifted my eyebrows, hoping she'd provide further details. When she merely gazed at me expectantly, I knew I'd get nothing more from her—it was likely she hadn't read the missive. I reached for the message and unfolded it gingerly; the parchment was damp and clung to itself, but most of the writing remained legible.

To the knight in charge —

Jennavere has been razed by an army of hooded ones and its docks destroyed by a monster from the lake. Few escaped alive.

I apologize for leaving a message rather than seeking you out personally, but Pine must be warned. I dare not tarry. I know not which direction the hooded ones will travel next, though I suspect it will be another city along the lakeshore. Warn the dockworkers and merchants of the creature in the water. Prepare your defenses or flee.

I ride for Pine to bring them warning.

—T. Opalhilt

I recognized the signature at the bottom of the page. Terrence Opalhilt was a fletcher of great skill based in Jennavere, and I'd had dealings with him in the past. He was a good man, even-keeled and stoic, but the contents of his message were baffling. By the gods, what were hooded ones? And a monster in the lake? None of it made sense.

I peered at Ina. "Did anyone read this message before you brought it to me?"

She shook her head. "The man was in a hurry. He said the knight in charge must see it straight away. You're the only knight here, Ser."

I nodded and forced a tight smile. "Yes. Thank you. When you return to the guard post, send your captain to me. There is much we need to discuss."

Her eyes widened and she swallowed hard. "Ser, the captain's home abed. Sick, according to his wife. I—"

I heaved a sigh and waved a hand dismissively. "It's no matter. I'll pay your captain a visit at his home." I pushed away from the table and rose. "Perhaps you'd be kind enough to escort me on your way back to the guard post?"

She nodded eagerly. "Of course, Ser."

I followed her to the door and paused to throw my cloak around my shoulders, then drew its hood up. As soon as Ina opened the door, I was forced to tug the hood back in place as the gale ripped it free. Icy rain lashed my face and soaked through my clothing in moments. I groaned and motioned to Ina impatiently as we trudged outside. I hoped her captain's home wasn't far.

The streets of Stone Hill were vacant due to the viciousness of the storm; we were the only souls unfortunate enough to be traipsing through the muddied lanes. Ina led me a short distance from the barracks to a residential street crowded with small brick homes. She turned toward the third on our left, and I followed her along a short gravel path that cut between a waterlogged garden on one side and a gnarled spruce tree on the other.

We huddled beneath the eaves as she rapped on the door, but the scant shelter wasn't sufficient to block the storm's unabated fury. I cast a glare at the leaden sky and silently cursed Maelstrom's temper.

Autumn was in its infancy; it was too early for weather of this nature, and the timing was damned unfortunate.

I mentally included a curse for Karmada as well. Misfortune was her purview.

After moments that seemed a rain-drenched eternity, the door swung open to reveal a middle-aged woman, her hair in disarray. She peered at us in confusion, but when she recognized the design on Ina's uniform and the snow leopard on my cloak, she stepped aside and held the door as we entered.

"I suspect you're here to see Matheson," she said. When Ina nodded, the woman pursed her cracked lips in disdain. "He's here. I'll wake the lazy bastard."

As she trundled away, I lifted my eyebrows in question. "Your captain isn't ill, Ina."

She fidgeted and averted her gaze. "He was out with some of the others last night. There's a tavern, or ah, brothel, near the eastern gates where we sometimes go after our shifts."

"Was it drink that has him waylaid, a whore, or did he get his fix with something stronger?" I demanded, unable to keep the edge from my tone. "Your *captain* has an obligation to this city, to the guard—to *you*, Ina. We all have our vices, and I won't fault him for that. But he should have avoided the place, knowing he was scheduled for duty today."

Her face flushed as she shifted uncomfortably beneath my scrutiny. I understood loyalty, but hers was misplaced. Matheson may have been her captain, yet he set a poor example for his underlings—and as the knight in charge, it was my duty to remedy the situation. I groaned inwardly; I didn't know the people of Stone Hill, and any action I decided on would be called into immediate question. I was obligated by the laws of the kingdom and my station to replace him and denounce him for dereliction of duty… But the timing couldn't have been worse.

"What will you do, Ser?" Ina asked in a small, tremulous tone.

I clenched my jaw. Her captain had placed me in an impossible predicament, though both were unaware. "I should strip him of his post and seek a replacement."

She eyed me warily. "But?"

"The message you delivered indicated there's trouble on the horizon, and we'll need every able-bodied soldier in this gods-forsaken city on the walls." I shifted my gaze as a disheveled man stumbled into the room, the woman of the house glaring daggers behind him. "Even *him*."

"Ser Owen?" the man asked, rubbing his eyes. "What brings you here?"

I crossed my arms and leveled him with a steely gaze. "You. We've received word from Jennavere, and I require your assistance immediately."

He blinked blearily. "But the storm—"

"The storm is irrelevant," I growled. "Jennavere has been *razed*, Matheson. Pull your shit together and meet me at the guard post within the hour. I'll hear no more excuses."

Matheson blanched. "Yes, Ser. I'll be there."

"Good." I motioned to Ina and strode toward the door, pausing with my hand on the knob. "And Matheson? Carry your sharpest blades. I've a suspicion you'll need them before long."

Once outside, Ina scurried to match my pace. "Ser? Is it true?"

I eyed her from beneath my hood. "Yes. I was sent here by the king to help prepare this city for an attack. Jennavere has fallen, though I'm not certain how. The message made little sense, but we'll learn soon enough, I fear."

I paused to take in her attire. A standard guard's tunic and trousers, leather bracers, and cloak.

"Does the city guard provide you with armor? Mail?" I asked.

She nodded. "Weapons too, Ser. I've a mace."

"Good. Collect your things and meet me at the guard post. If you see any of your comrades on the way, spread the word. I want every member of the guard present for what I have to say. I don't like repeating myself."

I returned to my office in the barracks to collect my own gear. Unlike many knights, I preferred hardened leather to plate mail. It provided a greater range of motion, and the lighter weight allowed me to fight for longer periods without fatigue. The leather was worn, yet held its supple luster, and the tooling around the edges had not faded with time.

I donned the armor, then picked up my pair of war hammers and slipped them through the loops on either side of my belt. I preferred them over swords or axes since I was expected to fight from horseback as often as I was on foot. They were versatile weapons and sported deadly spikes on one end.

I shook out my cloak before slipping it on, though it would be soaked again within moments once I stepped through the door. I grimaced at the window as another torrent of rain slashed across its surface, tugged my hood into place, then strode outside. As much as I detested the weather, there was work to be done—and little time in which to complete it if the enemy had chosen to march southwest from Jennavere.

Based on how my luck had unfolded since my arrival in Stone Hill, I'd be stunned if the enemy's army *didn't* make their way here. I'd prepare for the worst and be elated if I was wrong.

My second trek through Stone Hill was just as dismal as the first, but the streets were no longer as empty. Ina had been busy since we'd parted ways; city guards braved the storm wearing ring mail over their tunics and cursing Maelstrom under their breaths. I followed them to the guard post a block from the city's eastern gate, grateful to escape the storm.

Inside, little more than two dozen city guards were gathered, most congregated near the roaring hearth on the far side of the entry hall. I scanned the faces and smiled grimly as I spied Matheson amongst them. His eyes were bloodshot and his face was pale, but he'd donned his uniform and combed his hair. He leaned against a doorframe some distance from the hearth, his eyes hooded as he peered at the fire longingly. I strode toward him, nodding to those who greeted me on the way.

"Captain," I said as I approached, "it's good to see you here."

He snorted and crossed his arms, refusing to meet my eye. "I wasn't given a damned choice, *Ser*."

I swallowed my exasperation. "Listen closely, Matheson. We've received word from Jennavere, and I need to relay what I know to your people. Stone Hill is—"

The exterior door burst open, banging loudly against the wall as the wind ripped it from the newcomer's grasp. I shot a glare over my shoulder at the boy who now struggled to close the door and shield us from the elements. Once the door was secure, he surveyed the room until his gaze landed on mine. Eyes wide, had trotted toward us.

"Captain, and Ser Knight," he added with a nervous glance in my direction. "There's trouble at the docks. A beast destroyed the ferry bound for Pine, then demolished the merchants' pier."

Dread seized my gut in its frigid claws as he confirmed half of Terrence Opalhilt's message. "What manner of beast?" I asked.

The boy's eyes darted between us as the color drained from his face. "Ser, it's… I saw it with my own eyes, Ser. It's a scaly beast. Enormous. It dove beneath the water only to come up beneath one of the ships, and the ship splintered in two. What should we do?"

I glanced at Matheson. These were his people, the city his responsibility, but he stood rigid, paralyzed by unspoken fear. He'd be useless in mustering a defense.

"What's your name?" I asked the boy. I realized he was old enough to earn his place in the guard, but his rounded features and patchy stubble marked him as one of the youngest of their number. I couldn't help but think of him as a boy.

"Stonemark, Ser. Hensen Stonemark."

I nodded, then turned toward the rest of the room. Most of the guards chatted amongst themselves and seemed to pay us no heed. I raised my voice to be heard above the drone of conversation and pointed to the group near the hearth.

"You lot, follow Stonemark to the docks. I want every civilian evacuated into the city. Once you've returned, secure the southeastern gate. Don't allow *anyone* entrance unless you're certain of their identity." I turned to Matheson. "And you, Captain. Take some of the others with you to the eastern gate. Close it as well."

"Would you mind telling us what in the gods-damned hell is going on?" Matheson spluttered, finding his voice at long last.

"Jennavere was razed," I stated evenly. The room fell silent as they awaited my next words. "We received a message not long ago to prepare for the worst—and that is what we'll do. The message spoke of a monster in the lake, which Hensen has confirmed is true. It also spoke of an army of hooded ones. We're on the brink of a siege."

Matheson expelled an explosive breath. "Fuck. Hooded ones? The creatures from children's stories meant to frighten little ones into behaving? And we're not equipped for a siege, Ser."

"We'll do all we can," I replied. "Close the gates as I've ordered. Evacuate the docks. Gather every able-bodied person willing to hold so much as a broom handle in their defense and bring them to the gates. We need every defender we can scrounge. Now, go."

A flurry of activity erupted as guards made for the door. Matheson gripped my elbow as I began to turn away. "As I said, we're not equipped for a siege."

"I'm aware. I've looked over your supplies." I kept my voice low, hoping few would overhear our conversation. The last thing we needed was a blow to morale.

"I've fifty-seven guardsmen to watch over the entire gods-damned city," Matheson continued. "If we're facing an army—"

"Fucking gods, I *know*, Matheson. The odds aren't in our favor. I suggest you pray to Karmada with every waking moment you have that she'll smile upon us in the coming hours. Pray to Blademon as well, though he's as likely to find our defeat entertaining as he is to intervene." I grimaced at my own words; my cynicism wasn't helping the situation, but I couldn't take them back now. "We'll do all we can to protect the people of Stone Hill. It's all we can do. Now go—we need that gate closed."

2

SIEGE PREPARATIONS

"You'll want to look at this, Ser."

The guardsman saluted and offered a spyglass as I strode from the southeastern gate's tower to the wall's crenelated exterior. I'd made the journey directly from the guard post after my conversation with Matheson to evaluate the damage the docks had taken—and I hoped to catch a glimpse of the monster myself.

I accepted the spyglass and moved to the nearest vantage point. As I adjusted the focus, I noted with relief that sunlight glimmered on the choppy waters of Lake Jennavere some distance out from the docks. The storm was abating. Perhaps we'd mount a proper defense before the invaders arrived now that we'd receive a break in the weather.

I shifted the glass to take in the lakeshore and the docks. Four of the five docks remained intact. The fifth—the merchant's pier, I recalled—was splintered. Debris floated in the water amongst the shredded remnants of a sail from the ship that had been sundered, but there was no further evidence of the purported monster.

I sighed and turned away to hand the spyglass back to the guard. "Has the creature returned since its initial attack?"

"No, Ser. Do you believe it's finished with us?"

He clung to hopeful optimism as though it were a lifeline. I loathed the fact that I'd be forced to shatter it.

"No, it'll return. I suspect it's here ahead of the army." I peered over the wall at the intermittent stream of humanity fleeing the docks and the lakeshore. "What's your name?"

"Vandric Clay," he replied. "We met the day you arrived."

I managed a tight smile. "I'm sorry. I'm rubbish with names. Have you always lived in Stone Hill?"

"Yes, Ser."

I nodded thoughtfully. "This city is inaccessible from the north and west due to the cliff it's built on. The wall is in good repair, as are the gates. If you were an invading military commander, would you seek to storm the eastern gate or this one?"

Vandric blinked and looked away as he shifted uncomfortably. "I, ah… I don't know, Ser."

I lifted my eyebrows, nonplussed. He clearly had an opinion on the matter, but feared to share it. "You're a local, Vandric. Tell me what you know—it may just save this damned city."

Vandric flicked a glance in my direction before turning to gaze toward the docks. "I've spoken to the captain several times about defenses since the rumors about the Shadow Council started," he said after a time. "He said I was too green to know any better and to mind my place."

I frowned. *Of course*, Matheson would dismiss one of his people's concerns as unfounded. The man was as useless as he was inept.

"I'm not Matheson, and I'd like to hear your opinion."

"The eastern gate appears shabby, but it's reinforced better than this one—not that an enemy would know by looking at it," Vandric said without taking his eyes from the scene beyond the walls. "The path up to the eastern gate is steep and narrow. A small force may go that way, but it's unlikely. This gate requires repairs, and I've begged my gods-damned captain for weeks to approve the request. He refused. 'The gate's fine, and the threat's nothing.' He's said as much more than once."

"Your captain's a bigger fool than I'd given him credit for," I growled.

Vandric shrugged. "Not my place to judge him, though I suppose we all do. But my opinion, Ser? If I were a foe, I'd strike this gate. It's vulnerable, and the land outside is relatively flat. It's easier to march an army up a gentle slope than it is a cliff." He pointed toward the docks. "And the shore's undefended. Take the docks, and Stone Hill is cut off."

I nodded; it was as I'd suspected. "I'll give the order to have the bulk of our defenders stationed here. Your captain must defer to me—and I'll see to it he does." When Vandric turned, eyes wide with surprise, I chuckled. "Your captain's an incompetent ass, but you've been a great help. Thank you."

Vandric brightened. "You're welcome, Ser."

"Who is in charge of the gate at present?" I asked.

Vandric tilted his chin toward the gate tower I'd recently exited. "Camden Silverwood. He should be inside, on the top level."

I nodded my thanks and strode toward the door, then paused as a final thought struck me. "Vandric? If you see the monster again, send for me at once."

"Of course, Ser." He held the spyglass aloft with a grin. "I'll be watching for it."

As I ducked inside, I was enveloped by warmth. A hearth roared at the center of the room, and a pair of guards huddled near it, their cloaks spread on the floor nearby to dry. Recalling the glimmer of sunlight I'd spied, my spirits lifted. The storm would soon pass, and we wouldn't be forced to contend with the weather *and* the invaders. It was a small stroke of luck and one I wouldn't question.

The first rule of praying to the goddess of fortune—and misfortune—was to accept what one received and demand nothing more from her. Karmada always exacted a steep price for those who weren't appreciative of her gifts, however small they might be. And with an invading force looming in the lands nearby, I'd be a worse gods-damned fool than Matheson to evoke her wrath.

I gave silent thanks to the wily goddess as I made my way to the stairs, then amended it to include Maelstrom as well. It was his storm that had plagued us, after all, and the break in the weather was certainly welcome.

I took the steps two at a time to emerge in what appeared to be a small armory. Long bows and quivers lined one wall, while flasks of oil and pitch were arranged neatly on a nearby shelf. Three narrow windows looked out from the tower toward the road and the docks beyond, providing an unobstructed view of the rolling landscape south of Stone Hill and the expanse of Lake Jennavere to the west.

Unlike the room below, this one was cold, the window slits open to the elements. A lone man stood at the central window, his back toward the stairs as I entered. He wore the uniform of the city guard, with a burnished set of ring mail atop it. He turned at the sound of my footsteps, his gray eyes narrowing in recognition as he noted the blue of my cloak and the snow leopard designs tooled into my leather.

"I've been expecting a visit from you, Ser."

I lifted an eyebrow. "Camden Silverwood?"

He nodded. "Call me Cam."

"If we're dispensing with formalities, then call me Owen." I flashed a grin. "I spoke to Vandric. He believes this gate is the weaker of the two."

Cam crossed his arms and scrutinized me. "And you've listened to the boy? That's good. He's one of the few guards *from* Stone Hill. He knows his business."

"It sounds as if your captain dismissed his concerns."

"He has, on more than one occasion. The captain didn't take the post due to skill—as I'm sure you're aware. He's the cousin of some minor lord who pulled a dozen strings and more to see him placed in a notable position that cast their family in a favorable light. Fucking politics." Camden rolled his eyes and turned back to the window. "I'm thankful you're here to set him straight, though I wish His Majesty had sent more than a single knight. We lack the numbers to oppose an invading army, despite this city's natural defenses. And that gods-damned monster…" He shook his head and trailed off.

I strode to the window on his right and gazed outside. The docks remained quiet, save for the trickle of remaining civilians fleeing toward the city gates.

"Did you see the creature?" I asked.

He nodded. "Have you heard tales of the serpents from the Endless Sea?"

I pushed aside the swirl of unease that rippled through my core. According to Matheson, the hooded ones were figures from a children's story, a rumor and myth, nothing more. And now Camden, who by my reckoning was level-headed and reasonable, insinuated the creature in the lake was yet another storybook monster come to life? Fucking gods, this was madness.

"I've heard the stories," I replied with a frown.

"My mother was a scribe," Camden went on. "There were always books in our house, and one of my favorites as a child was The Traveler's Tales."

"I'm familiar with it." I'd skimmed parts of the book in my adolescence, but remembered little more than the traveler's penchant for landing himself in impossible situations.

"It was an illustrated edition and must cost a fortune now, but that's not my point." Camden turned to face me. "There was a painting midway through the book depicting the traveler's battle with the Serpent of Santine Harbor. A silver snake with a spined dorsal fin, fangs, and menacing yellow eyes. The creature in the lake… It was a near replica of that painting."

"You think it's a sea serpent?" I asked, unable to mask my skepticism.

Camden's eyes darkened as he frowned. "Impossible as it may seem, that's exactly what I think. And based on the reports we received earlier, I believe it's working with the invaders—whatever they happen to be. The timing isn't a coincidence."

I wouldn't argue with him about the timing; I felt the same. "How in hell are we supposed to fight a sea serpent? I may be a knight, but I can assure you my training did not include the slaying of mythical beasts or creatures of folklore." I raked a hand through my hair and shifted my gaze to the window. "*Fuck.*"

Camden chuckled. "For a knight, you're a bit unorthodox, Owen. I think I like you."

"Unorthodox sums up my career rather aptly." I grinned. "I don't believe it's necessary to feign superiority over guards, Cam. I was once a city guard myself, though far from this region of the kingdom."

"It's nice to know the king's promises aren't empty on that front," he replied dryly. "Some of the younger guards have been honing their skills for next year's melee at the king's court. I'd written them off as fools, but if you speak the truth, maybe they have a chance."

I nodded as my memories drifted to a time two decades past. I'd been a young guard—not even twenty—when I entered my name into the melee. Only the winner would be granted a place amongst the young nobles entering the ranks of the royal guard. It was the first step to true knighthood, but one of the most difficult for commoners like myself. I'd entered the arena determined to forge my path, seeking the purported glory and prestige that came along with the title of Ser.

I'd emerged the victor, but immediately realized my combat skills didn't grant me acceptance by the others. I wasn't nobility. I was beneath them.

Yet I persevered and proved myself worthy of the title six years later. The majority of the young nobles who entered the training regimen with me couldn't boast the same. Only two of their number eventually became knights, and despite our strained beginning, we'd become friends. The rest had returned to their opulent manors and silk-clad mistresses to do…whatever it was nobles did. I still wasn't certain what their functions were beyond irritating the masses and flaunting their wealth.

Both were things our kingdom could have done without.

"The melee isn't easy," I cautioned. "They don't turn would-be contestants away, and every teen and twenty-something in the kingdom who can wield so much as a carving knife can enter. Your guards will require true combat skill to succeed, and the king selects but one victor."

Camden grunted. "Perhaps they *are* fools, then. The trek there will cost them six months' wages alone."

I shrugged. "Perhaps after the threat to Stone Hill is past, you can introduce me to them. I may have a few pointers to share."

His gaze shifted to the docks. "Do you truly believe we'll survive an attack?"

I glanced skyward as my thoughts raced. "In truth? I don't know. The king assumed an attack from the Shadow Council was imminent, but we believed it would come in the form of human soldiers and their version of corrupted wizards. The message from Jennavere mentioned hooded ones." I raked a hand through my hair in frustration. "Fucking gods, I don't even know what the hooded ones are beyond yet another fable."

I turned away from the window to find Camden's eyes locked on mine. "What is your plan?"

"We'll bolster the defenses at this gate over the other," I replied. "Archers will be stationed here and along the wall at intervals. Foot soldiers will muster in the street just inside the gate. Then we'll wait. It takes time to disseminate orders through an army. We'll use the opportunity to learn what we can of the enemy."

"And what of the lake monster?"

I shrugged helplessly. "We've evacuated the civilians from the docks. There's little else we can do but pray the damned beast can't come ashore."

"Then the docks are lost."

"But the people may be spared," I replied evenly. "The docks can be rebuilt."

It was clear Camden wasn't happy with my reasoning, but he grudgingly accepted it with a terse nod. I'd take the blame for the loss of infrastructure if it meant even one civilian life would be saved. It was the right call and I wouldn't back down from my stance, no matter how brutal the backlash.

"I'll return before nightfall," I promised as I turned my back on the window. "I need to speak with Matheson and inform him of my plans. In the meantime, gather as many guards as you can at this location. We'll need more arrows, oil, pitch… The stores here won't last long."

Camden nodded again. "I'll see it done. Stone Hill will be ready for the bastards."

I smiled grimly. "I hope so."

3
THE INVADERS

I swept the spyglass across the hills to the southeast for the third time in as many minutes. The enemy numbered in the thousands, their ranks mere silhouettes in the darkness. A few glimmers of firelight shone amongst the distant shadows, but not in the quantity I'd expect from an invading army. Either our foes were attempting—and failing—to conceal their presence, or they could see better than we could in the dark.

"I suspect they're waiting for dawn," Camden stated from my left. "It's what I'd do."

I released a low growl of frustration. "Dawn's still two hours off. I'd hoped to see more than the hint of gods-damned shadows stalking the plains."

I dropped the spyglass from my eye and handed it to Camden. I'd gleaned nothing from my observations beyond a vague headcount. If the city's gates failed to withstand the assault, we'd be overrun. Stone Hill wasn't ideally located for escape; it was built on the cliffs for the singular purpose of defense. There were but two ways in or out of the city, and both were currently barred and barricaded as we awaited the enemy's next move. Even if I ordered an evacuation, the citizens would be forced to flee directly into the invaders' ranks.

It was a hopeless situation, and I was reduced to praying the damned gates would hold. They were our salvation, but I harbored little faith they were up to the task.

"We'll see what awaits us soon enough," Camden replied with a shrug. "It'll begin to lighten in an hour or so."

I suppressed a wave of unease. To be forced to wait another hour to glean even an iota of information was maddening. We were short on time, and the more I learned *now*, the better off we'd be. But without light to reveal the nature of our enemies, I could discern nothing of their nature.

The notion they might not be human continued to niggle at my mind. The monster in the lake had been verified. Why wouldn't the army that now crouched menacingly on our doorstep be comprised of an equally unlikely foe? If they were indeed hooded ones, the gods had a wry sense of humor.

I began to pace, my gaze fixed on the shadowed mass that marked the invading army. We were prepared for a siege. The archers were in position, clusters of guards were primed atop the gates with pitch, oil, and fire, the city's stores had been inventoried and allocated, our ground troops were gathered… There was nothing more to do but wait.

I strode past an archer who knelt against the wall, her head bowed as she murmured a prayer. Perhaps I should have added a silent plea of my own, seeking the gods' protection, their favor, their aid—but they'd vowed to remain neutral in mortal conflicts. There would be no divine intervention unless the Nameless god reared his ugly head, and that was as likely as a goat sprouting wings.

Stone Hill was on its own, and if the gates failed, we were well and truly fucked.

Perhaps, I thought wryly, this was my opportunity to make peace with Aeon before I entered his dark realm. The Underworld's caretaker was the only deity I'd consider speaking to—the others would only laugh, amused by our fears, as they sat back to watch the battle unfold. They'd see our struggle as entertainment at best, a mere footnote in the endless flow of history at worst.

I glowered over the wall as my thoughts continued to darken. I'd trained for this day for years, but I was only one man. Under my guidance, the city guard would put up what fight they could muster, but all of us—myself included—were untested in war. Our world had been at peace for over three hundred years, the Five Kingdoms operating in relative harmony while the lands to the east remained still. We'd grown complacent.

Even His Royal Majesty Brennan Silvermane hadn't realized the magnitude of the threat when he'd dispatched me to Stone Hill alone. A single knight, without a contingent of the king's soldiers or the aid of a wizard, could not hope to stem the tide against the sheer number of adversaries I spied from afar. It was hopeless, and I teetered on the brink of despair.

"Owen Greenwaters, Ser."

The voice broke through my grim reverie. I turned in my circuit of the wall to find a tall, lithe woman steps away. She wore the uniform of the city guard beneath a set of ring mail, a conical helm tucked in the crook of one arm and a short sword sheathed at her hip.

"Ser, Camden asks that you return to his location. He's seen something."

I nodded and strode past her, retracing my steps toward the gate. I hoped Camden's news would ease my unspoken dread.

The glint of his spyglass caught my eye before his silhouette became visible against the wall. As I approached, he dropped his arm and turned toward me, strain tightening his eyes and creasing his forehead. I knew before I voiced my question his news was dire.

"What have—"

Drumbeats began to pound a cadence to the east, the sound reverberating across the hills. A chill raced the length of my spine as I intuited its meaning: The enemy was on the march.

"I noticed increased movement," Camden said, his gray eyes clouded by fear. "But this means—"

"They're primed for an attack," I finished for him. "We've discussed our strategy. You know what to do. I'll send runners to Matheson at the eastern gate."

Camden nodded once, then dashed toward the gate tower. I drew a breath, steeling myself for what was to come, and followed in his wake. The runners would be awaiting orders at the base of the tower. I descended the worn steps as rapidly as I dared and made my way to the pair of runners huddled near the hearth. Their eyes were wide and faces pale; they understood the significance of the drums as well as I did.

"Go to the eastern gate and warn Matheson the attack is imminent. We anticipate they'll hit this gate first, but he must be prepared for anything. He knows what to do—and tell him I expect him to follow orders, or by the gods, I'll skewer his cowardly ass to the wall myself."

In the hours since I'd arrived at Matheson's home with news from Jennavere, I'd learned the man was not only a chronic drunkard, but he had a tendency to disappear when matters became tense or dangerous.

"And if you can't locate Matheson, give my orders to Reg Whitecastles in his stead," I added. "Reg is his second at the gate. He at least appears to be more dependable than your gods-damned captain. Now, go."

The pair saluted and darted through the door. One way or another, someone would be notified at the eastern gate while we finalized our meager defense in the southeast. Fucking gods, I hoped the gates held.

The distant drumbeats thrummed in my ears as I bounded up the steps to take my place atop the wall once more. The sky was beginning to lighten toward gray with the promise of dawn, and even without the spyglass to aid my eye, the scope of the invaders' army was daunting. And now I understood why they'd been so difficult to make out in the blanketing darkness of the night; most were garbed head to toe in black. As they marched nearer to the walls, it was as if a writhing mass of shadow had overtaken the landscape.

An elbow nudged my arm. Turning, I found Camden offering the spyglass to me once more. I nodded my thanks and lifted it to my eye.

My breath hitched as the nearest enemies came into focus. Our warning from Jennavere hadn't been a mere fabrication as I'd hoped; the soldiers wore deep hoods to match their attire. Most sported sheathed weapons of various sorts—maces, swords, axes, spears—and their armor was tinted the same dark shade as their hoods. A few carried shields, and still others hoisted ladders. They planned to scale the walls.

They appeared human in form, but on closer inspection, I spied several exposed hands. Their skin was as blue as the nearby lake on a clear summer day, inked in an array of light-colored tattoos. They weren't human, but I had no idea what species they *were*. Hooded ones was as apt a term as any.

With a shake of my head, I scanned farther into their ranks. A few of their number sported brilliant green garb, and beyond them, the drummers pounding their relentless cadence wore violet. Those in green were interspersed with the black-clad masses. Were they commanders of sorts, or did they serve another function?

I handed the spyglass back to Camden and raked a hand through my hair. "They're not human. Fucking gods, there are more than I'd believed." I drew a breath to quell the anxiety threatening to overwhelm my senses. "Are the archers ready?"

Camden nodded. "We'll take out as many of the bastards as we can."

He didn't voice his thoughts, but I understood from his tone that he believed as I did. The gates wouldn't last under a sustained assault, and with the numbers we faced, we'd be overrun eventually. It wasn't a matter of if, but when.

My hands sought the hammers hanging from my belt. "Let's make them pay for Jennavere's fall."

Even if I couldn't convince myself with my bravado, perhaps it would inspire some of the others. It was the best I could do.

An hour later, the invaders stood silhouetted against the rising sun, but they had yet to attack. The drums had fallen silent some time ago, though the army remained in rigid formation. I couldn't fathom what they were waiting for, but my answer arrived soon enough.

"Owen," Camden hissed, drawing my attention.

The spyglass was pressed to his eye, and he was fixed on a single point in the distance. I followed his gaze to a location in the middle of the enemy's ranks. A space had been cleared, and a shimmering bluish light shone from its center. I'd rarely been in the presence of wizards, but I knew magic when confronted with it.

"What do you see?" I demanded.

"Figures… Three of them, emerging from the light." He paused and spat over the wall. "I can't make out their features from here, but I'll be damned to Aeon's hells if I said they were human. They're…something else."

"Blue?" I asked.

He barked a laugh. "No. They're not like the soldiers. They seem…gray. Colorless. I don't fucking know." He thrust the spyglass in my direction.

I took it and focused on the point where I'd glimpsed the blue light. The trio he'd described stood alongside a pair of black-clad soldiers. None of the three hid their faces. Camden was right—there was something distinctly *different* about them, though they appeared human in form. Two were men, one tall and dark of hair, the other short and compact. The third was a woman who was inexplicably dressed in a red gown. Her dark hair was loose around her shoulders, but I could see nothing of her face; her back was turned toward us.

I had no doubt the woman was a mage—or whatever the Shadow Council deigned to call themselves. Her companions were an unknown, though I suspected they'd wield magic just as she did. I shoved aside another wave of unease and handed the spyglass back to Camden.

"Are you thinking as I am?" he asked, one eyebrow lifted in question.

I nodded. "They aren't here for peaceful negotiations."

He snorted a laugh. "That woman's a mage. Only a magic wielder would have the audacity to enter a battle wearing a gods-damned dress."

"And I was sent here alone," I growled. "Fucking gods, I've done all I can to prepare this city for an attack, but…" I shook my head. I wouldn't voice my misgivings nor my fears where the other guards could overhear. Morale was too fragile as it was.

"What I said to you earlier still holds true, Owen." Camden slid the spyglass into a pocket and turned to face me with a stern expression. "We'll give our all defending this city. We'll give them a brand of hell they won't be expecting. It doesn't matter their numbers or if the gates hold—we signed up for this duty, and most of the city guards will honor their oaths."

I nodded, heartened by his words. "Then we'll go down together."

Camden clapped my shoulder and nodded appreciatively. "I knew I liked you." His brief smile fled as he eyed the invaders once more. "I'm going to make peace with Aeon before the drums start up again."

I shifted my gaze to the ranks of black-hooded soldiers below. I should have followed Camden's example and offered a prayer or three to Aeon, but what good would it do? Our fates were likely sealed, and the Underworld's caretaker knew each soul who entered his realm intimately.

I considered my life before my arrival in Stone Hill, and realized I had few regrets. I'd proven myself capable years ago and made good on the promise I'd made to my teenaged self to achieve knighthood. I'd lived a happy, albeit lonely life, following the king's commands and ensuring the safety of countless civilians. It had been fulfilling.

My single greatest regret was that I'd forsworn a family of my own in favor of traveling the kingdom. I'd never settled down. But as I looked at the enemy army, the incarnation of my doom, I decided even that regret was minor. I had no family to mourn my loss, no children that would be forced to grow up without their father. Perhaps my life choices had been for the best after all.

Few would mourn my passing, but I was at peace with it.

I narrowed my eyes and drew my hammers from my belt as the drums resumed. I didn't fear death.

Let them come.

4

PRISONERS

The invaders flooded the dock district first. Since we'd evacuated most of its residents the previous day, there was little resistance—though I was dismayed to see a number of the more stubborn inhabitants herded into the muddy streets. Some fought their hooded foes, while others surrendered as they realized they were overrun.

While the invading army burned and pillaged the structures outside the city's ancient walls, the monster in the lake made its second appearance. It crashed through one of the docks, splintering the boards as though they were mere twigs. Silver scales glittered in the morning light as it dove beneath the surface to mount its next attack. Its body was longer than the merchant vessels bobbing in the waves, serpentine, with a spined dorsal fin just as Clay had described.

How had a gods-damned sea serpent found its way into Lake Jennavere?

It was clearly trained to attack when commanded—or it harbored a higher intelligence than its reptilian features portrayed. One of the black-hooded enemy seemed to be directing its actions against the docks, though the creature decimated some of its allies in the process. Its attacks were ruthless and efficient; within the first hour of the assault, the docks were reduced to splinters, while the boats that had plied the water now rested on the lakebed, marked only by the occasional shattered mast where one thrust above the surface.

The destruction was absolute, but I spied only snatches of the events along the shore. The invaders had encircled Stone Hill and begun to scale the walls while the docks were overtaken. I was too busy shouting orders and attacking the enemy forces that reached the top of the wall to truly take note of the serpent's movements.

Through it all, the invaders' drums pounded their relentless cadence, spurring the army on.

I adjusted my grip on each war hammer, pleased at how well the leather wrapping on the handles gave my fingers purchase even when the weapons were slick with blood. Until now, I'd used them only in training, often against straw-filled targets. It was a relief to learn the coin I'd spent to obtain them had been worth it. They were certainly being put to the test on this gods-forsaken day.

I kicked at the top of yet another siege ladder as it clattered against the rim of the wall. When it held firm, I released a snarl. Risking a glance toward the ground, I noted four invaders held its base while two others began to ascend its rungs.

"Draw!" Camden's voice bellowed above the din.

Along the length of the wall, our archers obeyed his command, nocking arrows. Our supply was dwindling, but I trusted the grizzled guardsman's judgment. He wouldn't waste our ammunition without good cause.

I smashed the blunt end of one hammer against the top rung of the siege ladder, then ducked behind the crenellations to await the first of the hooded attackers. Another guard stood opposite me, mace in hand, and nodded once. We'd strike from both sides when the invader reached the top.

"Loose!" Camden roared.

The twang of bowstrings was momentarily heard over the surrounding din. I drew a breath and focused on the nearby ladder, prepared to assail the first invader who appeared at its top.

"Owen."

I turned at the sound of my name, startled to find Camden a pace away. I'd believed he was more distant, near the base of the southern gate's tower.

"The guards can handle the ladders for a time. There's something you ought to see." He tilted his head toward the tower with a meaningful look.

I glanced toward the guard on the far side of the ladder. When she nodded her understanding, I rose from my half-crouch and slid my hammers into my belt, then followed Camden. Small clusters of guards huddled between crenellations along the wall's length as they prepared to face the invaders. A larger group was gathered near the tower's entrance, preparing to ignite a cask of oil before they shoved it over the edge.

Camden led me past them and into the tower, then up the steps to its top floor. A pair of archers stood at the narrow windows. One loosed an arrow as we entered, while the other paused to glance over his shoulder before returning to his duty. Camden led me to the central window and pointed to an area not far beyond the wall.

The two men I'd spied earlier stood within an eddy of the swirling invaders' ranks. They spoke briefly, then the shorter one disappeared into the masses.

"I believe the tall one is their leader," Camden said.

Without the spyglass, I couldn't make out his features from our present distance, though there was something distinctly *wrong* about his presence. The coloration of his skin wasn't natural, and his eyes…

I blinked as he seemed to focus his gaze on us. Crimson glittered in his eyes.

"What in Aeon's hell—?" I began, only to have my words cut off as the man lifted his arms and the tower began to shake violently.

"*OUT!*" Camden bellowed as the floor heaved and buckled beneath our feet.

"He's a fucking mage," I gasped as I scrambled toward the stairs.

"Worse," Camden replied as he stumbled and fell to his knees. He pushed himself upright as I reached his side.

A loud crack rent the air, drawing my attention to the windows once more. Fissures appeared in the tower's wall at the same moment the floor tilted precariously. I lost my footing and found myself sprawled across the floor, sliding toward the gaping hole the mage had created in the wall. I scrabbled for purchase to no avail. I was slipping toward a fall that would surely result in broken bones—if I survived at all.

The floor inexplicably pitched in the opposite direction and slid toward the stairwell as Camden clung to the railing. I crashed into him, unable to stop my momentum. His fingers dug into my shoulder as he hoisted me to my feet.

"We need to get out of the tower," he panted.

I grasped the rail and nodded. "Let's go."

When we reached the room at the base of the stairs, I began to sprint toward the second staircase that would lead to the lower level.

"Owen, there's no time!"

I spun to face him. He stood near the exit to the wall and pointed toward the roof. A single glance told me he was right. The timbers supporting the roof were cracked; they'd give way any second. I darted toward him as the floor buckled once more, sending me careening in his direction. My unexpected flight was arrested by the doorframe; my right shoulder struck with a sickening crunch, and I knew immediately something was terribly wrong.

I grunted in pain, then forced my feet toward the exit and the relative safety of the wall. I stumbled outside to lean against the nearest crenellation, even as the wall beneath my feet began to crack and shudder. My arm hung limp at my side, and my fingers were growing numb. It was likely broken.

I grimaced and pushed myself away from the wall with my left hand. Camden was a short distance ahead, but turned to motion frantically. I stumbled toward him only to be lifted from my feet in the same instant.

Brilliant white light seared my vision. A deafening roar filled my ears as I realized belatedly the tower and the nearby wall were collapsing. Wood splintered, stone fractured, men and women screamed.

I was falling. Instinctively, I twisted to land on my uninjured side, but the impact with the ground reverberated through every fiber of my body. My right arm shrieked with agony and I roared from the pain. Debris rained down as I sought to regain my footing.

I winced as the world was enveloped in white light a second time. What manner of magic was I witnessing? My battered body and exhausted mind refused to make sense of the scene. One moment, the remains of the tower teetered dangerously, and the next, it was reduced to cinders. It was more power than any wizard I'd ever encountered could boast.

I shook my head and stumbled away from the crumbling wall as the first of the black-clad invaders marched through the gaping hole that had once been Stone Hill's southern gate. I hefted a hammer in my left hand and prepared to face them. I wouldn't give in without a fight.

Pain split my skull as I collapsed to my knees. The invaders weren't to my location yet; what had struck me? Spots danced through my vision, but I attempted to shake them off. By the gods, I wasn't going to die like this.

I forced myself to stand and glanced behind me. There were others in the debris-strewn street, some relatively uninjured, others unmoving and possibly dead. There was no one near my present location, but there was a bloodied stone on the ground near my feet. More stones continued to fall around me as the wall continued its slow demise.

Darkness began to cloud my vision as I was struck again. The gods certainly had a sense of irony; the one thing that was supposed to keep Stone Hill safe would prove my undoing.

I stumbled forward. In my pain-induced haze, I didn't understand why the ground rushed toward me at an alarming rate. I couldn't piece together the sight of black boots stopped before my sprawled form, nor comprehend the lilting voice that spoke near my ear.

My skull thundered in time with my heartbeat, drowning out the words, while my arm shrieked a counterpoint. I needed to fight this but was unable to focus. I groaned as another burst of white light seared my vision. My eyes burned.

In that moment, I prayed to any god that might listen. I wasn't ready to die.

I fully expected to open my eyes and find Aeon's furred countenance peering at me as I looked upon his fabled jeweled gates.

Instead, I awakened to a wave of nausea so profound I nearly vomited. My right arm throbbed, my head pounded, and my vision swam dizzyingly as I blinked and attempted to take in my surroundings. My damned eyes refused to focus; everything remained a bright blur. My knees protested their contact with the stony earth. The left side of my face ached where it had been pressed against something uncomfortably hard. I groaned.

Aeon's realm would have been preferable to this hell.

"Owen?" The voice was a bare whisper, but one I recognized.

"Cam?"

"Not so loud," he hissed. "It's good you're awake."

I shifted away from the hard surface I'd been leaning against, only to realize it was his armor-clad shoulder. My right arm shrieked with the movement. My hands were bound behind my back, and even if the shackles hadn't been secure, I wasn't sure I'd manage to wrest myself free of them, given the state of my arm. My right hand was cold and numb, another sign the damned thing was broken.

"What happened?" I asked in a lower tone. "Fucking gods, I can't see."

"We're prisoners," he replied. "The hooded ones seem to have made a deal with their masters…" His voice faltered. He cleared his throat, then went on. "They're the Soulless, Owen. They've executed a number of us already, but the hooded ones intervened. It seems we've been chosen to return with them. They require laborers."

I grunted and swallowed a wave of panic. "My gods-damned arm is broken, and there's nothing but a white blur. Cam, *I can't gods-damned see.*"

I heard him shift beside me. "There were others who witnessed the magical light as you did. The hooded ones believe your vision will return in time."

"And my arm?" I pressed, trying to focus on anything but my present blindness.

"I don't know." He expelled a sigh. "I recommend you don't mention it until the Soulless are gone."

I grimaced and blinked several times, hoping my vision would clear. It didn't.

I swallowed another groan and considered Camden's words. I still wasn't certain who or what the hooded ones were, but if they'd intervened to save some of our number, perhaps they weren't merciless. But the Soulless…

That was a term I was familiar with, one that struck a chord of fear deep within my core. Our world had been plagued by a number of violent and destructive wars, each prompted by the arrival of the Soulless. They were servants of thc Nameless god—zealots, if the stories were true—granted inhuman power in exchange for their mortal souls. Perhaps their strange coloration was explained by what they were—the gray skin and crimson eyes were fitting for a human-turned-monster. And the blast of magic that had toppled the tower was certainly more than any wizard could have conjured.

"How long was I out?" I mumbled, desperate to change the subject.

"It has been a little more than an hour since I was brought here," he replied. "You were face-down in the mud. I convinced one of our captors to help you sit upright."

I forced a tight smile. "Thank you. After I fell from the wall, I was struck by…something. A rock, perhaps. My head feels like it's split."

"Hmm." Camden shuffled closer. "There's blood in your hair, but there's nothing I can do, Owen. I'm shackled just as you are."

"I wasn't expecting you to do anything," I replied evenly, "but it's why I passed out. At least, I believe it's the reason. After the wall collapsed, my memory is hazy."

Camden's elbow nudged my ribs. "Quiet. They're coming back."

I didn't have to ask who. The edge in his tone told me all I needed to know.

Footsteps crunched through gravel to our left. I turned toward the sound, though I could see nothing of the newcomers. There were two, perhaps three, pairs of feet striding toward us, but I couldn't be certain.

Gods-damn it, I wished I could see.

The white dimmed briefly to pale gray as a shadow passed over us. That meant it was still daylight, not that the time of day mattered while I remained blinded.

"On your feet," a gruff voice commanded.

The shuffle and scrape of dozens of boots erupted around me as I struggled to rise. It was disorienting without my vision to aid me, but I managed. Camden moved closer to my side, his elbow brushing mine in a silent promise he wouldn't abandon me, despite my injuries.

A crackling thrummed through the air and someone far to my right screamed.

"Learn to obey your betters," a woman's voice sneered. "Follow orders, or I'll send every one of you to Aeon's realm without hesitation, just as I did him."

I wanted to ask Camden for details, but feared to speak. I suspected the noncompliant man was dead and the woman was his executioner. I could seek more information later when it was once again safe to converse.

"Get in position, Dranamir," a man snarled. "You can take your gods-damned pleasure with others, but these go to the Murkor."

The woman snorted. "It's a pity the blue-skins refuse to see the value in their enemies' deaths."

"Dranamir…"

Cold laughter followed her footsteps as she moved away from my location. Her words had been callous and her mirth unsettling. I was grateful Camden had warned me into silence before she'd arrived, or it was likely I'd have become her victim in the other man's stead.

A wave of vertigo inexplicably washed over me, and I collapsed to my knees once more. But rather than landing on the hard stone and debris that was Stone Hill, the ground was softer. I shook my head in confusion and immediately regretted the action; the pounding in my skull intensified as my stomach roiled violently. I leaned forward and retched, unable to stave off the latest surge of nausea.

"Owen," Camden hissed through his teeth.

A pair of rough hands gripped my elbows and hauled me to my feet. I grimaced but stifled the scream that threatened as my right arm was jostled.

"Some do not tolerate the magic well," a lilting voice murmured in my ear. "The Soulless have gone, and you are safe now."

The hands released their grip as their owner stepped away. I bit my lower lip as pain continued to flood my arm, but I used the moment to piece together the meaning of the words. How was it possible we were safe when it was clear we'd been taken as prisoners of war? I was familiar with the laws of the Five Kingdoms, and there were few concessions made for people in our situation. I knew I should have been grateful simply to be alive, but what was the cost? And if my injuries prevented me from fulfilling my role as a laborer, would I be given to the Soulless to satisfy their bloodlust?

"I understand many of you bear injuries," the same lilting voice stated, addressing our group. "They will be tended before you are made to work. But before we enter the caverns, we must bind your eyes. Few outsiders are granted entrance to our home, but under the present circumstances, you have been made exceptions. The blindfolds will be removed when we reach the lower levels."

I stifled a bitter laugh. They'd blindfold me when I was unable to see more than passing shadows? I found the irony strangely amusing.

A thick strip of cloth was tied over my useless eyes, and a hand gripped my left arm. "This way," a different voice—though one with the same distinct lilt—said from my side.

We began to move forward, but toward what fate, I still didn't know.

5

UNDERSTANDING

"The arm must be reset."

I glowered at the green blur hunched before me. My vision was beginning to return since we'd been escorted through the Murkor caverns the previous day. Rather than a white expanse, I could now discern color, but my eyes hadn't regained the ability to focus. It was an improvement, but I wished they'd heal faster.

And Murkor… It was what the invaders called themselves. They'd been surprisingly gentle with us, though many—Camden included—had already been assigned to work details. My broken arm and my head injury prevented me from joining them until the Murkor deemed me fit enough for labor. The green-clad Murkor were healers of sorts, though the others referred to them as alchemists. I wasn't certain what the title implied, but if they could mend my arm, I wouldn't complain.

"Do not look at me so," the green blur said patiently. "If you'd rather I leave your arm as it is—to mend itself in the wrong configuration—there are many others who will benefit from my work. And most will be appreciative."

I released a sigh. "I'm not angry with you, but I know what resetting a bone entails."

"I will be quick," the alchemist promised, then said something to a pair of nearby black blurs in the Murkors' musical language.

One moved forward to unlock my shackles while the other gripped my left wrist firmly.

"Lay back. They will hold you in place while I work."

I clenched my jaw but did as he asked. I'd rather have my arm heal properly than be a plague to my existence for the remainder of my days. And it was my dominant arm. If I had any hope of escaping one day, I'd need it functional.

As I settled back against the mat I'd been given, the Murkor on my left kept a firm hold on my wrist. The other moved to kneel above my head. I was momentarily perplexed by his position until he placed one hand on either of my bare shoulders and applied pressure. I ground my teeth as the force sent a shockwave of agony through my right arm.

I felt something hard pressed against my lips.

"Bite down on this," the alchemist advised.

I grimaced but did as he asked; I'd likely need it. It was a block of wood wrapped in a thin strip of cloth. The bitter taste of pine sap coated my tongue.

"Brace yourself."

One cool hand slid beneath my arm, midway between my elbow and shoulder, while another rested gently atop it. I bit into the wood harder, anticipating the agony his next movement would bring. In one swift motion, the alchemist realigned my arm. My legs kicked reflexively as I released a muffled roar.

"Remain still," he ordered.

I managed a nod, though what he thought I was capable of in my present state, I didn't know. Fucking gods, it hurt more than I'd imagined possible. My arm throbbed in time with my heartbeat well after he dropped his hands. It was several seconds before I realized the pair of black-clad Murkor had released their grip, but I was in no state to attempt an escape.

I heard him shuffle away, only to return moments later. Gingerly, he lifted my arm and placed it in a padded contraption—I suspected it was a sling, but I could see nothing but a gray blur. He helped me to sit, then cinched it securely in place; one strap was fixed around my left shoulder, and another around my waist.

"Your arm must remain still while the bones heal," he stated. "It will take time. Weeks, perhaps."

I groaned but didn't put voice to my fears. Reduced to one arm, I'd be useless to my captors as a laborer. I'd be expendable, among the first casualties if they decided to thin our ranks. Instead, I focused on the more perplexing aspect of my captivity.

"Why do you help me?"

The indistinct green blur shifted slightly; I believed he shrugged. "It's the right thing to do. The Kal did not seek to harm your people, but our hand was forced. The commander struck a deal with the Soulless—you live under the pretense that we require workers. We do, but not everyone is fit to perform manual labor. You certainly aren't."

"Then why—?"

He chuckled. "You may have difficulty believing it, but we value life. *All* life."

I frowned, uneasy with my current prospects. I wanted to believe him, but remained skeptical—I was a prisoner, after all. What was I to do? And if the Soulless returned to find me unable to fulfill my promised role, how would they react?

"I believe I understand your concern," the alchemist said after a moment. "It is unfounded. Our caverns are protected from magic. Those who seek to control us cannot harm you here. And while many of the others who came with you have been assigned to work details, there is still a function you can perform for us, despite your injuries."

"And what's that?" I demanded. "My arm's useless, I've been advised against exertion due to my skull fracture, and I still can't fucking see clearly."

I loathed the feeling of helplessness that consumed me. I was reliant on my captors for treatment, food, water... It wasn't a position I'd ever expected to find myself in, and I wasn't prepared. I was floundering, and no amount of prayer had yielded results. In fact, the gods had been decidedly uncommunicative. I was on my own.

"Your vision has improved, if I'm not mistaken," the alchemist replied gently. "Your head is healing rapidly, but your arm will take longer. My caste always has a need for assistants, and despite my better judgment, I've taken a liking to your crass and forthright nature."

I snorted. Crass? I wasn't half as bad as some people. "You haven't met many humans, have you?"

"Only those like you." He paused, though I couldn't see his movements. "Many of those the commander rescued arrived injured. I have tended many wounds since the war began."

I frowned. "Rescued? I'm a gods-damned prisoner."

He sighed, clearly exasperated. "If the commander had not intervened on your behalf, you would be dead. The Soulless planned to kill everyone who stood against them, no matter their reasons for doing so. We've discussed this previously, and I grow weary of repeating myself."

"I've been shackled since coming here. Those who weren't hurt have been sent to the gods only know where, on the pretense of working for you. I'll concede you've helped me, but I know nothing of your people, your home, or what you plan to do with us." I shook my head and glowered at the dark blur that marked the ground. "Until I'm certain of your altruism—and that will take time—I can't trust you. Your people attacked and imprisoned *us*."

"I did not order the soldiers to cuff your wrist again," he pointed out.

"Some would consider that a mistake," I growled.

He laughed. "No. Even if your sight was restored, you have little hope of reaching the surface without a guide. Our caverns are vast, and you are presently several miles from the entrance. Your weapons and armor were confiscated, and the Kal has ordered they will not be returned. Your threat is baseless." He paused to poke one finger gently into my right arm. When I hissed from the pain, he said, "You are in no condition to fight."

I scowled and refused to look at him. I hated that he was right.

"We will speak again," he promised. "For now, you must rest."

I rolled my eyes as I heard him walk away, the pair of black-clad Murkor with him. There was a swish of fabric as they exited the little alcove I'd been assigned, then was left alone with my own dark thoughts and frustrated musings.

I ran my free hand over the straps securing my sling in place. They were made of a thick, woven material and ran through several metal rings in a pattern I couldn't decipher without the use of my eyes. The sling was padded and stiff; it enveloped my arm from shoulder to wrist and afforded little movement. If I were forced to wear it for any length of time—and I assumed I would, based on our earlier conversation—I feared I'd lose mobility in both my shoulder and elbow. But my arm didn't throb as fiercely as it had prior to the alchemist's ministrations. It would heal as he'd promised, given time.

I lifted my free hand to my scalp and gingerly explored the bandage wrapped around my head. The alchemist had focused on my head injury first, fearing it was the more grievous wound. There was a deep laceration, and he believed my skull was fractured. It explained the headache and nausea I'd experienced, but after a night's rest, it was immensely better. I supposed I had the alchemist to thank for that aspect of my recovery too.

I lay back on my mat and stared up at the indistinct ceiling. The behavior of our captors continued to baffle me. They believed they'd saved us, but I couldn't shake the sense of foreboding that gripped my heart. Every child in Balotica learned the history of the Five Kingdoms, and a large portion of it focused on our wars with the previous Soulless. I was convinced the Nameless god's minions weren't finished with us, and the Murkor had only granted us a temporary reprieve from their schemes.

We weren't saved. We were merely awaiting a more terrible fate than imprisonment. I suspected I'd wish for death before the war was over—unless I found the means to escape.

"You be him."

I flicked a glance toward the sound of the voice, though I could see little beyond a green smudge some distance from my mat. I stifled the urge to sigh and pushed myself upright as the green-garbed figure approached. Her voice was distinctly feminine and more heavily accented than the others I'd spoken to. As she knelt at my side, I noted she was much smaller in stature than her counterpart.

"Why have you come?" I demanded.

She was silent for a moment, then said, "Rej'vennar said your…eyes not healed yet. I…will help."

"Was that the other alchemist?"

"Yes. I am…not surprised he…not give you name."

She made a sound of frustration and muttered rapidly in the Murkors' musical tongue. It took me a moment to realize she struggled with the common language. When I spoke next, I did so at a slower pace for her benefit.

"None of your people have given their names. Nor have they asked mine."

She growled something that sounded akin to a curse. "I am Aj'ana. Alchemist. Come to…help. Your name?"

I considered giving her a false name, but if I was ever reunited with Camden or one of the soldiers from Stone Hill, they'd likely undo any false identity I attempted to create for myself. And if my suspicions about the Soulless proved correct, it wouldn't matter if the Murkor learned my name or the details of my past. I was doomed regardless.

"Owen."

"Owen," she repeated slowly. "I help with…eyes?"

I chuckled despite my best efforts to remain surly. Her demeanor was gentle, and it was apparent she meant no harm. The cynical part of my mind stated it was why the others had sent her; I was more likely to trust her than Rej'vennar or one of the soldiers.

And I needed to regain my sight. I was utterly useless without it.

"Yes, you may help."

She moved slightly and I heard the rustling of fabric and a clink of glass. "I make…salve. Place on bandage for eyes. You wear for…one day. Yes?"

"You'll bandage my eyes for a day?" I asked.

"Yes. When bandage…off, eyes are…healed."

I nodded absently. I couldn't see now, and if her remedy failed, I'd be no worse off than I was at present. One day spent in complete darkness was worth the gamble of having my sight restored.

"Will you return when it's time?"

"Yes, Owen. I can…*want* to help."

"Then I accept." I managed a smile that I hoped was encouraging.

"Rej'vennar say you not agree." The sound of a cork being pulled from a vial accompanied her words, and the aroma of lilac and pepper filled the space. "Rej'vennar wrong. And I help." Her words were triumphant.

"I couldn't bring myself to trust Rej'vanyar," I admitted.

"*Rej'vennar,*" she corrected. "He not trust you. You not trust him. Men are *velan'sta.*"

I didn't know the word, but based on her tone, I assumed it was akin to "stupid" or "stubborn." I chuckled.

"You think…amusing?"

"I don't believe you're wrong," I replied with a grin.

"Hmm." She was silent for a moment, then said, "Perhaps you not…bad. Now, I place bandage. Yes?"

"Yes."

"It cold," she warned as she moved to stand behind me.

I shrugged as well as I was able given the sling, then immediately regretted the action. My right arm began to throb for the first time in hours.

"*Velan'sta*," she hissed in my ear. "You ruin arm."

The word meant stupid, then. I grimaced. "I won't do it again."

She muttered in the Murkor tongue for a moment before an icy cloth was drawn over my eyes. I stiffened in response, but she continued to work undeterred, tying the bandage tightly behind my head. After a few moments, the chill gave way to a soothing sensation that I found inexplicably pleasant.

I heard her footsteps as she resumed her place at my side. "Do not touch bandage. I will…come in one day. Then you…see. Eyes healed."

Her words were confident, and I couldn't muster the desire to question her further. There was something about Aj'ana that garnered trust, something that had been missing from Rej'vennar. Was it simply that she was a woman, or was it more profound?

A rustle accompanied her movements as she rose. "I send…Tre'ana with…food. She help."

I turned toward the sound of her voice. "Thank you, Aj'ana."

"You remember…name." Her tone was pleased.

"Yes. We'll speak again tomorrow."

The indistinct blurs of color had been preferable to the complete darkness I now experienced. I feared to leave my mat for more than necessities, and each time, I sought the rough surface of the nearby wall as a rudimentary guide. Gods, I loathed this helplessness.

But Aj'ana returned as promised, and when she removed the bandage from my eyes, I gasped and stared around my alcove in wonder. The walls were natural stone, and a few jagged stalactites hung from the ceiling. A pair of pale yellow crystals were affixed to the wall near the curtained entry; they emitted a soft light that filled the space with a diffuse glow. The curtain above the entrance was gray in color, yet adorned with intricate embroidery. My mat was nestled a few paces inside; it was the same shade of gray as the curtain. A slight curve in the cavern wall led to a smaller area where the chamber pot was located, but it was hidden from view from my present location.

The Murkor had given me a measure of privacy I hadn't expected. It was a relief, yet added another layer of confusion to my perception of them.

I turned to face Aj'ana where she knelt at my side. She wore a loose tunic and leggings of brilliant green, and her face was shadowed by a hood of the same shade. Only her hands were visible. They were midnight blue and covered in a swirl of silver designs.

"You see," she said knowingly.

I nodded. "Yes. I am in your debt, Aj'ana. Thank you."

"You not help if you not see." She tilted her head slightly and crossed her arms. "I ask Rej'vennar for assistant. He say…if you…agree to my help, he give you…to me. He not believe I do it." Her tone was mischievous, but her words struck a chord of alarm.

I tensed. "What do you want with me?"

She dropped her hands and grew still. "I need…your help. I help you, you help me. Yes?"

I shook my head, inexplicably terrified despite her gentle tone. "What do you need *my* help with? What do you plan to do? I'm already a gods-damned prisoner."

"Ah." She nodded once. "You…mistake. I am alchemist, work in…*halasta.* I need help. Fetch things. Reach things. You tall, but hurt. You not work with…others. You help me. Yes?"

I frowned, unable to comprehend what she asked. Fetching and reaching I understood, but why did she require *my* assistance?

She muttered under her breath when she realized I didn't understand. "Wait. I return with…speaker."

She disappeared through the curtain, and I scanned my surroundings a second time. The glowing crystals were remarkable. I wondered if they were a natural occurrence or something produced by the Murkor. I'd never encountered anything like them previously.

Aj'ana returned moments later with a brown-garbed male in her wake. She spoke rapidly in their tongue while the other nodded thoughtfully. When she paused, he drew a breath.

"Aj'ana apologizes for the misunderstanding. She is only just learning the common tongue." He spread his hands wide. "The Kal has ordered all prisoners must be put to work in some manner. We assign your people to tasks suited to their abilities. Given your injuries, you've been chosen for light detail."

I nodded slowly. "I see."

Aj'ana spoke again, her hands in constant motion as she did so.

"She says she would like you to act as her assistant," the brown-clad man said after a time. "She won a bargain against Rej'vennar for your services. Otherwise, you'd be assigned to him."

"What does the work entail?"

"You will fetch chemicals and reagents while she works," he replied without consulting her first. "The alchemists' laboratories are in a remote section of the caverns. She will lead you there each evening and return you here in the morning."

Aj'ana spoke again, gesturing impatiently.

"She asks if you can read the common tongue."

I nodded. "It's required before becoming a knight."

I grimaced and looked away, angered by my lapse. I should have kept that detail to myself, but Aj'ana's manner was so disarming, I'd lowered my guard.

"You are…knight?" she asked, awe in her tone.

"Yes," I replied grudgingly.

"It's fortunate the Soulless weren't aware of your status," the brown-clad man said. "They would have murdered you."

I scowled. "Yet I'm a prisoner. Am I truly so much better off than I would have been if they knew?"

"You *live*," Aj'ana replied fiercely. "Life is…better. *Always*."

"It is why we help as we can," the man added. "To thwart the Soulless and gain our own freedom, we must not follow their bloodthirsty ways."

"You aren't free?" I asked, stunned by the revelation.

Aj'ana shook her head while the man said, "No. We are compelled to fight, to obey. If we do not, the Soulless will kill us too. We would not be the first people to be eradicated on the orders of the Nameless god, but we do what we can to subvert him."

"I didn't know."

"Few outside the caverns do," he replied with a shrug. "Now that you understand, will you accept Aj'ana's offer?"

I shifted my gaze to hers and smiled faintly. "Yes. I can see because of her. Fetching vials is the least I can do to repay what she's done for me."

6

THREE KNIGHTS

"So, this is the result of you winning a bet?" I asked Aj'ana as she led me away from the alcove I'd come to think of as my temporary home.

A soft laugh issued from beneath her hood. "Yes. Rej'vennar was…upset. He not like…losing."

"I can't say I blame him. I don't much enjoy it, either."

I glanced around the cavern as we walked, enthralled by the natural beauty of the striated stone. Stalactites dripped from the ceiling, columns rose from the floor, and colored crystals dotted the surface at intervals, providing soft illumination for our journey. The floor had been worn smooth along our path and shone faintly in the muted light. Whorls of tan, gray, and white were visible on the floor and walls, interspersed with occasional veins of black or red.

Aj'ana pointed to a vein of glittering black as we passed. "Obsidian. I need it sometimes. Remember."

I nodded but hoped she didn't expect me to dig it from the cave wall myself. I calculated the days until my arm would be free of the sling and scowled. Rej'vennar had said it might take weeks—was it two, six, ten? At best, it would be another twelve days, but I suspected it would take longer. At least my sight was restored and my head seemed to be healing well enough.

We passed a few other humans with Murkor escorts as we traveled. Each was dressed as I was in sturdy yet flexible garments designed for long hours of labor, accompanied by leather boots. Unlike our Murkor captors, we wore shades of gray, a drab counterpoint to their more colorful attire. I suspected the variety of hues worn by the Murkor were significant; Aj'ana and Rej'vennar wore nothing but brilliant green, and the soldiers in Stone Hill had been garbed in black.

The tunnels we traversed wound through an impossible maze of caverns and intersections, some busier than others. Aj'ana waved a hand as we began to cross a wide tunnel.

"Market that way. Maybe I take you later."

I turned to peer in the direction she indicated and was astounded by the sheer number of Murkor I glimpsed in the vast cavern beyond. Rows of stalls were erected, where merchants and craftsmen offered their wares and services. The Murkor threading their way through the space wore a rainbow of colors—red, violet, yellow, white, green… As I watched, a small Murkor, likely a young child, scampered toward the tunnel. It was the first Murkor I'd encountered dressed in shades of gray.

"What do the colors of your clothing mean?" I asked as we turned around a bend and the marketplace vanished from my sight.

Aj'ana was silent for a moment, her head tilted in thought. "This is alchemist." She pointed to herself, then aimed her blue finger at me. "Gray is…means no caste. Child color."

I raised my eyebrows. "The Murkor believe we're children?"

She laughed nervously. "No. Child wears gray. Not old enough for caste. You not Murkor. No caste. You wear gray."

I nodded. I believed I understood what she was trying to convey. As an outsider, I was made to wear gray, an indication of my status—or lack thereof—amongst the Murkor people.

"When does a child choose their caste?" I asked.

She shook her head. "They not choose. *Chosen.* They…test. Then caste accepts. We…we…celebrate? Yes, celebrate, on shortest night of year."

"The summer solstice?"

She nodded. "We call *salanar.* Choosing? Child must be…" She sighed in frustration. "Seven…teen?"

"I understand," I assured her.

I chewed my lower lip as I considered her struggle to convey her thoughts. I'd never fully understood the complexities of the common tongue until my interactions with her; I'd grown up with it, studied it, learned to read and write it fluently. Despite my status as a prisoner, I realized I wanted to help. She'd healed my eyes, after all—and I wanted to believe the story I'd been given the previous day. The Murkor were victims of the Soulless as much as we were.

"Aj'ana, perhaps I can teach you more of the common tongue? You've done so much for me—"

She spun to face me, fingers spread wide. "You would…teach?" Her voice was breathless.

"If you'd like."

"Yes!"

I laughed, delighted as she twirled momentarily in excitement. "I can teach while I assist you in your laboratory."

"Good. This good."

It was impossible to maintain my previous skepticism regarding the Murkor in the face of her unabashed enthusiasm. I knew so little of her people, and much of it stemmed from the vague stories Matheson had mentioned when we'd first received word from Jennavere. I wondered if the inept captain of the guard had survived the sacking of Stone Hill and where he'd been assigned in the caverns if he had. If the Murkor were as smart as they appeared, they'd keep him away from the ale—or whatever their drink of choice happened to be.

"I'm glad you won your bet, Aj'ana. I'd rather be working with you than Rej'vennar."

"You say, but you not know plans." She snickered. "You work hard. I have much to do."

"Nevertheless, I didn't like him," I replied. "Against my better judgment, I think I might like you."

She shook her head, amused. "You feared this…last night. Now you like? Humans are *caf a'zar.*"

"What does that mean?"

She groaned. "It mean…not make sense."

"Confusing?"

"Yes!" She laughed. "Humans are *confusing.*"

"And Murkor are *caf a'zar.*" I smirked.

"Ah, you learn Murkor too? Also good." She nodded. "Yes, we trade. You learn, I learn. You help, I help. You see?"

"I do."

I smiled. Perhaps understanding the Murkor language and their ways would allow me to better devise a plan for escape when an opportunity arose. It would take time, but at present, I had that in spades.

"This is *halasta*."

"Your laboratory," I stated.

Aj'ana nodded and swept one arm toward a long workbench littered with an array of glassware and tools I assumed were essential to her trade. At its center was a bowl-shaped depression filled with coals. Perpendicular to the workbench were a series of shelves filled with labeled bottles and jars. Some contained liquid, others dried herbs, powders, or dead insects. On the opposite side of the small room was another, smaller shelf lined with leather-bound books. The laboratory was lit by milky crystals inset into the smooth cavern walls.

"I make healing salve today."

She withdrew a thin wooden stick the length of her thumb from a box on the bench, then flicked her thumbnail against its end. I was startled when a tiny flame erupted from the stick, then gaped, awe-struck at what I'd witnessed.

"Fucking gods, is that magic?"

She shook her head and laughed as she dropped the burning stick into the coals. "No magic in caverns. Is sealed." She paused to blow gently on the flame. "This is...firestick. Scorpion Men name it."

"Your people make them?" I asked, leaning toward the depression.

"Yes, we make." She pushed me gently but firmly backward. "Stand away. Is dangerous, sometimes."

"I'm—"

She waved a hand at me impatiently. "You in way. Go to shelf. I need...dry...Argh!"

She pushed past me and stomped to the shelves lined with jars, then pointed at a large vessel on the topmost shelf. It was clearly above her reach. I pulled it down and examined the label before handing it to her; it was written in the common tongue, with a series of unfamiliar symbols beneath that I assumed were the corresponding letters in Murkor.

"Dried red trefoil," I said.

"We say *vassa'eral*." She took the jar to the bench, then drew a heavy mortar and pestle to her location. "*Vassa* is name. *Eral* is dry. Yes?"

The remainder of the night passed in much the same fashion, though I found myself flagging after a few hours. The Murkor operated according to a nocturnal schedule, and I'd been given little opportunity to adjust. I began to pace between tasks in an attempt to keep myself awake, and vowed I'd sleep the entirety of the day if it meant I'd be more alert the next evening. While I was once no stranger to brief overnight vigils during my time in the city watch, it had been years since I'd last been forced to undertake one.

Between the unfamiliar Murkor terms Aj'ana bombarded me with and my sleep-deprived fatigue, I was overwhelmed by the time she announced it was time to return to the residential caverns. My mind was muddled and weary, my arm ached despite its confinement in the sling, and I was developing a headache.

Gods, I was growing too old for this shit. Learning a trade—even as an assistant—was a young man's game, and I'd never had an interest in herbs or in becoming an apothecary.

I trudged alongside Aj'ana as we made the return trip to the alcove I'd been assigned. She didn't appear tired in the least; I envied her energy through the haze of my exhaustion. She bade me a good day as I stumbled through the curtained entrance and sought my sleeping mat, ignoring the tray of food that had been placed on the floor nearby while I pulled off my boots.

I knew I ought to eat before I fell asleep, but the fare I'd been provided so far was unfamiliar and often far too spicy for my palate. This morning's offering was soup coupled with a flat bread I'd come to recognize as a staple of Murkor cuisine. I drew the tray closer and lifted the spoon to investigate the soup further. Dark chunks floated in the creamy broth alongside the red of an acidic fruit the Murkor referred to as *mataj*, and the green of a pepper. I'd learned the peppers were at times mild, yet blazingly hot at others, depending on which variety the cook used. I hadn't learned to tell the difference by sight alone.

I took an experimental bite, then grinned with relief. The peppers were mild, and the dark pieces were mushrooms. An unusual array of spices flavored the soup, but it was still warm and I was ravenous. As I swallowed the first bite, my stomach grumbled for more.

A few minutes later, the bowl was empty, the flat bread was gone, and I was pleasantly full. I pushed the tray toward the entrance, then lay down on my mat, taking care not to jostle my right arm.

I was nearly asleep when the rustle of the curtain drew my attention. I snapped my eyes open, then grinned at the silhouette in the entrance.

"Cam?"

He nodded as he stepped inside. "They wouldn't allow me to visit until you'd recovered enough to be assigned to work. Their rules are so gods-damned confounding."

He sat down heavily a short distance away, gray eyes fixed on my sling as I pushed myself upright with my good arm. I studied him in the muted lighting of the crystals; he appeared to have been treated well enough by our captors so far, though he reeked of sweat and sulfur. I wrinkled my nose as he shifted in his seat and the odor was momentarily stronger.

"Fucking gods, what sort of work did they assign you to?" I asked with a laugh.

He shrugged uncomfortably. "Mining detail. And before you grow too excited about the prospect of obtaining weapons, the Murkor don't allow us near the picks or the…sandblasts, as they call them. We move carts loaded with ore—or in my case, yellow sulfur—from the depths to the mine entrance. The carts may have wheels, but it's gods-damned exhausting." He paused to pick at his fingernails, then said, "I imagine you've been dealt a more favorable hand, given your injuries."

I told him of Aj'ana and my determination to learn the Murkor tongue if it might help us escape. "But I've been relegated to the role of a trained dog," I grumbled. "Fetch this. Fetch that. Good boy, here's your supper."

He tilted his head back and roared with laughter. "When you put it that way, perhaps the mines aren't so bad. You know, you aren't the only knight down here, Owen. There are two in the mines who were taken from Jennavere, and they've mentioned a third—though they aren't certain where she is now."

"Perhaps I can learn something of her whereabouts," I mused. "Aj'ana has been forthcoming with information so far."

"They'll be appreciative." He nodded at my sling. "How is your arm?"

"They reset the bones, but I'm stuck in this contraption for a while."

"And your vision?"

I flashed a grin. "I can make out every detail of your ugly mug from here."

He snorted. "I'd take offense if I wasn't so relieved. And for the record, my wife always found me attractive." The note of sorrow in his tone was unmistakable.

I grimaced. "Gods-damn it, Cam, I'm sorry. I shouldn't have—"

He held up one hand for silence. "I've come to terms with it, Owen. There weren't many who survived Stone Hill, and I believe the Murkor when they say they saved everyone they could. Ianna and our girls aren't here, so I must assume they've gone to Aeon."

"Gods, I'm sorry."

"I never asked after your family," he replied after a time. "Were they—?"

I shook my head. "I never settled down, Cam. There isn't a wife waiting for me back home, nor any children. Perhaps it's fortunate." I shifted uncomfortably, then bit back a groan as my arm protested. "Who are the other knights?"

"Senna Coldcreek and Petric Stonewarden."

I nodded. I'd met Petric on several occasions; he'd taken a permanent post in Jennavere over a decade ago when he'd announced his betrothal. When last we'd spoken, he had three children. I hoped for his sake at least some of his family had been spared. I knew Senna only through her reputation. She was young and had been raised to knighthood only a few months prior, but had already impressed several of my veteran acquaintances.

"And Petric's family?" I asked.

Camden shook his head. "They aren't here. He's sworn himself to avenging them when we contrive our means for escape."

"Shit." I released a heavy sigh. "Why in Aeon's hells *were* we spared, Cam? Why us, when the children had their whole lives to look forward to?"

"The gods only know the answer to that." He groaned and glanced over his shoulder. "I've stayed long enough. One of our hooded captors is bound to learn I'm not in my cell if I don't return soon."

"We'll speak again," I promised. "And I'll try to pry the other knight's location from Aj'ana."

"Her name is Mona Greyplains." He rose to his feet and offered me a weary smile. "I'm glad to see you're healing, my friend."

7

VENOM

Aj'ana returned the next evening before the brown-clad Murkor who often brought food arrived. I'd been awake for some time; my body continued to struggle with its adjustment to a nocturnal schedule, though I'd done my best to sleep after Camden's brief visit.

Aj'ana carried a small sack in her hands and fiddled with its rolled top while I pulled on my boots. She appeared nervous, but she said nothing until I rose and made my way toward her. She opened the sack and held it out as a sweet scent wafted from within. Inside were a half-dozen yellow cakes the size of my palm.

"Honey cake," she explained. "My…ah, the woman live near me. She make sometimes."

I reached into the sack and pulled one out. I grinned as I realized they were still warm. "Your neighbor makes them?"

She nodded emphatically. "Yes. Eat while we walk." She withdrew a cake of her own.

I bit into it and lifted my eyebrows, pleasantly surprised. It was spongy, yet light, slightly sticky, and tasted of honey. "Delicious."

She swiveled her hooded head toward me. "What you mean?"

I chuckled. "It's good. Tasty. I could eat the whole damned bag if you'd let me."

She jerked the sack away from me and held it close. "We *share*, Owen."

I laughed through a mouthful of cake. "I'll share, Aj'ana, but I'd like some answers in return."

"Ask."

"Why did you arrive early today, and why bring the cakes?"

Her shoulders visibly tensed. "Cakes because I like. Early is… We go to *other* prisoner area. Need your help."

I narrowed my eyes. "There's another prisoner area?"

She nodded once. "Not for humans. Scorpion Men. They…struggle. Dangerous."

I considered the implications while I finished eating my first honey cake. I'd never encountered Scorpion Men, though I'd heard plenty of tales. They were purported to be taller than humans, faster, and trained in combat from a young age. The war god, Blademon, was predictably their patron. It was said the Scorpion Men were descended from humans, though I didn't know the details of how they'd come to possess the lower body of desert scorpions. It was rumored their venom was fatal within minutes of injection.

It was little wonder why Aj'ana was edgy at the prospect of paying them a visit.

"Why are we—?"

"Collect venom," she interrupted. "We use."

I gaped at her. "You want my help to collect Scorpion Men venom? Fucking gods." I shook my head. "This is madness. I won't do it."

She spun to face me and crossed her arms. "You help. You must."

"No."

She heaved an aggravated sigh. "You no choice. You help, or Kal send you to black tower. You die there. Scorpion Men are…bound. You not hurt. You reach…stingers. Tall."

I clenched my jaw, furious with her threat. "You'd force my hand? Gods-damn you, Aj'ana."

I understood her broken speech well enough to know the Scorpion Men remained shackled, denied the meager freedoms I'd been afforded. It was unlikely I'd be hurt during the process, but it didn't sit well with me. As a fellow warrior, I could only imagine the humiliation they must experience each time an alchemist arrived to harvest their venom. Despite her threat, I still wanted to deny her order, no matter the consequences. What she demanded was fundamentally *wrong*.

"Need venom for healing salve," she persisted. "I put salve on your eyes."

"*What?*" I spluttered, incensed.

"Salve work, yes?" She tilted her head to one side and widened her stance as though she knew she'd already won the argument. "You *see*. We need venom."

"This goes against every gods-damned oath I swore when I became a knight," I growled. "I'm supposed to *help* those who need it, not prolong their misery."

"You help us. Your people too." She shrugged. "Scorpion Men not work. Refuse."

"Then why haven't you sent them to the tower, as you've threatened to do with me? Or are your threats nothing but empty lies because you want that venom?"

It required every ounce of my restraint not to lash out in my rage, and I hoped she understood the magnitude of my present anger. I would not be forced, not for this. Fucking gods, it was wrong.

Her stance grew rigid as we both seethed. "Soulless not demand Scorpion Men. Soulless demand humans. You safe here. You would ruin? Why?"

"Because it's fucking *wrong*, that's why!"

"Your life not *wrong*, Owen. This is…small…inconvenience? Yes. For Scorpion Men." She shook her head. "Perhaps I ask too soon. Fine. We go to prisoner cavern, you see. I ask Mej'ranir to sample."

She spun on her heel and began to march away. When I didn't immediately follow, she peered over her shoulder. Though I couldn't see her eyes beneath her hood, I could feel her heated glare.

"If you not come, I speak with Kal."

Exasperated, I released a groan. "Fine. I'm coming."

As I caught up with her, she thrust another honey cake in my direction. "You eat. Need strength for night's work."

"And if I refuse to eat, you'll threaten me again?" I growled.

"Humans are *velan'sta*."

She said nothing more until we reached the other prisoners' cavern. I considered refusing the second cake simply to spite her, but my rumbling gut decided for me. I ate while we walked and studied the other Murkor we passed. Few took notice of me, and I wondered if they all chose to follow the same frustrating line of reasoning as Aj'ana.

As we neared a large cavern with black-clad soldiers at its entrance, Aj'ana handed the sack to me. "You follow. Do not speak, only listen. Watch. Next time, you do this."

I clenched my jaw and resisted the urge to roll my eyes. "Fine."

She marched to the nearest soldier and began to speak rapidly in Murkor. He laughed after a moment, then his hood turned in my direction briefly before he replied. They conversed too rapidly for me to follow, though I understood *velan'sta* well enough when it was uttered. My rage simmered as I watched the pair.

Finally, Aj'ana beckoned me to follow as she and the soldier entered the cavern. I forced myself to obey, though it went against my every instinct.

The cavern was vaguely rectangular in nature. Along its two larger sides were two dozen Scorpion Men, each chained and shackled securely to the stone walls. Their hands were bound behind them, and thick metal chains looped around their waists to hold them in place. Many sported bruises and lacerations, bandages, and splints. There seemed to be an even split between men and women; the men were bare of clothing, though the women had been given loose shawls to cover their breasts. Each bore the muscled physique of career soldiers on their human upper bodies. Below the waist, they sported the chitinous form of a scorpion. The stingers at the end of their tails were encapsulated in strange glass structures, rendering their natural weaponry harmless.

My footsteps faltered only a few paces into the room. I was stunned and appalled by their treatment. Why did the Murkor shackle them while we humans were allowed relative freedom by comparison? Did they truly think so little of my people, believing we weren't a threat? Or were the Scorpion Men truly as ferocious as the stories made them out to be?

Aj'ana paused when she realized I'd stopped following and spun to face me, arms crossed. "Owen. You come. *Now.*"

I forced my feet forward as every eye within the cavern focused on me. I detected wary curiosity from some of the captives, mistrust and anger from others. Aj'ana exuded impatience as I made my way toward her. I didn't want to be there, didn't want to be complicit in her business, didn't want to make enemies with the fearsome warriors chained to the cavern's walls.

Yet if I failed to obey, I knew she'd make good on her threat. A trip to the black tower could only end in death, and I wasn't ready to enter Aeon's realm.

We approached one of the shortest captives, but he still towered several inches above me. His dark eyes were wary, though I sensed no hostility from him. Aj'ana spoke with the Murkor soldier in their own tongue, then withdrew a stoppered flask from one of her pockets.

The captive rolled his eyes, then focused on me. "For your benefit, they require venom to make healing salves—as well as the black metal they forge their weapons from. We aren't here willingly, but it's better than the alternative. I suspect it's the same for you."

Aj'ana made a sound of frustration beneath her hood. "You not speak to human."

The captive laughed, a deep, resonant sound. "I doubt you could stop me, even bound as I am, little alchemist. It's clear you're frustrated with him, but it's also clear he doesn't understand half of what you're attempting to do." To me, he said, "The Murkor are in a difficult position. Despite what you may believe, they *do* have your best interests at heart."

I wrinkled my brow in confusion. "Fucking gods, how can you say that? You're chained like a common criminal."

He laughed again. "The Murkor know we'd escape if allowed the freedom you've been granted. Unlike you, we speak their tongue and have learned the navigation signs of the caverns."

"No more," Aj'ana hissed. "We come for venom. Then leave."

He rolled his eyes. "Then go about your business, little alchemist. I'd rather be finished with this particular brand of humiliation quickly."

Aj'ana pushed the flask into the soldier's hands, then leveled a blue finger at me. "You watch. He take sample, yes? Next time, you do it."

I shot an apologetic glance to the captive, who merely shrugged his massive shoulders in response. No matter how I tried, I couldn't puzzle out why he seemed to accept his treatment. If I'd been in his position, I would have been furious, lashing out at any Murkor who came near.

Aj'ana tugged at my left arm. "You not watch, Owen."

I clenched my jaw and focused on the Murkor soldier. He uncorked the empty vial, then pressed it against the base of the glass apparatus encasing the captive's stinger. He twisted the vial a half-turn clockwise, and almost immediately, a viscous yellow liquid began to drip inside. The soldier stood nearly the same height as I did, but the apparatus was still a handspan above his head. It was no wonder why Aj'ana sought help with the process; the top of her head didn't even reach my shoulder.

"Simple, yes?" she asked. "You see?"

"Yes, I understand," I replied grudgingly, "but I maintain my earlier stance. This isn't right, Aj'ana."

The captive's rumbling laugh drew my attention once more. "It's better this than death, my friend, and I suspect we'll return to the Stronghold well before the Soulless' war ravages this land. But your compassion is welcome. Owen, was it?"

Aj'ana hissed, but I ignored her. "Yes. Owen Greenwaters."

He smiled knowingly. "A Balotican, then. So much of your behavior makes sense now. I'm Thedrak."

The Murkor soldier twisted the vial again, and it detached. He handed it to Aj'ana with a nod and growled something in his tongue to Thedrak, who smirked and responded in kind.

Aj'ana tugged at my sleeve fiercely, clearly hoping to leave.

"We'll meet again, Owen," Thedrak promised.

I nodded. "I hope it will be under better circumstances next time."

I followed Aj'ana out of the cavern. As soon as we were out of earshot of the soldiers keeping guard, she rounded on me. "You not watch! Only want to talk with Scorpion Men. No. You here for work."

"What harm is a little conversation?" I asked, arching an eyebrow.

"If Kal learns you not work, he send you away. I promise you watch today, but next time? You work." She heaved a sigh. "You say last night, you like me. You *velan'sta*, but I like you. I not want you hurt. I not want...you dead. If...guard say to Kal you not work, what happen? You sent away. I blamed."

I blinked, startled by her revelation. "They'd blame you for *my* refusal to cooperate?"

"Yes." She crossed her arms. "And you die. I not want that."

"Why didn't you tell me sooner?" I asked.

She snorted and tossed her head. "I *try*, Owen. You not listen, and…it difficult. Sometime, I not know human words."

I expelled a breath and shook my head. "Shit. I'm sorry. But you have to understand my position too. Your people razed Stone Hill—yes, I know the Soulless demanded it," I said when she tensed. "I understand acting on orders. I'm a gods-damned knight. Orders have been my life for nearly two decades. But I'm a *prisoner*, Aj'ana. I couldn't reach the surface if I wanted to. We were blindfolded and led to…wherever we are, and I was sightless as it was. My weapons and armor were taken. Yes, your people have tended our wounds, but it's damned difficult to trust you after everything that happened in Stone Hill. Entire families were killed, murdered in the streets. Those who survived don't believe the Soulless are finished with us—and I suspect you feel the same."

She was silent for a few moments. I wasn't certain if she was upset or merely contemplating my words. In my frustration, I'd spoken rapidly, heedless of the communication barrier hindering our tenuous progress.

Finally, she said, "I know. You not wrong. The Kal think they return for you too."

My heart plummeted at her admission. "Then why do you care if I'm sent away?"

She reached out and took my left hand. "We hope to be wrong. We hope you safe here." She squeezed my fingers gently before releasing her grip. "Life nothing without hope, Owen."

Hope. After the events of Stone Hill, I'd given up on the notion of *hope*. But Aj'ana's words rekindled its flame.

"You're right."

She tilted her head thoughtfully. "Yes. We go to *halasta* now? You help make salve?"

I nodded. "We may as well make the most of that venom."

She bobbed her head and beckoned for me to follow. "You have last cakes while we walk."

I managed a smile. It was a peace offering of sorts, but I was grateful. I'd been too harsh with her, unable to shake my suspicions until the confounding conversation with Thedrak. I didn't believe I'd ever fully comprehend the dynamic between the Murkor and the Scorpion Men they held captive, but I trusted Thedrak's word.

"We need to work on our communication," I said as I withdrew the last pair of honey cakes from the sack. "I don't know if there's a better way than what we've done so far, but I don't want to argue any longer. Thedrak was right when he said I don't understand. There's *so much* I don't understand, Aj'ana. And it's not only your language."

She swiveled her hood in my direction. "Ask, Owen. I answer."

8

NEBULOUS PLANS

"Do you…ah…ever…remove your…hood?"

I stumbled over the familiar words and hoped Aj'ana understood—and that I hadn't said anything considered offensive. After spending nearly a fortnight in her company, she'd become more fluent in the common tongue and had begun teaching me to speak Murkor. Their words flowed in a different pattern than I was accustomed to, and at times, the same word might have multiple meanings depending on the speaker's inflection. I paused often while I fumbled through the words as my mind struggled to recall what I wanted to convey.

Aj'ana's reply was rapid, but I understood most of her response. It was progress, which was more than I could have said ten days ago.

"Yes, but not outside my home." She paused to add several drops of an oily substance into the flask on her workbench. "No one sees our faces beyond immediate family, Owen. It is a show of great respect, trust—and often an intent to partner—when a Murkor shows their face to someone not of their kin." She pointed at the shelves behind me. "Ground willow bark."

I turned to scan the jars and flasks as I sought the one she required. I still hadn't made sense of the Murkors' written language, but mercifully, most of the items in her collection were labeled in common as well. I located it in the center, a tall jar filled halfway with a gray-white powder. I pulled it carefully from the shelf and placed it a short distance away from her on the workbench.

I'd been reprimanded several times for coming too near. At first, I'd believed she was upset that I crowded her, but as our communication strengthened, I realized some of the compounds she worked with were volatile, flammable, or toxic. It wasn't *safe* for me to draw too near, untrained as I was. I spent most of my nights standing sentry near the shelves, observing her work as we spoke and taught one another.

I was no longer mistrustful of Aj'ana, something I hadn't believed possible during my first nights in her laboratory. She was genuine and cared deeply for everyone she met, even captives like myself. Our early arguments had stemmed from a mutual lack of understanding, coupled with our language differences, but we were overcoming both obstacles. She had a sharp intellect, a witty sense of humor, and a deep-seated compassion for all life that I was wholly unfamiliar with. Despite my initial misgivings, I now understood how fortunate I was to have been assigned to work with her.

Perhaps Karmada had been listening to my reluctant prayers after all, but I hoped I wouldn't come to regret it. Karmada was as fickle as she was beautiful, and most would have labeled me a fool to seek her aid. Yet I had, and I'd deal with her price when she arrived to demand it.

"Ask me something else, Owen." She opened the jar of willow bark and tipped a small amount into the flask.

"When I…can be rid…of sling?" I scowled at my broken attempt at the question. The string of words didn't sound right. "Gods-damn it," I muttered under my breath in common.

She laughed softly. "You're too hard on yourself. Say it this way," she said before repeating my question in Murkor.

I nodded and restated my question. "When can I be rid of this sling?"

"Better." She paused to swirl her flask, then placed it into the bed of coals inset in the workbench's center. "While I wait for the next phase of the reaction to take place, I will look at your arm. I doubt it has healed enough to be free of the sling. A break like yours takes time to mend, but perhaps I'm wrong."

"It does…not, ah…"

I groaned and raked my left hand through my hair, unable to recall the proper word for *ache*. My hair was growing too long, but the Murkor refused to allow me anything sharp with which to trim it—nor had I been allowed to shave. The beard was less irritating than the strands of brown hair that seemed to constantly fall into my eyes.

"It doesn't what?" she pressed.

"Ache," I said in common. "I don't know your word for it."

"We say *va'aj*." She gestured to the unoccupied stool to my left. "Sit down. I can't reach the clasp over your shoulder while you stand."

I sat and studied the silver designs on her hands as she unbuckled the sling. "What do…the marks?...mean?" I asked in my stilted version of Murkor.

She paused to peer up at me, and I spied a glimmer of pale eyes within her hood. "What marks?"

"Your hands," I tried again. "The…marks?"

She laughed again. "They are tattoos, Owen. They indicate my name and my family's, as well as my profession. It is how we identify one another without removing our hoods."

Gently, she pulled the sling away from my arm. I tried to extend it, but both my elbow and my shoulder protested the motion. The joints had been locked in the same position since Rej'vennar had reset the bone. In the same instant, the site of the break began to throb dully, though its pain was less severe than that of my joints. I winced and returned my arm to its previous arrangement.

Aj'ana had not failed to notice my reaction. "It still pains you."

I nodded once. "My…arm—"

"Speak in common, Owen," she cut me off in Murkor. "I need to understand precisely where the pain is located, or I may cause you further injury."

I forced a smile, grateful for the reprieve. "My arm hurts, but not as badly as my damned shoulder. Or my elbow."

"I feared your shoulder would suffer during the healing process, but there is no other way." She shook her head and reached toward my sleeve. "May I pull it up?"

When I nodded, she pushed the loose sleeve of my tunic up to my shoulder. My arm was a mottled mass of purple, green, and yellow bruises around the site of the break. It didn't appear swollen, but it was clear I was far from healed. She pressed her fingers gently into my flesh, and I hissed as a jolt of pain shot through my arm. She shook her head and stepped back.

"It's not ready, Owen. I'm sorry."

I sighed, unable to hide my disappointment, though I knew she was right. I tugged my sleeve back into place with a grimace, then said, "You have nothing to apologize for. I should have said this to you sooner, but I appreciate your help."

She laughed softly as she gently replaced the sling and began to fasten it in place. "You've thanked me previously, but I'll admit I don't grow tired of hearing it. You and your people are in a difficult situation. It's my duty as an alchemist to assist as I can." She tightened the strap around my shoulder and stepped back, her hood tilted to one side. "I think that's enough of a respite for one night. Go back to practicing Murkor."

I groaned dramatically and elicited another laugh.

"I thought…the sling…torture," I muttered, feigning hurt, though the effect was diminished by the brokenness of my words.

"I didn't believe humans possessed a sense of humor before I met you," she replied. "I'm pleased to know I was wrong."

She turned toward the workbench and leaned toward the flask in its bed of coals. "It's nearly ready for the next phase. Fetch the venom—and be *very* careful with it."

"I know," I replied as I stood and scanned the shelves.

She'd cautioned me each time she'd requested it since the evening we'd collected the sample from Thedrak. In its pure form, Scorpion Men venom was so potent, a single drop could kill an adult human—or Murkor—in the span of a few minutes. I'd learned the alchemists prized it for uses beyond the healing salves and the infusion they used to create the black metal of their weapons. Tonight, Aj'ana was making a batch of antivenom, but she'd also used it to create a paste that numbed the skin on contact, and once to create a powder that would incapacitate anyone who breathed it in.

I located the vial and placed it carefully on the bench. There was only a small amount of the viscous, yellow liquid remaining.

"Almost…empty," I told her.

She released a sigh. "We'll need to collect more in the evening. I hope you don't plan to argue over it again."

"Are all…Scorpion Men as…" I closed my eyes as I searched for the word I needed. "As…*amiable* as Thedrak?"

"No, but given your injury, we'll only visit those who won't fight us. My colleagues can deal with the more unruly captives."

I was relieved, yet I loathed the upcoming task. It would never sit well with me, and gods-damn it, I prayed one day I'd be granted the opportunity to make amends to the Scorpion Men.

"Are you prepared for the task this time?" Aj'ana asked when I didn't respond.

I looked away, unable to meet her hooded gaze. "Yes."

Camden stood outside the entrance to my alcove when I returned with the dawn.

I'd learned the subtle brightening of the crystals lining the cavern walls coincided with the rising sun in the world above. I missed the sunlight, missed the sting of wind against my face, missed the open expanse of the sky above. A fortnight in the cavern may not have seemed long to some, but I was beginning to pine for a brief glimpse of the world I'd been snatched away from. Gods, what I wouldn't give for a mere five minutes outside.

I shook off my longing and focused on my visitor. I knew why he'd come, and the news I bore wasn't good. Mona Grayplains had succumbed to her injuries three days prior, despite the Murkors' best efforts to save her life. I'd been forbidden contact with her, though Aj'ana had never elaborated as to why. Perhaps the Murkor feared what she'd tell me, or perhaps it was merely their way. There was still much I didn't understand regarding their culture.

"Good morning, Cam."

He nodded and followed me inside. "I'm never certain what time it is," he grumbled. "It's always dim up here, and even darker in the mines. Thank the gods for those crystals."

"The Murkor treat them to glow as they do."

I settled against the wall and leaned my head back against the rough stone as Camden sat cross-legged a short distance away. I was avoiding his unspoken question, but I knew he'd eventually come to it. I hated bearing bad news—and Mona's death would be a blow to the other knights. I hadn't known her in life, though I suspected they may have.

"How is your arm?" Camden asked as he did each time he paid me a visit.

I grimaced and told him of Aj'ana's examination a few hours before. "It's healing, but not as rapidly as I'd like."

Camden lifted his eyebrows and smirked. "You're not a young man any longer, Owen."

I snorted. "I'm not *old*, either. Not like you."

He barked a laugh. "And I was under the impression we were the same age."

I grinned. "Perhaps you'll never know."

In truth, Camden was two years my junior, but the banter served as a welcome distraction. It brought a sense of normalcy to our lives, one I sorely needed. Working with Aj'ana had its benefits, but she wasn't human and often didn't fully comprehend my attempts at humor.

"You're right—particularly if you keep that scruff you call a beard after we're free," Camden shot back. "You look like a damned barbarian."

"I could the say the same of you." My grin faltered as I pushed a few wayward strands of hair from my eyes. "I'd give my right arm for a barber."

"Don't go sacrificing any limbs yet." Camden chuckled. "A number of us have been petitioning the mining caste leader for exactly that. If they won't allow *us* to trim our hair or shave, Petric pointed out they may be willing to do it *for* us if given cause. He's been attempting to convince them long hair is a safety risk for those in the mines—he's not wrong, but he's exaggerating a bit to press his point. The Murkor seemed willing to listen, but nothing has come of it so far."

"I hope his luck runs better than mine," I replied bitterly.

Camden narrowed his eyes. "Is this about Mona?"

I nodded and looked away. "She was injured before her capture—severely, from what I was told. Aj'ana said the Murkor did their best to save her. I believe she spoke the truth. I've watched her and some of the other alchemists at work. Our apothecaries are novices in comparison."

"Owen, you're skirting the gods-damned subject." Camden crossed his arms and shot me a pointed glare. "She didn't make it, did she?"

I shook my head. "I'm sorry."

"Senna will take the news hard," he said. "Mona was her mentor."

"I didn't know."

We fell silent, lost in our own thoughts. I wondered how Senna fared; if she had a mentor, it meant she was from a noble family. The rigorous training required to become a knight often transformed nobles from arrogant and pompous asses to more compassionate souls, but I knew little of Senna beyond the first impressions of others. To be torn from knighthood's prestige and thrust into the role of manual laborer was a sore blow for anyone, but I suspected those of noble birth would struggle more than most. Or perhaps I was merely jaded by my own experiences and unable to shake my innate mistrust of those born into positions of power.

The rustle of the entry curtain drew my attention. A brown-clad Murkor appeared with a tray of food; bread, an array of baked root vegetables, and what appeared to be strips of steamed white fish. My stomach rumbled at the aroma wafting from the tray as the Murkor placed it before me.

"That's my cue to leave," Camden said as he rose to his feet. "I'm fucking famished."

"Your tray…in…cave," the Murkor managed before he ducked outside.

"Cam," I said before the other man disappeared, "do the others—Petric or Senna—have any ideas yet?"

He shook his head. "I believe both were waiting for news on Mona's whereabouts. If we can arrange it without drawing suspicion, it might prove beneficial if the three of you met. Perhaps you'll form a plan then."

I nodded. "Tell them I'll be waiting."

I pulled the tray closer once he was gone and tore into my meal as I contemplated my future—and that of the other human prisoners. We couldn't remain trapped in the Murkor caverns; Balotica needed us. Hell, the whole of the Five Kingdoms needed us. I no longer considered the Murkor enemies, but their position in the burgeoning war was complex, and I doubted the human rulers would understand without some of us vouching for them. And I would—I owed them that much for tending our wounds.

But I wouldn't formulate a plan that ignored the other prisoners' plight. The Scorpion Men deserved their freedom as much as we did, and I certainly didn't want to make an enemy of them. If even half the stories I'd heard were true, it would be a fatal mistake to cross them. After seeing them in person, I couldn't help but be intimidated by their size and apparent strength—and aiding them was the right thing to do.

My plans were nebulous, yet better than nothing.

I grimaced around a mouthful of bread as my thoughts triggered the memory of my conversation with Aj'ana. I was expected to extract venom the next evening. I now understood its significance to the Murkor, why they coveted it as they did, but the process had been humiliating for Thedrak. I loathed that I must be complicit in their plight, but what choice did I truly have?

I didn't believe Aj'ana would warn the Kal if I refused to assist her, but she'd been adamant that not all Murkor would understand my position. There would be witnesses in the cavern; the soldiers who stood guard, other alchemists, and potentially the brown-clad ones who often delivered food.

Gods-damn it, I was in a difficult situation. I prayed the Scorpion Men would understand.

9
THE KAL

Aj'ana arrived early the next evening bearing honey cakes.

"If I didn't know better, I'd think you were trying to bribe me," I said in common as I accepted a pair of the pastries.

She laughed softly. "Perhaps I am."

Her use of the common tongue had grown more fluid, and she rarely stumbled over her words any longer. She still preferred to speak in Murkor, but we'd agreed to alternate languages each night. Tonight was mercifully reserved for common.

"Damn, these are good. Your neighbor has a gift." I flashed a grin as we began the trek toward the Scorpion Men's cavern.

"I'll be sure to tell her." Aj'ana took a bite of her own cake and made a sound of contentment. "I hope this is…sufficient payment for what you're required to do."

I swallowed a mouthful, then released a sigh. "I know your reasons for collecting the venom, Aj'ana, and I'll never be comfortable with the task. *But,*" I said with emphasis before she could interrupt, "I gave you my word. I'll do it as promised."

I'd sworn an oath to uphold my promises when I became a knight, and I'd always followed it. I'd never been one to break my word, even before I'd signed up for the melee so many years ago. I wasn't going to start now.

She visibly relaxed. "Thank you. I would never have asked it of you if I could reach the apparatus myself. The process is…demeaning for the Scorpion Men. Asking them to kneel is cruel."

"I know. I didn't understand before, but I do now."

"Your kind adapt rapidly," she mused. "I have considered how Murkor would react if placed in the same…circumstance. I fear we would falter and lose our way. But humans do not. You lash out and grumble, but you *try*. You adapt, then begin to thrive."

"Hmm."

I frowned as I considered her words. While I agreed with portions, I didn't believe we were thriving. Based on my brief conversations with Camden, most of those sent to the mines were too exhausted to voice their opinions, though he'd related few were pleased with their situation. Others were tasked to carry water from the lake in the depths to the upper caverns, another grueling job that left our people weary and sore. Few were as fortunate as I was—and I doubted my luck would last once my arm was healed. Karmada may be smiling on me at present, but her mood would sour eventually. It always did.

"You disagree?" Aj'ana asked.

"We don't thrive, Aj'ana. We work for you because we've been given no other choice. As you've stated before, if I don't help you, I'll be sent away. It's a death sentence." I paused to brush crumbs out of my beard. "None of us have been allowed to bathe since we arrived. I'm aware how damned badly I reek at present. I need my hair cut, and I'd do nearly anything to be allowed to shave. We've been denied basic amenities. Perhaps we'd be more forthcoming, more willing to listen, and less prone to 'lashing out' if we were granted some of these things."

She was silent for a time, and I wondered if I'd spoken too rapidly, impassioned as I was. But it was true—my hair was too long, my beard was unkept and beginning to itch, and I smelled worse than a privy at high summer. Petric may have been working on the mining caste's leader to arrange for the same standards, but I believed it wouldn't hurt to press the issue with Aj'ana as well. The more voices that clamored for it, the more likely we'd be heard by those in power.

"I believe I understand *bathe*," she said. "You wish to wash? Clean?"

I laughed with relief. "Yes."

"The other things… I don't know words for them."

I shifted my remaining cake to my right hand and tugged at my hair with my left. "My hair is too long. It falls in my eyes. I'd like it shorter."

"Oh!" She nodded emphatically. "I see. My people don't have *hair*, but the Scorpion Men do. They ask for trimming? Is that the right word?"

"Yes. They had human ancestors. Their needs aren't so different from ours," I replied.

"But *shave*… What does that mean?"

I frowned as I realized I hadn't spied any of the Scorpion Men with facial hair. Perhaps they weren't capable of growing it, despite our common lineage?

I moved my hand to the side of my jaw. "Most human men either trim their beards or shave them off," I said slowly. "It becomes itchy after a while. It's uncomfortable."

She tilted her head thoughtfully. "How do you *shave*? What is needed?"

"At minimum, soap, water, and a razor. Or a sharp knife."

"The Kal won't give you knives," she replied, "but perhaps the same people who trim hair for the Scorpion Men can help with *beards*. I will ask."

I blinked, stunned that it may have been so simple. I should have asked sooner.

"You would do this for us?"

"Yes. It would have been offered when you arrived if we knew. But human needs are…foreign to us, sometimes. As I said, we don't have *hair*."

I grinned, delighted by the simple prospect of a bath and a shave. "Is it too much to hope you might arrange this tonight? I'll collect all the gods-damned venom you want in exchange, and without a single complaint."

"If it means you won't argue any longer, then yes," she replied with a laugh. "After we collect the venom, I will take you to the Kal. He may have questions I cannot answer about your people's needs." She withdrew a trio of flasks from the pouch at her belt. "But I must hold you to your promise first. Three flasks filled, and we have a deal."

The task of collecting venom wasn't as simple as I'd hoped. I struggled to remove the stoppers without the use of my right arm, but after several fumbling attempts, I managed. Placing the flask against the apparatus affixed to the first captive's tail went smoother; there were ridges molded into the flask that locked in place when twisted against the tail piece, and the collection began automatically.

The first captive was a woman, though she was as tall and heavily muscled as the men. She said nothing throughout the process and maintained a stern expression that I was certain was meant to intimidate me. It worked, though I'd never admit it aloud.

With the flask nearly filled, I removed it from the apparatus and turned toward Aj'ana. I wasn't certain I was capable of balancing the flask and replacing the stopper one-handed, and I didn't want to spill the venom. I wasn't concerned about its value to the Murkor; I feared what would happen if it splashed on my skin.

Self-preservation was a stronger motivation than pleasing Aj'ana.

She seemed to intuit what I needed before I opened my mouth to ask and beckoned me to move toward her. She stood a few paces away from the chained woman, who continued to glare menacingly at us both.

Fucking gods, I hoped I'd never be on the receiving end of her wrath. I suspected she was capable of crushing my skull between her hands without breaking a sweat.

"One finished," Aj'ana said as she pushed the stopper in place.

I risked a final glance at the woman as Aj'ana led me away. Her eyes remained hard, her expression steely. I sensed she was memorizing my face, storing it in her memory for later when I'd be forced to speak to my perceived crimes. I shuddered and increased my pace. There was no doubt I'd just made an enemy by assisting Aj'ana.

The second captive was a shorter man with meaty hands that marked him as a smith. He released a sigh and stared at the ceiling as we approached, his jaw set and his dark eyes unreadable.

"One flask wasn't enough for you?" he demanded of Aj'ana in Murkor.

"There are many wounded. We must make healing salves."

This time, she uncorked the flask for me, and I merely had to attach it to the man's tail.

"Does he realize Valri will never forgive him for helping you?" he asked as we waited. "She doesn't care if he's a prisoner."

I flicked a nervous glance toward Aj'ana, but could read nothing of her emotions from her posture.

"He understands our words, Travin," she replied coolly. "The humans have been made to work, but until he heals, he assists me. Your people understand why we collect the venom."

"It's fucking humiliating," he growled in common.

"I'm fully aware," I snapped. "I didn't want to do this, but the alternative was worse."

He fixed his gaze on Aj'ana. "What was the alternative, alchemist?"

"The tower." Though I couldn't see beneath her hood, I sensed she met his eyes unflinchingly.

"That's an unusually cruel punishment by your people's standards," Travin replied icily. "When my brother arrives—and I'm certain he will—he'll hear of this. He'll learn of your treatment of us, and of them. He'll know of your threats."

Aj'ana released an exasperated sigh. "You speak of your brother each time I visit you. He hasn't come."

"Not yet, but he will. You don't know the depth of Patak's stubbornness. Even the Warleader won't stop him."

"We'll see." She crossed her arms, then nodded to me. "Owen, it's nearly finished."

I moved to detach the flask. "For what it's worth, I hope your brother comes. I hope he'll free you."

"Owen…" Aj'ana said in a warning tone.

I handed her the flask with a scowl. "Fine. I won't speak to them."

"If the soldiers weren't nearby, I wouldn't care," she whispered as we moved away. "But they are watching. If one of them decides to inform the Kal—"

I held up my left hand in surrender. "I understand. We've been through this. It's just so gods-damned difficult to stand by and do this to them without saying *something*, Aj'ana. The guilt gnaws at me."

"You have a good heart, Owen."

I snorted. "It feels damned rotten right now."

"One more flask, and we're finished. Yes?" Her tone was compassionate.

I heaved a sigh. "Yes."

We repeated the uncomfortable ritual for the final time with a woman shackled near Thedrak. She seemed less hostile than the first, but as promised, I completed the task in silence. She spoke with Aj'ana briefly in Murkor while pointedly ignoring my presence. It was just as well; I wanted this portion of my evening finished without further complications.

With the final flask filled, we exited the prisoners' cavern. Aj'ana stowed the precious venom in her belt pouch, and I could hear the glass clink as we walked. I hoped I'd never be forced to go through this embarrassing ritual again—for the Scorpion Men's sake as well as my own.

"We'll visit the Kal now," Aj'ana said once we were away from the sentries. "You upheld your portion of the bargain. I will do the same."

I nodded but made no reply. I should have thanked her for her help in potentially securing basic amenities for my people, but after the distasteful role I'd been forced to play, I was unwilling to muster the words. I'd violated the Scorpion Men on a fundamental level and cursed myself for it. It didn't matter that I'd been blackmailed into the task—what I'd done was *wrong*.

Fucking gods, I craved a bath for more reasons than mere cleanliness. I needed to scrub the foul stench of betrayal from my skin.

I trudged alongside Aj'ana, lost in my thoughts. She offered me another honey cake, but I declined. I was no longer hungry, my appetite replaced with self-loathing. I was undeserving of the sweet pastry after the crime I'd just committed.

After a period of tense silence, Aj'ana expelled an exasperated sigh and muttered rapidly in Murkor, her tone low enough I couldn't make out her words through the fabric of her hood. I clenched my jaw as fury began to replace melancholy. Her frustration was misplaced—she should have focused her irritation on her people's practices, their need for the venom, or the Soulless for forcing them to acquire it in the first place. I wanted to lash out, to express my own dissatisfaction in a bloody haze, but it would serve no purpose.

And I'd feel even worse after a rage-fueled outburst. Gods-damn it, I needed to *hit* something.

Instead, I swallowed the bitter anger that threatened to consume me. I would never strike an unarmed person, and since I was no longer permitted the luxury of venting my pent-up fury in the practice yard or with a hopeful squire, I must learn to seek a different outlet.

I squeezed my eyes shut, focused on my breathing, on slowing my rapid heartbeat, and counted to ten. I went through the process again. Tension dissolved, rage dissipated, and an unexpected calm settled over my heart. I counted a third time. As my breathing slowed further, I relaxed. Rational thought returned, and I knew I could focus once more.

When I opened my eyes, Aj'ana stood several paces ahead, her hood fixed on my location. I'd stopped walking as I sought to control my temper.

"Owen?" her voice was uncertain, laced with fear.

I drew another even breath, then released it slowly. "I'm fine."

I walked toward her, but she remained still.

"I don't understand," she said after a few moments. "You were angry, and now…"

"I'm still angry," I replied, "but I'm calmer now. Let's visit your Kal."

"I should not have said what I did." Aj'ana crossed her arms and seemed to shrink into herself. "I am sorry, Owen."

I hadn't heard her muttered words, but I'd accept the apology. Her tone had told me enough. "Thank you."

I followed her in silence through another set of broad tunnels to an immense cavern, larger than any I'd been through previously. At one end was a set of broad steps leading up to a series of ornately carved columns. Beyond the columns were several openings sealed from the main cavern with the first true doors I'd seen since my arrival. Glowing crystals in a rainbow of hues were embedded in the cavern walls or suspended from the stalactites above. The overall appearance of the structure was one of significance to the Murkor people beyond my meager comprehension.

"Aj'ana, what is this place?" I breathed, unable to tear my eyes from the impressive sight.

"This is the Matriarch's dwelling. As her *ujar'havel*, the Kal lives here too." She swept her arm across the space. "On the summer solstice, our people gather here to witness the Choosing. We spoke of it once."

I nodded. Tens of thousands of people could fit inside the cavern with room to spare.

"Come," she said, beckoning for me to follow. "The Kal is not only the Matriarch's partner, but he is our people's spiritual leader as well. He was once an alchemist and still has many ties to our caste. I believe he will see us and will agree to your request."

"Why?" I asked. Her confidence in the outcome mystified me.

"You were not brought here for punishment, Owen. The commander bargained with the Soulless for your lives in exchange for labor. The Kal knows this. It is common knowledge amongst our people that he works with the commander for a favorable outcome—not just for the Murkor, but for all peoples affected by the Soulless' warmongering." She tilted her head and crossed her arms. "That includes *you*. But we know very little of humans, of your needs…" She trailed off with a shrug.

"And you believe if I explain them, the Kal will understand." I shook my head, baffled. "Why must the request go through him? Why not—?"

"You also do not understand *our* ways," she interrupted firmly. "All important matters must be presented to the Kal, who in turn will discuss them with the Matriarch. Without his approval, she will not hear of it, and without her approval, nothing will be done."

"I see." I chewed my lower lip in thought. "They are akin to the king and queen of my homeland."

"Perhaps. They govern and lead my people."

She led me to the base of the steps, then paused as a pair of red-clad Murkor appeared from behind the columns. Both carried multiple weapons.

"Stay here. I will state our business, and if the Kal has time—and interest—he will send for us." She turned to ascend the steps, but I reached forward and grasped her elbow.

"Will they attack, Aj'ana?" I whispered, nodding toward the duo in crimson.

"Not without cause," she replied. "They are the Matriarch's personal guards—and by proxy, the Kal's. Sit down and remain calm. They'll do nothing to harm you unless you give them reason. I won't be far away."

I dropped my hand and nodded, then seated myself on the lowest step to watch her interact with the guards. They spoke rapidly in Murkor, but from my position, I could not make out what was said. Aj'ana gestured impatiently, and after several moments, one of the guards nodded and sauntered away. He slipped through the doors and disappeared inside. Aj'ana remained at the top of the steps with the remaining guard, her arms crossed. Her posture exuded tension, which didn't bode well for our request.

I clenched my jaw and looked away, determined to place my trust in the alchemist's judgment. Even if my petition for a bath and a shave were denied, my circumstances couldn't get any worse—so long as I didn't give the Murkor reason to pack me off to the black tower. Interfering when I'd been forbidden would certainly have been reason enough, and I'd pressed my luck with Karmada's favor too much since my arrival at Stone Hill as it was. The goddess of fortune was likely growing weary of my constant pleas, which would only result in one outcome.

She'd exact her payment, and I'd find myself wishing I'd spent more time silently seeking another god's assistance. Karmada wasn't known for her mercy or her kindness.

I stared down at the sturdy gray boots I wore, a constant symbol of my position within the Murkor society. An outsider, casteless, easily forgotten. Why should the Kal, in his purported wisdom, waste his precious time or allocate resources for the betterment of someone like me? To him, I was a laborer, disposable once my tenure was complete. I wanted to believe Aj'ana when she claimed the Murkor simply didn't understand our needs and genuinely believed they'd saved our lives. But what if it was merely her optimism speaking? What if the Kal didn't feel the same?

I suppressed a groan and glowered at the stone beneath my boots. I'd gone this long without proper hygiene, and while I detested my own stench and the itching of my beard, neither would kill me. It was inconvenient, nothing more. I'd adapt, bide my time, and when the opportunity arose to break free of the Murkors' hold, I'd seize it without hesitation. There was nothing more I could do.

The scuff of boots on stone drew my attention. I looked up to find Aj'ana and another Murkor, clad in shimmering copper, descending toward my location. A quartet of crimson-clad guards flanked them.

I rose and dusted myself off, certain the figure in copper was someone of importance. A thick chain hung from their neck, and a curved saber was sheathed at their side, but it wasn't these items that drew my attention. This was the first Murkor I'd encountered wearing copper, a sign their rank was significant.

"Owen Greenwaters?"

The voice that issued from beneath the shimmering hood bore the telltale signs of age, yet was strong, confident, assured. I nodded once.

"I am Kal Aran'jandah. Aj'ana has related your request, and I would like to discuss it further." He paused to gesture at the guards. "They will search your person for potential weapons. If you pose no threat, we will speak privately."

I snuffed out the brief spark of anger that arose within my heart and nodded again. Rage would not serve me here. I understood if our roles were reversed, he would be forced to do the same before speaking with my king. It was simply a matter of course.

Aj'ana moved forward with two of the guards and assisted with the removal of my sling. My shoulder and elbow sent jagged bolts of pain through my arm, unused to movement without the sling's support.

I was inspected, prodded, and made to remove my boots before they were satisfied. One assisted Aj'ana with replacing the sling, while the other whispered to the Kal. As I sat down to tug my boots on once more, the Kal spoke.

"You are not considered a threat on this occasion. I will speak with you, as you've requested."

10

THE MURKOR PERSPECTIVE

The crimson-clad guards escorted me into the main structure behind the Kal. Aj'ana remained outside; the needs of the human prisoners were not truly her concern, but they *were* mine.

The room immediately inside the stone doors was an enormous dome with dozens of small, arched doorways ringing its perimeter. Suspended high above was the largest crystal I'd ever seen, glittering with a milky luminescence along every facet and elegant spine.

I paused to gape at the sight, only to be jabbed firmly in the back by one of the guards. Admiring the cavern's natural wonders was clearly not part of my brief tour of the Matriarch's compound. I bit back a growl and refocused on my escorts as they led me toward one of the arches.

Beyond the arch was a short corridor that ended in a curtained alcove. I was ushered inside by one of the guards, who remained at the entrance while the aged Kal seated himself on a padded bench. He gestured to the vacant bench across from him.

"Sit down, Owen. I don't like to conduct business on my feet unless I'm given no other choice," he said in flawless common.

I settled on the open bench and waited for his next words. I wasn't certain what the proper etiquette was when speaking to the Kal, and silence seemed the best option at present. I should have asked Aj'ana what was expected of me before we made the journey here, but I'd been preoccupied. Fucking gods, I hoped I wouldn't make matters worse in my ignorance.

"Aj'ana explained that we've overlooked several matters of basic decency in our treatment of your people." The Kal steepled his gnarled, blue fingers as he spoke. "Your discomfort was not our intention. Tell me what you require, and I'll consider your request."

I relayed what I'd said to Aj'ana in an even tone and managed to avoid lacing my words with the common profanities I often used. I didn't want to offend the Kal, and I sorely needed a bath, a shave, and a haircut. I needed to make a good impression, and if it meant acting the part of a more noble spirit, then I'd do my damnedest to excel.

The Kal was silent as I spoke, but nodded thoughtfully on occasion. When I finished, he leaned back, his hood tilted toward the ceiling as he contemplated my request and his subsequent actions. Finally, he released a sigh and looked in my direction.

"I will provide what you seek, but not without conditions."

I nodded; I'd expected this outcome. "I understand."

"Your people cannot be allowed to leave the caverns, nor can they be given items that may be used as weapons against the Murkor. I will arrange for a group of water-bearers to assist with the bathing, and I believe our shepherds are best suited to help with shaving." He paused and studied his hands. "I will allow these amenities under two conditions. First, your people will be taken individually under armed escort, then returned to their places immediately afterwards. Those who struggle or cause distress during the process will be detained and sent to the Soulless' tower."

"That's…fair," I replied, unable to mask my unease. "And your second condition?"

"I would like you to continue your assignment with Aj'ana after your arm is healed. She mentioned you have been teaching her to speak the common tongue, and she teaches you our language in return."

"Yes…"

"There is much my people can learn from yours, and much you can learn from us. I believe knowledge is a powerful gift, and I would not see it wasted."

"I don't understand."

What could the Kal possibly hope to learn from me, from *us*? The Murkor alchemists knew how to create things I'd believed only magic could conjure, their soldiers were as efficient and well-equipped as ours, and it was clear they'd devised the means to thrive in their subterranean world without need for the sun. The human world seemed primitive in comparison.

"I was once an alchemist," he replied with a chuckle. "After I was named Kal, I became something of a scholar. Your arrangement with Aj'ana is mutually beneficial. Through her, our people will learn to understand yours. Through you, the humans will learn to do the same. Perhaps you will never fully accept your place here, but I pray to the gods each night that this arrangement will be temporary. For the Murkors' sake, as well as your own."

I shifted uncomfortably in my seat. "I don't share your optimism."

"There are forces at work that I cannot speak of," he replied cryptically. "But know this: The Soulless will fall. It may take time—months, or perhaps years—but they will not prevail."

I looked away. I'd watched as one of the Soulless toppled the gate tower in Stone Hill without aid from the Murkor or any of his brethren. I'd been atop the gods-damned wall when he'd rent a hole in the stone, and I knew my limited experience had been less catastrophic than some of the survivors from Jennavere. They'd spoken of whole families cut down and exsanguinated by magic, their corpses left to rot in the streets, while others described earthquakes and fires that destroyed entire sectors within moments. Some of the captives from Stone Hill had mentioned the same—as well as the spectacle of the sea serpent shocked and tortured to death after it displeased one of its masters. I'd missed most of the devastation when I'd suffered the head injury.

"I've seen some of what they're capable of," I said in a low tone. "I've heard stories from the others that detail far worse than what I witnessed myself. How can you be so certain they'll fail?"

"There is much the Soulless do not know, though they believe otherwise. I'll say nothing more, lest my words find their way back to them."

I snorted. "They'll hear nothing from me."

"Nevertheless, it's a risk I will not take." He gestured to the silent guard in the doorway. "Mev'ranel will see you outside. I will speak with the Matriarch, but I know she will understand. The arrangements for your people will be made tonight."

I rose, then hesitated, uncertain if I should say anything in parting. I settled on a simple "Thank you."

He nodded once while the silent guardsmen shifted impatiently from his post at the door. I turned to follow him out the way we'd come, and a second guard accompanied us from the corridor. I was once more forbidden to pause in my trek and managed only a fleeting glimpse of the massive crystal suspended from the cavern's roof. I decided I'd ask Aj'ana more about it later.

She was pacing along the top step when we exited the compound. Mev'ranel relayed my conversation with the Kal to her in Murkor, clearly unaware I could understand his words. He said nothing offensive, but his tone indicated he was displeased by the Kal's decision.

"It isn't our place to judge the humans, nor is it proper to question the Kal," Aj'ana replied once he'd finished. "I'll return him to work."

Mev'ranel snorted. "If that's what he does for you. I suspect there is more between you than a mere prisoner and his captor, but the Kal has placed him in your charge indefinitely. It's *mesj*." He spun on his heel and marched back toward the compound.

Aj'ana clenched her fists and stiffened, visibly angered by the exchange. After a moment, she drew a shuddering breath and motioned for me to follow. She said nothing as we traversed the immense cavern, and I sensed she wouldn't appreciate my questions. I held my tongue.

We traveled through several winding passages before I began to recognize the stony landmarks that led to the alchemists' laboratories. The Murkor caverns were a veritable maze, and I didn't believe I'd ever learn to properly navigate them without a guide.

Aj'ana still hadn't spoken by the time we reached her workspace. She removed the flasks of venom from her belt pouch and arranged them carefully on the shelves, then silently began the task of heating the coals in the depression. Despite my situation, I'd come to understand her, to *like* her. It was clear the guard's parting words had hurt her deeply, but I wasn't certain what I should do.

"I need the cactus flower," she said without looking in my direction.

I located the jar amongst her collection and placed it on the workbench. "Are you alright?"

She forced a laugh. It was a hollow sound brimming with despair. "No. Mev'ranel has always been...what is the word?" She shook her head. "Envious. He has asked to partner with me more than once, but I...denied him. He accuses me—*us*—of a forbidden act. Murkor do not pair with other...species. He knows this, yet he falsely claims I have chosen you."

"Oh, fucking gods." I ran my free hand through my hair and barked a laugh. "And I thought he was merely pissed that I wasn't being sent to the mines with the others. I like you, Aj'ana, but not...romantically. It has never crossed my mind."

"I know." She took the jar of cactus flowers and wrenched the lid open more forcefully than necessary. "Mev'ranel has never trusted other men in my presence, not even my kin. He is...possessive. It's why I will never join him."

I'd encountered Mev'ranel's type before. Fueled by jealousy, prone to anger, swift to act with their fists or their blades. I was immediately concerned for Aj'ana's safety.

"Will he become a problem?"

She pushed away from the workbench and turned to face me. "What do you mean?"

"Will he try to hurt you? To force your hand?"

She looked down, and I wished I could see something of her face. It was impossible to know what she was thinking beneath her hood.

Finally, she drew a breath and looked up. "The Murkor people do not act in that manner, Owen. I am granted the freedom to make my own decisions, and any man I choose to partner with must defer. When I denied him the first time, he sought his mother's intervention. I spoke with her as an equal. When she repeated his request, I explained my reasoning, and the matter was done." She sighed. "He remains bitter, but he can do nothing but seek someone else's favor. He will not earn mine."

I frowned as I contemplated her response. I didn't fully understand the dynamic between Aj'ana and Mev'ranel—did his caste relegate him to a lower status than hers? Was Mev'ranel's mother a fellow alchemist? Or was it something else that determined power amongst the Murkor?

"You are confused," she said after a moment. "I see it in your expression."

"I..." I shook my head. I didn't know where to begin.

She removed a dried cactus flower from the jar and dropped it into her stone mortar while she awaited my response. I knew from experience her patience was limitless while she was at work in the laboratory, but she would not forget our conversation or where it had broken off.

"You said he must defer," I said slowly. "Why? Is it due to his caste?"

She chuckled softly, then turned to face me, her task momentarily paused. "I often forget human society does not follow the same rules as ours. He must defer because he is a *man*, Owen. If a woman denies him, his only option is to seek his mother's aid and hope she can convince the woman to change her mind. A man's path is dictated by the women in his life. It is simple."

"Oh." It wasn't the answer I'd been expecting, but so many of our interactions now made sense.

"You are Balotican, yes?" When I nodded, she said, "Your land sees all people as equals, but I am told it is to the detriment of decision-making. Too many voices seek to be heard while nothing is accomplished."

I frowned, uneasy with her assessment, though I knew she wasn't wrong. "I suppose that's true."

"My people believe women are better decision-makers," she went on. "Sons, brothers, fathers—all of them must defer to the women of their household for important matters. Unity is one such matter, as is the selection of a caste to work toward."

"And where does that leave someone like me?" I asked. "I'm a prisoner and a man."

"You are human," she replied with a laugh. "Our societal rules don't apply to you."

"That doesn't make sense."

She tilted her head to one side as she studied me. "It doesn't have to make sense. You are here to work, and each of your people are assigned a task based on their apparent aptitudes. If you hadn't been injured when you arrived, I suspect you'd have gone to the mines or been tasked to aid the water-bearers. What you do beyond your work is not my concern."

My frown deepened. "And what of the Kal?"

"He speaks for the Matriarch," she said with a dismissive wave of her hand. "The Matriarch's word is as law. She is old, frail… It is difficult for her to meet with everyone who seeks her wisdom."

"They must have spoken of my placement with you prior to our meeting today," I replied.

"Yes, it is likely they did."

"Why did they choose this for me, Aj'ana? I'm no scholar. I have no…aptitude for herbs or salves, or any of your work for that matter."

"What did the Kal say to you? I know only what Mev'ranel said."

"He said, 'There is much my people can learn from yours, and much you can learn from us.' He didn't want to see the knowledge wasted." I sighed. "I disagree. There is much *I* might learn from *you*, but I doubt you'll uncover anything from me that you don't already know."

"That is not true." She crossed her arms and faced me directly. "You have taught me to speak common. That is something, is it not? You have spoken of your homeland, the ways of your people. I learn new things from you each night."

"And what have you learned this night, Aj'ana?"

"The hair on your face itches and you don't like the way you currently smell. I don't either," she added with a mischievous laugh. "I've also learned you *care*, Owen. Your concern for my safety regarding Mev'ranel was unexpected, but appreciated."

"I've encountered his type before," I replied. "If he were human, he'd have tried to force himself on you by now. I won't stand for it. It's wrong."

"Ah, this is another thing. You have a keen understanding of what you believe is right or wrong. You act according to your beliefs."

"You've learned much about *me*," I conceded, "but I fail to see how knowing one man's mind is beneficial to the Murkor."

"We seek to understand your people in order to be better protectors," she replied. "We believe in empathy, in compassion, in preserving *life*. When faced with the Soulless, there is little else we can do but cling to hope and pray our actions will one day undermine their goals."

"I see."

Her perspective—the *Murkor* perspective—was in some ways not so different than my own. I'd organized the defenses in Stone Hill to protect its citizens, to spare as many lives from the Soulless' devastation as I was able. I'd become a knight to travel the kingdom and assist others when they required aid. I understood compassion and empathy. I understood the desire to protect and defend.

It was the first time since I'd arrived in the caverns that I began to truly understand the Murkor people. I wanted to learn more. I'd be better for it.

11

A GRIM WAGER

"Shit. What did they do to your face?"

I lifted my eyebrows at Camden's jibe. "This has always been my face, Cam."

He chuckled. "So it has. I've merely forgotten what it looked like beneath that scruff you called a beard."

I rubbed my jaw in response. The Murkor had been fearful of harming me when I'd asked for a shave and had refused to go too near my skin with a blade. I was left with short, scratchy stubble, but it was better than the unruly and greasy mass I'd sported before. They'd trimmed my hair as well; it was shorter than I would have preferred, but it would regrow in time. For the first time since I'd awakened a captive, I felt something akin to my usual self.

Camden had opted to keep his beard, though it had been trimmed significantly. His hair had been lengthy before our capture, and it appeared untouched by the Murkor.

"How the hell did you manage this, *Ser*?" he asked with a grin. "I thought Petric had finally made some headway with the mining caste's leader, but the Murkor claimed it was your doing."

I shrugged. "Let's call it my brand of magic."

He snorted. "Magic? If you're a wizard, then I'm the gods-damned king." He leaned against the cave wall and sighed contentedly. "However you did it, we're all in your debt. And because of it, we've been granted a day of rest as well. It's more than I'd hoped for."

"Likewise. But it's evening, Cam." I flashed a grin at his momentary confusion. "The Murkor are nocturnal."

"I still haven't learned how to tell night from day down here." He shook his head and pushed away from the wall. "Petric should have returned by now."

I nodded and rose from my seat on the floor. "It would be nice to speak with him again. It's been a few years, and when you mentioned his family, I—"

"I wouldn't bring it up today," Camden replied. "Tonight. Whatever the hell time it is."

"I understand. Grief strikes everyone differently."

Camden crossed his arms as we began to walk. "And what do you know of grief, Owen? You've no family in Balotica to mourn your disappearance, no children slain in the streets, no wife—"

"I've borne my share, Cam," I growled, cutting him off. "You don't know my past prior to my path to knighthood. Few do, and I'd rather keep it that way."

His gray eyes were hard, but after a moment, he relented. "Fine. I'll take you at your word. I suppose I owe you that much."

In the span of four months, I'd lost my father to an inexplicable accident in his forge and my mother to illness. I'd been fourteen, but the pain of their combined loss had never fully dissipated. Not long after, I joined the city guard of Crystal Isles and was assigned a grizzled veteran as my mentor. Selwin taught me to fight—and fight well, as my success in the melee could attest—but he passed of old age less than two years later. I was once again on my own.

I suspected this was why I'd never harbored the desire to settle down or start a family. Few things in this world lasted, and time was fleeting. I couldn't bear the thought of leaving a child to fend for themself as I'd been made to do. I became a knight, opted to travel rather than remain confined to a city, and visited the occasional brothel when the need for release overcame me. But there had never been a constant woman in my life, and given my current situation, I doubted there ever would be.

Camden knew none of my early history, and it wasn't a topic I'd willingly share with anyone. I'd worked for years to bury my grief. I didn't need a pointless conversation to rip the fragile wounds open anew. There were other, more pressing matters to contend with.

I followed Camden to a corner of the prisoners' cavern and an alcove closed off with a tattered blue curtain. Other humans milled about the space, some in conversation, others merely surveying our surroundings. Most appeared in good spirits, despite our status. It was a wonder how much a bath and basic grooming could improve one's mood.

Camden slapped the palm of his hand against the stone several times. A muffled voice answered his summons, and moments later, the curtain was pushed aside. Petric Stonewarden was not a tall man—he stood only chest-high compared to myself or Camden—but he was muscular, with biceps easily twice the diameter of mine. His hair was cut short and he sported a beard, trimmed in a similar fashion to Camden's. He nodded to Camden in greeting, then smiled as he saw me.

"Owen! By the gods, it has been too long. I'd heard from this scoundrel that you were here." He jabbed a thick finger at Camden, then motioned for us to follow him inside.

Petric's alcove was marginally larger than my own, but organized in the same utilitarian manner. It seemed the Murkor treated us all equally.

"Sit down. We've much to discuss." Petric seated himself on the thin sleeping mat, while Camden took up a position near the door. I sat equidistant between the pair.

"I asked Senna to join us," Camden stated after a moment. "I saw her as I was on my way to fetch him. She was...preoccupied."

Petric harrumphed. "I've no doubt I know the source of her 'preoccupation,' Cam. It's that Coldwater boy again. I can't bring myself to chastise her behavior, though. She's young, and we've all suffered since Jennavere was attacked. If she needs him for the diversion, then let it be."

"And what good would it do any of us if she finds herself with child?" Camden groused. "The Murkor will likely ensure her welfare, but a newborn is a liability we can't afford."

They both had valid points, but as the outsider in the conversation, I felt it wasn't my place to interject.

"If she fails to moderate her behavior, she'll be forced to live with the consequences." Petric shrugged and turned to face me. "That's enough about Senna. She'll join us if she chooses, and there's nothing more to be done about it. How are you faring, Owen? Cam mentioned you were hurt in the attack."

"I'm well enough. The Murkor reset my arm, and it's still not healed to their satisfaction—nor mine." I chuckled. "I've never excelled in sitting idly by. With only one arm to work with, I've been assigned to assist an alchemist."

"So I've heard." Petric leaned back, his hands splayed behind him. "I'd like—"

His words were cut short by a commotion outside. I pushed myself to standing and strode to the entrance, where Camden peered into the larger cavern beyond. Petric pushed between us a moment later to take in the scene.

A line of Murkor, some clad in red, others in black, filed through the cavern. I recognized the copper attire of the Kal at their head. The guards escorted all two dozen of the Scorpion Men between them, three Murkor to each one of the prisoners. The captives' hands remained bound, and the glass apparatuses were still affixed to their stingers, yet there was a gleam in their eyes and a determination to their steps that indicated they were being led to their freedom. When the Kal turned to follow the passage that would lead toward the bustling marketplace some distance away, it confirmed my theory.

"I'd heard rumors there were Scorpion Men held here," Petric breathed. "Gods, I didn't realize they were so tall."

"Which is why I was assigned to work with Aj'ana," I murmured. "The alchemists were harvesting venom, but she's a head shorter than you are."

Camden snorted a laugh. "And I thought you'd been gifted your work detail because you'd started to pick up their language. She only needed your gods-damned reach."

I jabbed him in the ribs with my good elbow and feigned indignation. "At least I'm good for something. I can't say the same for you."

"You wound me, Owen." Camden pressed one hand to his heart while Petric chuckled.

"It's good to see you haven't lost your sense of humor. Gods, do we need it," Petric said. "Some of us more than others."

My smile faltered, and I focused on the Scorpion Men as they marched to their freedom. Camden had warned me away from the subject of Petric's loss, but it didn't seem right to avoid it.

"Perhaps I'm only distracting myself from all that's happened," I replied somberly. "Rage didn't serve me years ago. It led me along a dark path, one I don't wish to return to."

Petric nodded in understanding. "Jannis mentioned you were a difficult squire, but she never spoke to me of your past."

I nodded once, grateful to Jannis—another mentor and friend I'd lost during the years—that she'd kept my history to herself. She'd been the one to introduce me to Petric after I was knighted, but by that time, she was aged and frail, though she stubbornly refused to retire. She knew her time was nearing its end, and she'd attempted to soften the blow with her own brand of wry humor. Gods, I missed that old woman at times.

She would have taken charge, organized our people, and seen to it their needs were met within days. It had taken me nearly three weeks to accomplish only one item on the list. I'd wasted too much energy on anger and pointless spats with Aj'ana before I understood it gained me nothing. Jannis would have remained calm and assertive, whereas I continued to struggle with my volatile temper. I lashed out and growled, cursed the gods for our collective misfortune, and wallowed in despair. She would have done none of those things.

Faced with her memory, I was forced to confront my failures. I should have sought the Kal sooner, should have spoken with Petric as soon as I learned he was alive, should have begun planning a course that would lead to our freedom. But I'd done nothing. I was a pale shadow of what she'd been, a disgrace to her legacy.

I drew a breath and resolved to do better. I was in a position to help the others, whereas Petric and Senna were often too busy to affect change. Their work in the mines left little time for conversation—and Senna was apparently too enamored with her current paramour to spare even a few moments to meet with us.

Internally, I relented. We all had personal demons to confront; perhaps hers were simply more visible than most. And Petric was right.

An escape from our dark reality, however brief, might be better for her morale than any alternative we might conjure.

Belatedly, I realized the Scorpion Men were gone, and the cavern outside had quieted. Petric had returned to his seat, Camden leaned against the wall, and both studied me with a measure of concern as I turned from the door.

"I should not have brought up Jannis," Petric said as I resumed my seat across from him.

I shook my head. "I needed to hear it. I haven't thought of her in years, and I'm worse for it."

"She was the embodiment of a true knight," Petric continued, a sad smile pulling at his lips. "Few will ever attain her level of compassion, her sense of duty, nor nurture her ability to take charge and say *precisely* what was needed for any situation she found herself in."

"She took me on after I won the melee without question," I replied. "Few of the other knights present that day would even look me in the gods-damned eye. I wasn't nobly born. I was beneath them. Worth less than the mud on their fucking boots."

"You proved them wrong, Owen," Petric said firmly. "You surpassed everyone's expectations, overcame your anger—or at the very least, learned to contain it—and excelled where few of the nobles your age did. And Jannis saw your potential. She wouldn't have allowed it to be wasted, despite your humble origins."

"I know." I looked up to meet his gaze. "It's past time I stopped praying for divine intervention or an errant stroke of luck. Of the three of us, I'm the only one in a position to *do* something. And I will."

"Which brings us to why we're here," Camden said with a smirk. "We need you to learn how to navigate the caverns. The alchemist seems willing to explain the Murkor culture to you. Why not seek information on a means of escape?"

"I'll learn what I can, but she's more guarded about certain topics than others," I warned. "And if the Murkor begin to suspect what I'm working toward, they'll chain us like they did the Scorpion Men."

Petric narrowed his eyes. "They were chained? Shackled?"

"Yes. One of them told me it wasn't because the Murkor feared them, but because they knew how to escape." I sighed and looked away.

I'd come to understand Aj'ana, I *liked* her, and I didn't want to jeopardize her position, nor her people's. I needed to be subtle when I sought information, and subtlety wasn't something I was particularly good at.

"I believe I understand," Petric said after a time. "A successful escape would land the Murkor in a more difficult situation with the Soulless. Their relations are fraught with tension as it is."

I nodded, relieved I wouldn't be forced to explain my concerns. "I don't believe they mean us any harm, and they're willing to accommodate our needs. Things could be worse."

"Are you suggesting we sit by while the fucking war unfolds above our heads?" Camden spluttered.

"We aren't sitting by," Petric replied evenly. "We're assisting the Murkor."

"And they're our gods-damned enemies!" Camden's fist struck the stone wall with a solid crack, eliciting a string of curses.

I waited until his litany subsided before I spoke again. "Cam, when I spoke with the Kal, he alluded to a plan to subvert the Soulless. Or perhaps to defy them, I'm not certain. His words were vague, and he refused to offer any details when I asked, but I don't believe the Murkor are truly our enemies."

He flexed his fingers and winced. The knuckles were red and beginning to swell. "Everything's gone to shit, hasn't it?" He slumped against the wall and would not look at either of us.

"I don't believe escape is feasible at present," Petric replied slowly, "but I believe learning to navigate the caverns will be beneficial when the time comes."

"I'll learn what I can," I promised.

"Good. In the meantime, take Cam to your alchemist. He's likely broken his hand." Petric shook his head, though amusement twinkled in his eyes. "We'll get through this, Cam. You have my word."

"And mine," I added as I rose to my feet.

Camden groaned as he pushed away from the wall, then shot me a smirk. "We're well on our way to Aeon's gates with you in charge."

I rolled my eyes in exasperation but was silently pleased he'd replaced frustration with dry humor. "I'll race you there. I'll wager I meet Aeon first."

"It's a bet, Owen."

12

THE DISPLACED BARKEEP

"You know I cannot tell you that, Owen." Aj'ana tilted her head and placed her hands on her slender hips as we paused in our journey. As I'd suspected, she would not reveal the secret to navigating the caverns easily.

I shrugged, then winced as my shoulder protested the movement. "It was worth trying."

"Have you performed your exercises tonight?" she demanded.

I shook my head. "When have I had time? You woke me this evening and demanded I follow you straightaway. As I recall, you claimed it was urgent business."

She crossed her arms, her stance unyielding. "You could have performed them after you returned to your alcove last morning."

I expelled a frustrated sigh. I'd been elated the night before when she'd deemed my arm healed enough to be rid of the sling, and I'd promised to perform the series of strengthening exercises she believed were necessary after weeks of inactivity. *Five weeks*, to be precise, not that I'd been counting.

During that time, my shoulder and elbow had become stiff and sore. I'd lost the range of motion I'd taken for granted throughout my life. Lifting my arm even halfway sent shockwaves of pain through my shoulder, and extending my arm caused my elbow to shriek in agony. Aj'ana believed I'd regain function in both joints given time and proper exercise. I hoped she was right.

"You can work through them after we reach the laboratory," she said. "I need to begin mixing healing salves soon. The army will be in need of them later this week."

She turned on her heel and began to march forward. I quickened my steps to catch up.

"What do you mean?" I asked. "Are they preparing to strike again?"

"That is the rumor."

"Rumor? Aj'ana, you *know*. You're a gods-damned alchemist."

She made a sound of frustration beneath her hood. "You are persistent today. I liked you better when you understood only half my words." Her tone was not unkind, but was laced with a grudging fondness I rather enjoyed.

I flashed a self-satisfied grin. "I think you like me more than you let on."

"Ugh. Fine, I will tell you." She paused to glance at our surroundings, but early as it was, there was no one nearby to overhear our conversation. "The army was driven away from Pine. They were met with greater resistance than they anticipated, and the Soulless were away on other business. The commander called a retreat. This was over two weeks ago."

"Before the Kal released the Scorpion Men?" I asked.

"Hmm, perhaps. It was near that time." She shrugged. "The army is now some distance south of Pine, in the mountains that mark the border between your kingdoms."

I frowned as I tried to recall my geography lessons from two decades past. Delucha was south of Balotica, but I was unable to remember the names of any cities along the border. There weren't many, but if the army had requested further supplies, I assumed they must have a target selected.

"They are nearing a city at the base of a fire mountain," she said. "The commander is concerned they will incur Flariel's wrath with the attack and has requested double the amount of salves."

"Daesan."

The word escaped my lips before I realized I'd spoken. It was the only city that fit her description. As the home of a venerated smith's guild and the source of much of the Five Kingdoms' steel, it was a strategic target. Without Daesan's forges, the Five Kingdoms would be hard-pressed to replenish damaged armor and weapons.

Petric needed to know this piece of information, though there was little either of us could do at present. Certainly, there was nothing we could do to stop the attack.

Fucking gods, I hated feeling so helpless.

"Perhaps. I do not know the city's name." Aj'ana shrugged. "It is likely more captives will be brought here as well. We have space for some, but you may be forced to share your quarters, Owen."

"I don't mind, so long as your people continue to allow us to bathe." I shot her a rueful grin in an attempt to mask my discomfort with the news of Daesan. "I don't know how you withstood *me* for as long as you did, and my work isn't as physical as some of the others'."

She laughed softly. "You *did* smell horribly. It was the true reason I brought you before the Kal."

I snorted. "And I believed you arranged the meeting out of the graciousness of your heart."

"You were wrong." She laughed again, then beckoned me to follow as we neared the entrance to her laboratory.

She bade me sit while she gathered implements on her workbench. "Exercise your arm. It will never regain its full function if you do not."

I sighed and began to work through the motions she'd shown me the previous night, a grimace plastered on my face as my joints protested. My shoulder was decidedly worse off than my elbow. I growled a string of curses, but persisted; I believed the activity would help, despite my present pain.

"Are you always so disagreeable when it comes to things that are *good* for you?" Aj'ana demanded after a time.

"I'm doing as you asked."

She crossed her arms with a shake of her hooded head. "Must all men be so difficult?"

I glowered at her. "I'm hardly a study of *all men*, Aj'ana."

"No, perhaps that was unfair. Are all *warrior* men so difficult?"

I rolled my eyes and straightened my arm as far as I could manage. I would not dignify her question with a response. She'd clearly formed her opinion and wouldn't be swayed, and I was in no mood for an argument. I hoped for both our sakes these damned exercises would prove worthwhile—and soon.

I'd vowed to myself I'd do better, that I'd stop wallowing in sorrow and accomplish something worthwhile despite my captivity. Two weeks and three days after speaking with Petric and Camden, I'd managed little more than a provocation of Aj'ana's temper. It was clear she wouldn't divulge the secret of navigating the caverns, no matter how subtle my probing. I'd anticipated the task would be difficult, but I hadn't counted on the sheer depth of her guile. I'd made no headway and had little to share with the older knight when we next met.

Petric arrived at my alcove alone and smacked the flat of his palm against the stone to announce his arrival. It was unnecessary; I'd left the curtain pushed aside in a gesture of welcome while I finished my evening meal. I waved him in, and he sat across from me as I cleared the last of the root vegetables from my tray.

"It's good to see you're healing," he said after a moment's silence.

I rolled my shoulder and managed to avoid wincing as a jolt of pain lanced down my arm. "The bones have healed well enough, but I doubt I'll be wielding a hammer any time soon."

He chuckled. "I'd forgotten you preferred those to a decent sword."

I shrugged. "My father was a smith, and war hammers are versatile. They suit me."

I pushed my empty tray to one side and leaned forward to rest my elbows on my knees as I faced him. "I'm afraid I don't have any information yet on our escape route."

He chuckled. "I didn't expect you would. The Murkor aren't very forthcoming, but that's not why I've come. There are rumors of an attack—"

"Daesan," I confirmed, cutting him off. "Aj'ana told me that much."

His face fell. "Truly? They've targeted Daesan?"

"Yes."

"By the gods." Petric released a heavy sigh and pushed himself to standing. "Walk with me, Owen. Your news has made me restless."

I rose and followed him out the door. The cavern beyond was a hive of activity as our fellow captives gathered in small groups to converse. A larger group clustered around a trio who tossed dice, placing whispered bets of their own on the results. I couldn't fathom what they were betting with—all our coin had been taken when the Murkor searched us—but perhaps it was merely the act of gambling they sought, the pretense of normalcy amidst the strangeness of our surroundings.

"Where's Cam?" I asked as I scanned the space.

Petric shrugged. "Perhaps he's found a diversion. By the gods, he needs one."

I nodded. "He lost his family at Stone Hill. I'm amazed he's kept himself together as well as he has."

"Yes, we've spoken. I lost mine as well. It has been…unimaginably difficult at times." He shook his head, his expression drawn with unspoken sorrow. "And now Daesan. How many other families will be destroyed in the Soulless' quest for blood?"

"I wish there was something we could do."

"There is." He paused to gesture at the other captives gathered in the cavern. "The Murkor will likely barter for the lives of those they believe they can save, just as they did previously. When those people are brought here, we must help them settle in, tend their wounds, assuage their fears as best we can. There is work to be done beyond the labors the Murkor have assigned."

I nodded. "I know, but—"

"There is nothing *we* can do about the battle, Owen. Even if we managed an escape, how many days would it take for us to reach Daesan? And how effective would we truly be without proper armor or weapons at our disposal?" He shook his head. "No, we don't even know where these caverns are located. We could be anywhere."

I looked away. His point was valid and brought a new wave of questions to my mind. Aj'ana may refuse to tell me how to navigate the caverns, but would she be averse to explaining our present location in relation to the Five Kingdoms? Perhaps not.

Petric was right. There were still tasks we could accomplish, no matter how far away from the fighting we presently were. And despite my desire to join in the defense of our lands, I'd be unable to wield a weapon in my right hand for some time.

"I feel so gods-damned *useless*," I growled after a time.

"You aren't alone in that," he replied evenly. "But seeking action when it will do nothing will not help our situation. We must gather what information we can, bide our time, and only when the right opportunity arises, make our move. We lack knowledge, but we have plenty of time to gain it."

"I'm not renowned for my patience." I crossed my arms and released a sigh. "If Jannis were here, she'd tell me now is the perfect opportunity to work on it."

He chuckled. "She wouldn't be wrong."

"I know."

We continued to walk, making a circuit around the cavern several times. We spoke of our lives before the Soulless' attack, our present situation, the people we'd met, and those we'd lost. It was at once mundane and therapeutic. I suspected Petric knew it was exactly what I needed in order to carry on.

We were nearing the end of our fourth circuit—or perhaps it was the fifth—when the sound of raised voices drifted toward us from the passage I believed led toward the surface. We paused in our walk to listen.

We weren't the only ones to take notice of the commotion. The cavern gradually fell silent as human faces turned toward the tunnel's shadowed exit. The black-clad Murkor assigned to oversee our activity moved away from the rock walls and toward the sounds, blue hands grasping hilts as they crossed the space.

I met Petric's gaze, certain I knew the origin of the noise. "More prisoners."

He nodded once, his expression guarded. "Undoubtedly."

Several guards conversed nearby, though they were too distant for me to make out their words. Moments later, one broke away and began to clap his hands above his head for attention. The quiet that had descended over the cavern deepened as we awaited his words.

"Return to your quarters," he ordered, his tone gruff and unyielding. "After we've finished our task, you may return to your present activities."

Petric gripped my elbow briefly. "We'll speak again later."

I nodded and turned away to retrace my steps to the alcove I'd begun to think of as mine. My thoughts were troubled, muddled by the Murkor's unusual command. I recalled little of my own journey to this cavern and didn't know if they'd done the same to Petric's group of survivors when mine had arrived. I'd been in significant pain, fighting to remain conscious, blind and blindfolded… My senses had been focused on the simple act of pressing forward, and I remembered nothing but obeying the soft-spoken commands of my Murkor escort as I was led to my alcove.

I ducked inside my space and noted the breakfast tray—or was it a supper tray, since it was evening?—had been cleared away. I wasn't certain if the Murkor had a term for the first meal of the night. It wasn't a topic I'd discussed with Aj'ana.

I settled on my mat and lay back to study the dimly lit ceiling and its now-familiar pattern of stalactites, my left hand supporting the back of my head. While I waited, I began to move through the series of exercises that would one day restore my shoulder to its former state. I ground my teeth through the pain as I attempted to lift my arm above my head and succeeded in reaching the halfway mark.

I groaned and repeated the motion. My progress was agonizingly slow, but at least the bone had reknitted in the proper configuration. It was a small victory in the otherwise tedious blur of my present existence.

Some time later, the curtains at the entrance rustled. I pushed myself into a sitting position as a dark-haired woman was led inside, a sleeping mat cradled in her arms. She wore unadorned gray garments, as all Murkor captives did, and her hair was loose, falling in tangled waves below her shoulders. Her black-clad escort said nothing as she trudged inside, and he promptly disappeared.

I studied her as she unrolled her mat a few paces away from mine. She wasn't tall, but she appeared strong and self-assured. Bruises marred her pale skin, and a thin laceration arced across her brow. She sat cross-legged on the mat and turned to face me, her deep blue eyes unreadable as she scanned my features. I believed she was close to my age, though I couldn't be certain.

I knew I should say something to break the silence, but my voice eluded me. What did one say when meeting a beautiful woman for the first time under such circumstances? Fucking gods, had I just acknowledged I thought her beautiful? Yes, I had. And the words that had been attempting to coalesce into a proper introduction evaporated as soon as I made the realization.

I averted my gaze as heat flooded my cheeks. It had been two days since my last shave; I prayed the stubble on my face would hide the reaction. Gods-damn it, I'd rarely found myself so tongue-tied.

"The soldier said I was to bunk here," she said after a time. "I hope it's not an inconvenience."

I shook my head and forced myself to meet her eyes. "Not at all. We're both prisoners."

"You're Balotican, by that accent. From the Crystal Isle, if I'm not mistaken."

I blinked. "I… Yes. Not many would have picked up on that."

She laughed, though the sound was hollow. "I've an ear for such things, and I've met my share of Baloticans." She extended a hand toward me, and when I shook it, she said, "I'm Tessamir Lontess. Barkeep by trade. Former proprietor of The Smith's Hammer, the finest tavern in all of Daesan. Or it was, before those gods-damned hooded bastards burned it to fucking cinders."

"Owen Greenwaters," I replied. "Knight…Or I was. My name has likely found its way onto the damned death registry by now."

"And what do our captors have *you* doing for them, former Ser-Knight?" she mused, her tone mischievous.

"I'm assigned to an alchemist," I replied with a shrug. "Most of the time, I'm ordered to reach things for her."

Tessamir laughed, a carefree sound unlike any I'd heard since my arrival in the caverns. "Truly? A waste of obvious talent, that."

I lifted an eyebrow. "I'm afraid I don't know what talent you speak of."

"Oh, I think you do." She flashed a knowing grin, and I felt my blush deepen. "According to the guard who dumped me here, I'm to work with the alchemists as well. Our hooded overlords seem to believe my tavern duties have made me uniquely qualified for the post."

I shrugged. "Perhaps. I've watched Aj'ana mix various concoctions, but I'm not allowed to interfere. As I said, I reach things… She's not very tall."

Tessamir laughed again. "Tell me, Owen: How did you come to be here?"

"It's a long story, Tessamir."

"Call me Tess. And we have all night."

I smiled. Despite my initial failure to speak, she'd set me at ease. I was certainly enjoying the conversation since I'd found my voice, and like Camden, I could use a diversion.

And gods-damn it, she *was* beautiful.

"That we do, Tess. That we do."

13

HISTORIES

I was on my feet the instant Petric arrived in my doorway, a bloodied and bruised Camden leaning heavily on his arm. Camden's right eye was nearly swollen shut, his lower lip was split, and he appeared to have a tenuous hold on consciousness.

"Shit. What happened?"

Camden grunted while Petric shot him a scowl. Tessamir remained seated, her eyes riveted on the pair. I'd finished reciting my story only moments before; she'd proven a rapt listener prior to our interruption.

"This lout thought it was a brilliant idea to attempt an escape while the Murkor were busy with Daesan's captives." Petric narrowed his eyes, irritation and disdain warring across his features. "The Murkor were forced to subdue him. Armistral must have stayed their hands, else he'd have been dead."

I raked a hand through my hair. "Gods-damn it, Cam. We had an agreement."

He eyed me sullenly. "Your plan was to sit here and do nothing while our lands burn. I never fucking agreed to it." His words were slurred and indistinct.

I clenched my jaw but swallowed the litany of curses I wanted to spew at him. Camden was the last person I would have anticipated trying to take matters into his own hands. The vengeful portion of my mind hoped the thrashing he'd received at the hands of our guards would be a deterrent for the others.

"I may not know what the three of you agreed on," Tessamir cut in as she rose gracefully to her feet, "but I've met my share of disagreeable and gods-damned stubborn men. You, sir, fit that description more aptly than most, and you're making an ass of yourself at present. Perhaps you ought to return to your little cave and sleep off the beating you've taken."

Petric's eyebrows rose at her words, while Camden sneered. "And who are you to tell me what I ought to be doing, woman?"

Tessamir bristled. Her hand lashed out before either man could react. Her fist connected solidly with Camden's jaw, and his lip began bleeding anew.

"Perhaps the hooded ones were justified in their treatment of you," she said, a dangerous undercurrent in her tone. "I hope for your sake your mind is addled and you didn't treat your family in this manner, for if I learn otherwise, your escape plans will be the least of your gods-damned worries."

Camden's eyes widened but seemed to clear. He muttered a half-hearted apology and pushed away from Petric, intent on fleeing the scene of his latest confrontation. I shook my head, unable to hide my exasperation with his behavior.

"I'll make certain he reaches his mat," Petric said quietly before he darted out the door.

Tessamir massaged her right hand as the pair departed. "I hope he doesn't suffer any lasting damage, the bastard."

"Cam hasn't handled his grief well," I muttered. "You may have saved us further trouble with that right hook of yours. Will you be alright?"

She laughed softly. "He's not the first unreasonable man I've been forced to set straight. I was a barkeep, if you recall."

"You didn't answer my question," I said evenly. "Are you hurt?"

She smiled faintly and continued to massage her knuckles. "I'll be fine. It's your friend you should be concerned for." She returned to her mat and sat cross-legged, her eyes fixed on mine. "I believe you were going to tell me what I should expect from the alchemist tomorrow night."

I was too restless to resume sitting; instead, I paced the short distance between my mat and the entrance to our alcove as I began to speak. "It likely depends on which alchemist you've been assigned to. Aj'ana often makes salves and poultices for healing, but I've heard others often work on more dangerous tasks."

"I'm familiar with their exploding devices," she replied with a frown. "They used them to breach the walls of Daesan. There was little we could do to stop them."

"At Stone Hill, one of the Soulless did the same, but with magic." I shook my head, recalling the frantic moments I'd spent trying to escape the gate tower, only to be tossed from the wall seconds later. "Were they present at Daesan?"

"I don't believe so, or fewer of our number would have survived. We heard rumors of what they did at Jennavere, but nothing was ever confirmed."

"I can confirm your rumors," Petric said from the doorway, startling me and causing Tessamir to twist in her seat. "Jennavere was razed, her buildings toppled and burned, her citizens slaughtered by the hundreds, her docks destroyed by that beast in the lake. Very few survived, and those who did owe their lives to our present captors."

I lifted an eyebrow in question, my thoughts on Camden. Petric shook his head subtly, unwilling to discuss our mutual friend's condition at present.

"The Murkor spared you?" Tessamir asked.

"Yes. They did the same at Stone Hill," he replied. "The Soulless would have killed everyone without their intervention."

She rose to her feet and offered her hand. "We weren't properly introduced. Tessamir Lontess."

"Petric Stonewarden."

They shook, and she stepped back to assess him with a smirk. "Petric sounds a bit pretentious. And your bearing... Another knight, if I'm not mistaken. Might I call you Ric?"

Petric's face turned several shades of crimson as he spluttered for a response. "I prefer Petric, thank you. And yes, I'm a knight."

She shifted her gaze to meet mine. "Your friend is the true embodiment of what I'd always envisioned a knight to be. Strong, intelligent, and too damned proper for his own good." She turned back to Petric. "You've never been in a real tavern, have you, Ric?"

I stifled my laughter with a feigned cough. Tessamir would not be deterred, and she was clearly enjoying his reaction to her teasing. As was I.

"Proper tavern? Why would you ask that?"

She flashed a grin. "I'm a barkeep by trade. It's rare to see your sort in my establishment, though I suspect *he*—" she jerked a thumb in my direction, "—wouldn't be averse to its unique ambiance."

Petric cleared his throat uncomfortably. "I suspect not. Owen isn't a typical knight."

"I'm aware. It's refreshing."

Heat rose into my cheeks for at least the fifth time since her arrival. Fucking gods, I didn't know how to react to her brash personality or her less-than-subtle insinuations. Was this her bizarre method of dealing with grief, or was she always like this? I'd rarely been reduced to helplessness, unable to form coherent speech simply from another's presence. Yet I could do nothing but stare at my boots and blush like an adolescent faced with the prospect of his first kiss. Gods-damn it, I was too old to react like this.

Tessamir's effect on me wasn't lost on Petric, and he released a hearty laugh. "I assume your presence here means you've been assigned to bunk with Owen?"

"I have," she replied. "It could be worse, all things considered."

I risked a glance in her direction. Her eyes were fixed on mine while a knowing smile played at her lips. Despite her bruises from the recent battle, she was captivating. With a start, I realized I'd been staring and forced myself to focus on Petric.

"How's…" My voice cracked, and I cleared my throat. "How's Cam?"

"You ought to work on your recovery, my friend." Petric shared a laugh with Tessamir at my expense.

I grimaced and felt my face flush further, though I didn't truly mind. Perhaps she was worth enduring a few jibes? I certainly couldn't keep my eyes away from her for long, and Petric knew it. I stared pointedly at him instead.

"Cam's most severe injury was to his pride," he went on. "The rest are superficial, with the exception of the barkeep's punch. He lost a tooth, but he'll be fine."

"Will he do as we've agreed from here on?" I asked.

The older knight shrugged. "I hope so, but I can't be certain." He flicked an amused glance between Tessamir and myself. "We'll speak later. I believe the two of you were in the midst of an important discussion before I interrupted."

"No, I—" He was gone before I could finish the sentence.

I looked down and groaned. They must have both thought me a gods-damned fool. Perhaps I was.

"I believe I owe you an apology," Tessamir said softly after a moment. "I meant no harm by what I said, but your reaction was irresistible. I've been told on numerous occasions that I'm a shameless flirt, even when circumstances shouldn't permit it."

I forced a nod, though another wave of heat rose into my cheeks. Fucking gods, was there no end to my reactions? It had been *years* since I'd last been affected by a woman's presence in this manner, and I couldn't fathom what made Tessamir Lontess different. It was humiliating, yet strangely enjoyable.

Gods-damn it, I didn't have time for this. Not now.

I cleared my throat and forced myself to look at her, to peer into those midnight blue eyes. "They weren't wrong."

"But?" she pressed.

I released an explosive sigh. "But there are other matters I need to focus on, and you're…" I gestured helplessly at her. "Shit, I don't know."

She arched her dark eyebrows. "I think you do. Why don't we try a different path? You've shared your story, now I'll share mine. We have a few hours before dawn, do we not?"

"We do," I replied hesitantly.

She grinned and resumed her seat. "Very well. Sit down, and I'll share my tale, as the traveling bards so often say."

She shared her story, and I listened. There was nothing more between us that night, though each moment I spent in her presence addled my brain even further. She was stunning. Intoxicating. Witty and confident…

And the distraction I definitely did not need.

I was helpless against her innate charms—and she knew it. I didn't doubt she'd exploit it at every opportunity. A large part of me didn't fucking care, but the other part, the one that had shunned entanglements for more than two decades, shouted in warning. Rather than give in to either, I focused on her story alone.

Lontess wasn't her birth name; she'd been married twice. Once to a smith, who helped her establish her tavern, and then to a merchant with a penchant for gambling. The smith had collapsed one day at Daesan's famed forges and never awakened. She'd been widowed at twenty-two, childless, and the sole heir to the smith's considerable assets. Her newfound wealth had attracted the merchant, who she kicked to the curb when she learned he'd wasted a small fortune on card games. Their marriage was annulled three months after they'd wed.

Lontess had been the smith's surname, though she never mentioned his first name. The merchant she referred to only as "the thieving bastard."

She spent the next decade as her own woman, tending the bar of The Smith's Hammer and befriending Daesan's working class. She'd been polishing glasses when the Murkor attacked, but rather than hide or flee, she'd collected the stout club she kept as protection and took to the streets to defend her establishment. She'd been subdued not long after by the invaders.

"And then I was led here." She leaned back, stretching her arms behind her. "Compared to your tale, mine is relatively boring."

I snorted. "My life as a knight wasn't terribly eventful before Stone Hill."

"You don't consider the melee 'eventful?'" she asked.

I shrugged and winced as my right shoulder protested. "It was more than twenty years ago, Tess. It's old history."

She tilted her chin to gaze thoughtfully at the ceiling. "Based on your story, that would place you in the latter half of your thirties."

"And?"

"Most men your age have families—or, at the very least, a steady partner."

I hadn't spoken of my past prior to the melee, and I didn't plan to.

"Perhaps I haven't met the right person."

Her laughter filled the alcove. "If that's your attempt at flattery, it's a poor one. I've heard that line before."

I groaned and shook my head, flustered. "No. That wasn't what I meant—"

She interrupted me with another peal of laughter. "I know, but I couldn't resist."

"Fucking gods…" I swore under my breath and looked away. Why did *she* have this effect on me, when so many others didn't?

I was spared further torment by a Murkor in brown, who entered the alcove bearing a large tray laden with an assortment of roasted root vegetables and mushrooms. On one side were a quartet of small, golden honey cakes, and on the other, two flagons of water. The Murkor placed the tray on the ground between us and silently backed out of the room.

Tessamir lifted her eyebrows in question. "If we ever manage to free ourselves, perhaps I ought to hire some of them to wait tables when I rebuild the tavern." She leaned over the tray and poked a finger into a bit of mushroom. "What is this?"

I chuckled. "We're served vegetables most of the time. And that is a mushroom." I picked up one of the cakes and flashed a grin. "These we don't see often, but they're delicious."

"No meat?"

I shook my head. "We're served fish on occasion. There's a lake somewhere in the depths, but that's the closest I've seen since coming here."

She frowned at the flagons. "And clearly, no ale."

"I'm not certain the Murkor drink anything but water," I replied.

She popped a chunk of mushroom into her mouth and gazed thoughtfully at the tray. "Perhaps I can convince the alchemists to allow me to brew something. I'll be the first human to introduce them to ale."

"I think most of us would be grateful for a pint or two now and again." I sank my teeth into the cake and closed my eyes, relishing the sweet flavor. It wasn't as fresh or as delectable as those Aj'ana sometimes shared, but it was a close proximity.

"Damn, I'd best try the cake," Tessamir said. "Based on your expression, they must be divine."

"They're good."

She snickered. "I can't believe I'm jealous of a pastry. Causing you to blush is well and good, but that smile of yours is heart-stopping."

I opened my eyes, abruptly and acutely aware of my inadequacies. She'd admitted to being a shameless flirt, but her tone hadn't been teasing. She'd *meant* it. My expression tightened and I looked away.

"Owen?"

I shook my head. "While you were listening to my story, did you wonder why I never settled down? Why I chose to travel in service to the king, rather than tie myself to one location?"

"I'll admit I've been curious," she said slowly, "but I didn't want to pry."

"I've lost too many people in my life, Tess. It's my way of avoiding another cycle of grief." I released a breath and stared at the tray between us, avoiding her gaze. "When I say it aloud, it sounds gods-damned selfish, doesn't it?"

Rather than agree, chide me for my choices, or deny my words, Tessamir reached over the tray and placed one of her hands atop mine.

"Did you ever wonder why I didn't remarry after I rid myself of the thieving bastard?" she asked. "For the same reason. Love can be wonderful while it lasts, but the ending is always painful. I didn't believe I'd ever meet someone who fully understood."

I looked up to find compassion in her gaze. Her previous teasing demeanor was gone, replaced by a woman as grief-stricken and lonely as I'd been, yet one whose determination and spirit had driven her to persevere. I'd recognized something of my own pain in her, though I'd been unaware of it until now.

"Tess…"

She squeezed my hand once and rocked back on her heels, pulling away. "I think we understand one another, Owen. We both require time, space… But I hope you don't mind me teasing you now and again."

I smiled and picked up another cake. "I'm not certain you can resist."

She laughed, a bright, joyous sound. "I can't, and I won't."

14

AN IMPOSSIBLE TASK

"Where's your girl?"

I suppressed a snarl and turned to face Camden as he filed in line behind me. It had been six weeks since the prisoners from Daesan arrived, and while Tessamir and I had come to an understanding, she was not "mine" by any definition of the word. We spoke often—a side-effect of being assigned to the same sleeping quarters—and I still fumbled my words on occasion when she began to tease, but there was no romance between us.

"We've been over this," I growled. "More times than I can count. Her name is Tess, she's not *mine,* and she doesn't need to queue up for a shave like we do."

Camden smirked. "Your defensiveness says otherwise, Owen."

I rolled my eyes and turned away. "Since you won't leave me be, she's with Rej'vennar."

He snorted. "Why? It's our day of freedom."

"She's trying to brew ale."

I didn't understand the details, though she'd attempted to explain them to me several times. She'd convinced Rej'vennar the fermentation process wouldn't disrupt his laboratory space and that we'd all benefit from her labors if they proved successful. Rej'vennar had been skeptical at first, but he'd relented a few days prior. Tessamir claimed it was due to her feminine charms, though I suspected he'd simply become exhausted and overwhelmed by her persistence.

I'd learned that when she set her mind to a task, she'd push forward until she achieved what she'd set out to do. She was a force of nature, and I'd become caught in the whirlwind.

I didn't mind. She was attractive and intelligent. I *liked* her, and she understood me in a way few others did.

"And she adds yet another temptation to my growing list of things I must avoid," Camden said with a sigh.

I glanced over my shoulder to look at him sharply. "You abstain?"

He shook his head. "Not typically, but given my history with the Murkor, it's best if I keep my wits about me. Alcohol will only fuel my desire to attempt another escape, which will piss Petric off to no end. He hasn't forgiven me for the first time." He shrugged. "It's best if I keep away from your girl's project."

"Fucking gods, Cam, she isn't *my* anything."

My temper flared, and I was tempted to unleash it. He'd been provoking me, prodding me since his tumultuous first encounter with Tessamir. He didn't understand my hesitation, didn't know my past, and certainly hadn't taken the time to learn hers.

If we survived to see the end of the Soulless' war, perhaps I'd act upon my suppressed desires, but now wasn't the time. I was unwilling to give my heart to someone who I might lose in an eye-blink if one or both of us angered our captors, and I knew she felt the same. It was simpler to wrangle grief if there was no foundation for it.

Camden could march his ass straight to Aeon's hells if he continued to press me. Perhaps I'd even send him there myself.

The line moved forward, and I stalked away from him, fuming. Our friendship had been strained since his escape attempt, and my patience was at its limit. I was finished with his goading. For his sake, I hoped he sensed the dangerous undercurrent stirring just beneath my exterior.

He growled something under his breath that I couldn't hear but maintained his distance. It was the wisest course of action; I was on the brink of losing control. Another word, another snide comment, and there would be blood.

The line rounded a bend in the tunnel. I was abruptly faced with a pair of black-clad Murkor bearing an array of weapons. Both stood resolutely across the path, their arms crossed and hoods focused on the string of captives behind me. Their presence wasn't unexpected—there were always guards blocking access to the chamber where we were allowed to bathe and groom—but in my anger, I'd failed to realize how far I'd traveled.

I was made to wait until another of the captives exited before they allowed me to enter. I strode forward, glad to place more distance between myself and Camden. Perhaps my rage would be quelled before I was forced to speak with him again.

A Murkor clad in dark blue ushered me toward an alcove in the cavern wall, not unlike my sleeping quarters. I'd been through the process numerous times now and wasn't surprised when I was greeted by another trio of similarly garbed Murkor inside. A stone tub sat in the center of the space, the water steaming faintly in the dim light.

I grinned. I'd arrived early enough that the water was still warm. I'd endured several ice-cold baths during the intervening weeks—this was an unexpected treat.

The Murkor spoke amongst themselves as I disrobed and climbed inside. One thrust a chunk of grainy soap into my hands while another offered me a soft cloth. I scrubbed hurriedly, despite my desire to languish in the warm water for a time. There were many others in line outside, and the Murkor wouldn't permit me to waste their time as I idled.

"A trim?" one of the trio asked as I finished and rose to accept an offered towel. The cloth was worn and rough but was sufficient to dry my skin.

"And a shave," I replied as I pulled my trousers on.

"No shaves today," another replied in Murkor. I recognized his voice from previous visits, though I'd never learned his name.

"Why?" I asked, pausing to peer at him, my gray shirt in hand.

"The craftsmen have been called away. The army returns to the tower." He shrugged. "No one present dares to wield a knife so near your skin."

I heaved a sigh as I tugged the shirt over my head. "If you'd allow us to do it ourselves, it would solve a number of problems."

He shook his head with a chuckle. "You say this each time. My answer does not change."

"I'm told I can be persistent." I managed a weary smile as he gestured toward another Murkor with a pair of sharp, but blunt-tipped knives.

"Persistence is good sometimes. But not this time."

I grunted and strode toward his companion, who bade me sit on a low wooden stool. "Why did the army return?" I asked as she began to trim my hair with slow, measured strokes of her knives.

"They attacked a great city and were repelled. There were wizards, or so I hear," she said softly in Murkor. "There were many injured on both sides. That is all I know."

"Which city?" I pressed.

She paused in her work and stepped around the stool to face me. "I do not know, and it is not your place to pry."

I returned to the main prisoners' cavern alone. I hadn't seen Camden since we parted ways at the bathing chamber, and I hadn't waited for him after I'd finished. I needed time without his pointed brand of antagonism.

I sought Petric when I returned, but he was absent. Tessamir hadn't returned from her ale experiment, and I doubted she would until dawn was near. I scowled and began to pace, making a circuit between my quarters and Petric's.

Others clustered throughout the cavern, some engaged in dice games, others in conversation under the hooded gazes of our captors. A few gathered in one corner with a pile of small, polished rocks divided between them, engaged in a game akin to marbles. Others remained ensconced within their sleeping quarters, napping perhaps, though I suspected more than a few sought private moments with fellow captives.

The days of rest occurred once every two weeks. While they bolstered morale, some people were easily bored. I studied a group near the center of the cavern who seemed more boisterous than the rest. They were young men, most still adolescents, and several shot glares at passersby. They exuded an aura of danger that we couldn't afford, but unless they acted out, I'd leave them be.

I didn't want to fight *them*, even though Camden had left me itching to bloody my knuckles. I'd reserve my rage for him. Perhaps then, he would realize he'd pushed me too far. Grief-induced or not, I was done with his jibes.

"Owen."

I stopped mid-stride and turned. "Petric. I've been waiting for your return."

"No doubt. I've likely heard the same news you have." He motioned for me to follow him across the cavern. "We'll use your quarters. Evorin wanted some time alone with his wife."

I nodded. "Tess is with Rej'vennar. We shouldn't be disturbed."

"And Camden?"

I growled low in my throat. "He's not with me."

Petric expelled a weary sigh. "You've both been acting like bored teenagers. He uses grief as an excuse, whereas you… I'm not certain why your temper has been unstable of late, but I wish to the gods you'd both move past whatever obstacle has grown between you and act your age."

I narrowed my eyes. "Tell him to keep his gods-damned thoughts to himself, and maybe I can be reasonable."

Petric looked toward the ceiling, exasperation written clearly across his features. "This isn't about you or him. It's about Tess."

"He—"

"I don't have the patience nor the desire to listen to excuses, Owen. You're a knight. Act the part." He shook his head, disappointed. "And I'll speak with Cam."

Chastised, I fell silent. I didn't want to argue with Petric. He was one of the few people I could count on, and like it or not, I needed the stability he represented.

We entered the alcove I shared with Tess and closed the curtain for the illusion of privacy. I leaned against the rough wall near my sleeping mat while Petric remained near the entrance. He glanced at the curtain a second time before he began to speak, as though concerned someone might decide to eavesdrop on our conversation.

"Tell me what you've learned," he said as he leaned back and crossed one ankle over the other.

I relayed what the Murkor woman had told me and hoped he knew more.

"I know the name of the city that was attacked," Petric said after a moment. "While it doesn't help our present situation, knowing the Soulless' army was repelled gives me hope. They attempted to take Delucha."

"The capitol?" I asked, stunned.

An attack on Delucha's capitol had been a bold move, though I wasn't surprised it had failed. The Soulless had razed Daesan, but we'd received no news of other attacks, which meant the bulk of the kingdom's defenders should have been present in the city at her heart. The news that the wizards had finally joined in the defense of our homeland was a relief as well. Perhaps the Soulless truly could be stopped.

Petric nodded. "It seems both sides took heavy losses, though I can't be certain the Murkor aren't skewing the numbers in their favor. Even so, they've been recalled to the tower." He frowned as a troubled expression crossed his face. "I've learned where we are in relation to the tower, Owen. It's… We're much nearer than I believed possible."

I peered at him sharply. "How far?"

"We're within a day's easy march."

Ice shot through my veins at the news. "Shit. Then Aj'ana's threats—"

"They were not baseless," he confirmed. "If any of us stirs unrest and the Murkor come to see us as troublesome, they can and likely *will* deliver us to the Soulless."

I slumped and slid along the wall to a seated position, then raked a hand through my hair. "*Shit.*"

"Indeed. Which is why I—*we*—cannot afford a petty spat between you and Camden to explode into violence. Reconcile with him, Owen. Set aside your anger and *think*. We must find a way to escape, and sooner rather than later."

"I've yet to learn how to navigate these gods-damned caverns. Aj'ana won't speak of it, and since I asked, she's refused to escort me anywhere beyond the alchemists' laboratories." I released a wordless snarl of frustration. "I don't know what more I can do."

"Don't give up," Petric replied firmly. "It may appear hopeless now, but the longer we remain here, the greater the chances are that we'll uncover a means to free ourselves. Focus on the immediate needs of our people as you've done in the past."

"I can't claim to share your optimism."

I stared at the floor as the enormity of our location and my role in our survival weighed heavily upon my soul. I'd sworn an oath to protect those who couldn't defend themselves, yet I was just as helpless as the others. It was expected for knights to act as the rallying force behind Balotica's armies, yet we weren't an army—and half of the human captives weren't Balotican. Most of the others were craftsmen, traders, merchants, barkeeps… They weren't trained to fight as we were. Camden was in the minority with his post amongst Stone Hill's city guard.

If we learned the secret to navigating the caverns, would the others follow us? And how would we survive the journey home? Now that I knew where we were, the task seemed even more daunting. Leagues of barren landscape separated the black tower from the Gray Mountains in the west. How many would die in the attempt as we ran out of water, scalded by the relentless sun? And if we managed to reach the mountains, what then? It was autumn, and the passes would soon be thick with snow. The Murkor garb was lightweight, meant for use in the heat of the Wasted Land and the temperate climate of the caverns.

It was an impossible task borne of desperation. Yet the alternative terrified me. The Soulless weren't known for their mercy and had a history of condemning their prisoners to fates far worse than death.

"Don't give up," Petric said again. "Together, we'll find a way."

I nodded absently, overwhelmed by a palpable sense of dread. I could see no way out of our situation, no end to our forced servitude without incurring casualties.

"Do you have something in mind?" I asked, my voice roughened by unspoken fear.

"Not yet, but I have faith we'll get out of this. Keep listening for any clue to our survival. You're in a better position than most since you've learned their tongue."

He pushed away from the wall and paused to study me for a time. I said nothing in response—what was there to say? I didn't share his outlook, and the gods had been silent to our collective pleas and prayers. We were alone and vulnerable.

He crossed his arms and said, "You've overcome darkness in the past. You can do so again. I can't save the others without you."

I forced another nod. "I'll do my best."

"That's all anyone can ask of you."

I looked up as I heard the curtain swish open. Petric was gone, and I was alone once more.

I didn't believe I'd learn anything of use from Aj'ana, and I rarely encountered other Murkor except on our days of rest. My conversation with the woman as she trimmed my hair had yielded nothing more than vague news and a reprimand when I'd asked too many questions.

Gods-damn it, I could see no way out.

I sighed and did the only thing I could think of in that moment. I knelt on my mat and prayed.

15

CHANGE

"I see you've caved to Ric's way of thinking and decided to keep the beard."

I opened my eyes a sliver and turned my head toward the sound of Tessamir's voice. She lay on her side, propped on one elbow, her blue eyes fixed on mine. When I'd fallen asleep the previous morning, she hadn't yet returned from her brewing experiment.

I groaned and forced myself to a sitting position. "Is it afternoon already?"

"Yes, and you're avoiding my question." She flashed a knowing smile and rose gracefully into an overhead stretch.

A pang of jealousy shot through me as I watched her. I couldn't yet lift my right arm that high, but it had improved over time.

"There weren't any Murkor available and willing to provide a shave," I grumbled. "In this state, it's beginning to itch. I'd rather be done with it."

She stepped toward me and placed one hand along the side of my jaw. I lifted my eyebrows, stunned by her action, but I didn't pull away. I could feel the warmth of her palm through the growing mat of brown stubble; I closed my eyes momentarily, reveling in the sensation.

"It suits you."

I opened my eyes to level my best skeptical gaze in her direction. "I disagree."

She dropped her hand, and I immediately missed her touch. Gods-damn it, I yearned for her, and friendship wouldn't suffice forever. It had grown increasingly difficult to keep my distance as the weeks crawled by, but I would maintain it, if only to prove Camden wrong. But I honestly believed it was the necessary and *right* thing to do given our circumstances, regardless of Camden's unwanted opinion.

I stood and began to work through the series of exercises that would one day restore my arm to its former mobility. Tessamir smiled and disappeared into the back area of the alcove while I focused on my task. We had an unspoken agreement that she would have access to the makeshift privy first each evening.

"How is the ale coming?" I asked when she exited a few minutes later.

"Not as well as I'd hoped." She collapsed onto her mat with a frown. "The Murkor don't know what hops are, and the grain they use is a different variety than what we're accustomed to. It doesn't ferment as readily. It's too soon to know how this first batch will taste, but I fear it will be horrendous, only suited for use in cleaning wounds."

"I doubt it'll be *that* bad."

She snorted. "I've been brewing since before I opened The Smith's Hammer. I *know* when a batch is questionable, and this one certainly is." She crossed her arms with a smirk. "It's a shame the thieving bastard isn't around. This batch might be suitable for revenge."

I laughed. "Remind me never to cross you, Tess. Bad ale is the worst of punishments."

She grinned. "I knew you were a smart one."

We went about what had become our typical afternoon routine; waking, my exercises, conversation and banter, breakfast, then more banter as we awaited the alchemists. Today's meal consisted of mushrooms that appeared to have been fried, and a crusty bread with a nutty flavor. I'd lost count of the number of meals that had contained mushrooms since I'd arrived in the caverns. They seemed to be a staple of the Murkor diet.

"Did you know mushrooms are a type of fungus?" Tessamir asked, her mouth half-full.

I grimaced. "I didn't."

She snickered. "The yeast used to make ale is too. Fungus isn't so bad, is it?"

I made a face and swallowed the bite I'd been in the process of chewing when she posed her first question. "I'm not sure I want to eat any more."

She flashed a triumphant grin. "Good. I'm hungrier than usual today, which means there's more for *me*. I'll take advantage of your misplaced squeamishness."

"I'm not squeamish—"

"That's right, *Ser*, you can stomach blood and gore, even when it's spattered across your face, but the notion of consuming fungus is just too much to bear." She rolled her eyes dramatically. "It hasn't harmed you so far, and the Murkor aren't malicious. If they wanted you dead, they'd feed you the red or orange varieties."

"How is it you know so much about gods-damned *fungus*?"

She shrugged. "I was curious once and read a book. Perhaps you ought to try it."

"Hmm." I feigned hurt and crossed my arms. "And I thought we were friends."

The slap of a palm against stone interrupted our discussion, and I looked up to see Rej'vennar pushing the curtain aside. Aj'ana stood a few steps behind him, her hands clasped tightly and her posture rigid. Something was amiss.

"Finish your meal quickly. We have much to do," Rej'vennar said by way of greeting.

I nodded and stuffed another mushroom into my mouth with a pointed glance at Tessamir. She smirked but said nothing more as we ate hurriedly. Despite being fungus, they tasted good—and I'd be of no help to anyone if I starved myself due to a ridiculous principle.

A few minutes later, we followed the two alchemists from our alcove toward the now-familiar tunnel that would lead to their laboratories. Rej'vennar remained silent, though his movements were sharp, edged in anxiety. Aj'ana clasped and unclasped her hands repeatedly.

"We know about the recent defeat," I said after a time. "Is this why—?"

"I *told* you the rumor would spread," Aj'ana said sharply to Rej'vennar in common, who grunted noncommittally. "If they know, we may as well discuss our work."

"What work?" I pressed.

"The army requires as many healing implements as we can produce," Rej'vennar replied over his shoulder in a begrudging tone. "Additionally, we're to make flares, fire-sticks, sand-blasts, antivenom…"

"It will be a very long night," Aj'ana added. "I hope you are rested."

"And the black substance?" Tessamir asked from my side.

Rej'vennar grunted again. "Yes, but that is handled by others. The Kal didn't believe it safe for *us* to create it, given that *you* assist us. It is a dangerous secret, one we do not willing share with anyone."

"So I've heard." Tessamir crossed her arms and frowned at the alchemist's back. "Even the donors of your precious venom don't know what you do with it. It's rather unfair."

"It has long been our agreement," Aj'ana replied smoothly. "During peacetime, the Scorpion Men trade their venom for some of our other wares."

I glowered as I recalled the Scorpion Men I'd met, chained to the cavern walls and forced to give up the venom in their tails. "And in times of war, you treat them like shit."

"Owen—" Aj'ana began, only to be cut off by Rej'vennar.

"Humans know nothing about the ways of our people, or theirs. Your ignorance has cost us greatly." He peered over his shoulder, and his eyes glimmered balefully beneath his hood. "The commander should have allowed the Soulless to end you all."

"You are *velan'sta*!" Aj'ana shouted. "You do not mean it."

"Are you certain?" he countered in a low, dangerous tone.

"Go to your laboratory alone, Rej'vennar," she hissed in Murkor. "I will take the woman today. You are unfit for company."

"I have my orders—"

"Your orders be damned. Go. If you do not, I will bring this matter before the Kal."

He clenched his fists, then huffed angrily and spun on his heel to march toward an adjoining tunnel. It didn't lead to the laboratories, and I wasn't certain where he planned to go, but I wasn't going to question his departure. I stared after him as I attempted to puzzle out his motivations. Our previous encounters had been far less hostile.

"Come," Aj'ana said wearily, switching back to common. "You will both assist me tonight."

"I may not fully understand what just happened," I replied slowly, "but I believe we owe you our thanks, Aj'ana."

"Rej'vennar blames your kind for the army's defeat. His brothers were among the fallen."

"Shit. I'm sorry."

"Do not apologize. How many of your people have been killed by ours? All of it is wrong. When Rej'vennar is finished grieving, he will understand he has erred and his blame is misplaced." She drew a breath and beckoned us. "Come."

We didn't see Rej'vennar again. I never learned if Aj'ana had spoken to the Kal as she'd threatened, but it turned out his rage didn't matter. Nothing did after another ten nights had passed.

Tessamir continued to work alongside Aj'ana, while I stood to one side and fetched vials and jars for them. I enjoyed the additional time I'd been granted in Tessamir's presence, though we didn't speak of our burgeoning feelings. That constant, sickening sense of dread refused to abate, and I couldn't allow myself to grow any closer to her. If anything happened, if I lost her, I knew what remained of my heart would be shattered. If we became intimate, my loss would be absolute. I wouldn't recover. I'd succumb to my long-suppressed darkness and turn my back on the world.

I never uncovered the secret to navigating the caverns, much to my eternal dismay. We would have been better off braving the Wasted Land's harsh environs than facing the fate the Soulless had in store.

But we didn't know what they planned, and I'd long operated on the assumption that every living being possessed empathy, even if it were only a meager thread. I'd never been so fucking *wrong.*

Empathy wasn't a characteristic the Soulless possessed. I know that now, but then… I was naive. Stupid. *Valan'sta.*

On the afternoon of that fateful tenth day, a day that will forever be burned into my memory as the beginning of an unspeakable atrocity, we were awakened hours earlier than the norm. A brown-clad Murkor shook me awake, then gestured toward Tessamir, indicating I should wake her. He disappeared through the curtain without a word, but I knew something was terribly and irrevocably wrong.

I placed my hand on Tessamir's shoulder, and her eyes flew open at my touch. Confusion and irritation flashed through her eyes as she sat up, and I rocked back on my heels.

"Owen? What—?"

I held up one hand. "A Murkor was here. He roused me. Something has happened, and I don't believe it's good."

She ran her hands through her hair while her eyes darted toward the curtained entrance to our alcove. "They've been on edge since the army returned. This can't be a coincidence."

"As a rule, I don't believe in coincidence," I replied wryly.

My gut churned and roiled uneasily. I'd failed to find a means of escape. Petric hadn't done any better, and now we would face the consequences of our deficiency. I simply didn't understand the stakes—none of us did—and I feared we'd pay for it dearly in the days to come.

She drew a steadying breath and moved toward the rear of the alcove. "If things are about to go to shit, I'd rather walk into it with an empty bladder."

I nodded and began to work my arm while I awaited my turn in the privy. I couldn't shake the palpable sense of dread that gripped me, despite my best efforts at reasoning the feeling away. Our lives had become routine, the Murkor a constant, but now something had changed inexplicably. The only variable that made sense was an order from the Soulless.

When Tessamir emerged, I took my turn in the privy. There was wisdom in her off-hand declaration. After I finished and returned to the alcove, we exited to the main cavern together.

All of the prisoners were being gathered, it seemed. Standing sentinel along the perimeter of the chamber were countless black-clad Murkor soldiers, each armed with at least one visible weapon. A quick scan told me they'd outnumber us two to one, and after Daesan, we were nearly one thousand strong.

We were herded into the beginnings of a long line, prodded into place at sword-point, while one of the soldiers bound our wrists. Tessamir faced forward, her jaw set with a determination that was diminished by the sudden pallor of her cheeks. Others were moved into place and bound as soon as they emerged from their quarters. I searched our ranks, seeking a glimpse of Petric or Camden, but could not locate them.

At least Tessamir was at my side. It was a comfort, albeit a selfish one.

"Where are we going?" a man somewhere ahead of us demanded loudly.

His words were met with silence from the Murkor, but in my heart, I knew the answer. I clenched my jaw, refusing to speak the name aloud lest my fears become reality.

"The gods have a twisted sense of humor," Tessamir whispered. "To spare us certain death and bring us here, only for our lives to come to this…"

I nodded my agreement. It seemed we'd been forsaken, sworn off as collateral damage to be remembered as a mere footnote in the history of the Soulless' war. It certainly wasn't the fate I'd imagined when I took my oaths as a knight.

Someone not far ahead of us darted away from the line and made toward the tunnel we believed led to the surface. Within moments, she was subdued in brutal fashion as one of the soldiers struck her temple with the handle of his mace. She crumpled instantly and was carried roughly to a position near the center of the chamber where she was visible to most.

The soldier deposited her unmoving form in a heap and pointed the mace's head in her direction. "She has ensured her death," he stated loudly in Murkor. "If anyone else wishes to share her fate, then by all means, follow her poor example."

"What did he say?" Tessamir hissed.

Before I could form a response, the mace arced toward the woman's skull with deadly accuracy. The crunch of bone as the weapon struck was sickening. The soldier's mace came away bloody, and he brandished it menacingly.

"He said if anyone else attempts to escape, they'll die," I summarized in a whisper. "I'm not certain what they or their masters want with us, but perhaps it isn't death."

"There are fates worse than death, Owen."

"I know. I pray we aren't walking into one of them."

She released a heavy sigh. "I don't believe the gods are listening to our prayers at present."

I shrugged awkwardly. "Perhaps they aren't, but what more can we do? I'm not ready to follow that woman into Aeon's realm. Not tonight."

"Then we must face our fate, whatever it may be."

Perhaps the change in our situation emboldened my tongue, or perhaps I was merely unable to keep the magnitude of my desire internalized any longer.

"I'm prepared to face it, Tess. With you at my side, I can face anything."

She looked down as a warm smile crept across her face. "I knew I liked you. But promise me this: Don't do anything to get your stubborn ass killed. I've become rather fond of it."

A strangled sound, something halfway between a laugh and a sob, escaped my throat as heat rose into my face. "I'll do my best. I've always been a survivor."

16

THE BLACK TOWER

The fading sunlight seared my eyes after weeks spent in the caverns. The sun was a hair's breadth from the western horizon, wreathed in orange and gold wisps of cloud. The sight was breathtaking, and I realized I'd always taken the sun and the open sky for granted.

I paused to take in the view, though I was forced to squint as my eyes struggled to adjust. My efforts were rewarded with a rough jab to my right shoulder that sent a fierce jolt of pain through my arm. I ground my teeth and moved forward while the hooded countenance of my captor and present tormentor looked on.

"I've missed the sun too," Tessamir whispered once I'd resumed my position at her side. "But it's not worth dying over."

I shook my head and cast a final, longing glance toward the horizon, where the sun was beginning to sink. "I didn't plan to stop. It was a thoughtless reaction."

How many weeks had passed since my capture at Stone Hill? I'd lost count, but it was the last time I'd spied the sun. I reveled in its warmth during the few minutes before it disappeared behind the distant mountains and prayed to the apathetic deities who ruled our world that I'd never be forced into perpetual darkness again. Based on the lack of response I'd received from them so far, I doubted they'd pay my latest request any heed.

We trudged on, through a harsh landscape made alien in the descending twilight. Behind us, the entrance to the Murkors' cavernous home loomed, a shadowed recess in an unforgiving and barren rockface. Ahead, the land flattened and sprawled for countless miles; dry, parched earth was broken only by the occasional rough stone or the twisted and gnarled remnants of plant life that had once aspired to become trees. There was no greenery, no water, no shade.

The air was warmer than I was accustomed to, but after taking in the scenery, I was grateful we were making this journey at night. The daytime heat would have been unbearable. For the first time in my life, I understood why we referred to this arid and inhospitable place as the Wasted Land.

As the night darkened, the temperature dropped significantly. Tessamir began to shiver, but there was nothing I could do to alleviate her discomfort. I was garbed in the same light-weight cloth as she was, and our hands remained bound. The Murkor didn't appear concerned over our welfare any longer and merely shouted orders to continue the march to anyone who began to lag.

I was certain we were traveling to the black tower and our captors were working under orders from the Soulless. There was no other plausible explanation.

I expected to die within hours. The Soulless had wanted us dead when they initially attacked, and the Murkor had spared us for a time. But their protection had come to an end, and with it, so had our lives.

Few of the captives spoke, and most who did whispered desperate prayers to one god or another. The gods remained maddeningly silent, and internally, I cursed them. I wasn't fucking ready to die, and they'd yet to intervene. I doubted they would.

It was nearing midnight when the Murkor called a brief halt. Soldiers strode down our column, offering skins of water. I was allowed only a few sips before the skin was wrenched away and passed to the woman behind me. It wasn't enough to ease the parched state of my throat, but it was better than nothing.

My feet were sore, and my gods-damned shoulder had begun to ache again. It had been a few weeks since it had last pained me, but my wrists hadn't been bound during that time. I was beginning to wonder if it would ever fully heal.

Shouts roused me from my miserable thoughts, and I peered over my shoulder to seek the source of the commotion. A knot of Murkor were gathered around a single man who had attempted to flee, their weapons drawn as he stood defiantly in their midst. Two Murkor stood slightly apart from the rest, torches clutched in their fists, while the grayish countenance of the Soulless—the same Soulless who had destroyed the wall at Stone Hill—looked on, grim amusement twinkling in his crimson eyes.

A chill raced the length of my spine as some of my fears were confirmed.

I shifted my focus to the man in their midst. I'd recognize the human face that stared toward our line in challenge anywhere. My heart sank as I watched the Murkor force Camden to kneeling. They weren't gentle when he refused to comply with their spoken demands. One kicked him savagely from behind, while another struck his knees. His eyes scanned the column of prisoners as he fell forward, but I don't believe he spied me. It was likely for the best—I was not complicit in his scheme, and I wouldn't be made to appear so.

And to reiterate, I wasn't fucking ready to die.

The Murkor to his rear grasped his ponytail and yanked him upright into a kneeling position. His head was tilted back, exposing his neck as he gazed defiantly toward the midnight sky. His eyes shone momentarily, though I wasn't certain if he shed tears or if it was merely a trick of the torchlight. I hoped he'd made peace with Aeon.

One of the Murkor moved forward, a double-bladed axe gripped in his hands. Another stepped away and raised his voice to be heard along our section of the column.

"The Soulless have business with you lot, and escape will not be allowed. Let this man's actions be a lesson to you all. We take no joy in this death, but it is necessary." He pointed his mace toward Camden's location, and I wondered if he was the same Murkor responsible for the woman's death earlier in the evening.

Their Soulless overseer nodded in approval.

The axe-wielding soldier edged nearer to Camden and prepared himself for his next strike. He spoke softly in the Murkor tongue, though I was too distant to make out his exact words. His tone was laden with sorrow, even as he placed the axe blade carefully against Camden's throat.

Beside me, Tessamir turned away. "Gods, I can't bear to watch, even if he was an ass."

"He doesn't deserve this," I replied, though I could not tear my eyes from the spectacle as she'd done.

Camden had chosen to follow his darkness of late, but he'd still been a friend. I was obligated to witness his last moments, despite the rift that had been gradually growing between us. He'd lost everything with the fall of Stone Hill, and now he'd chosen to end his life by the only means available to him.

The Murkor drew the axe back, then arced it forward in a dark blur. It hit its mark and cleaved cleanly through the flesh and bone as blood spurted from the stump of Camden's neck. The Murkor behind him held his head aloft, ensuring it was clearly visible to the line of captives. The man who had once been my friend wore a grimace into death, his face frozen eternally in an expression of pained acceptance.

Someone nearby retched audibly while another began to sob. It was too dark where we were to make out who had reacted, and truly, it didn't matter. Camden was dead, another casualty of the Soulless' gods-damned war.

The Murkor dragged his body away as their leader began to speak once more. "If you hope to live, do not follow his example."

"What did he say?" Tessamir hissed.

I turned away from the Murkor and shook my head as I repeated his final words. "They believe we'll live, but I have my doubts."

"If not execution, what could the Soulless possibly want from us?"

I shrugged. I could imagine nothing beyond a bloody and brutal end, and she deserved a more hopeful answer than anything I'd manage to provide. Aj'ana had believed a trip to the tower was a death sentence. I was unable to conjure a reason to disagree.

The march resumed at an increased pace. The air continued to grow colder as the hours crawled by, and I could no longer feel my hands by the time the sky began to lighten toward dawn.

With the first pale glimmer of sunlight, the black tower came into view. It thrust skyward from the parched landscape, a glittering black rectangle of magically carved obsidian. Some distance south of the tower sprawled a vast array of tents, and striding amongst them, the hooded figures of Murkor. I assumed it was the army's camp.

Farther away, the landscape fell abruptly into the dark abyss that was Blackstone Chasm. It ran south in a jagged line, a tremendous scar upon the damaged earth. Legend claimed the chasm was the result of the tower's construction, but the truth of the matter was likely lost to the annals of time.

We were halted again as we neared the base of the tower. I glanced up, taking in its full height from close range, then immediately averted my gaze. A tremor ran the length of my spine as primal terror squeezed my heart in its icy grip. This was a place of unspeakable evil, the stronghold of the Nameless god and his followers.

I cursed myself for a fool. I should have followed Camden's lead, should have fled, even if it meant my life was forfeit. It was too late to act now, pinned as we were between the tower and the Murkor army.

I shuddered and stared at my dusty boots. "*Fuck*."

Tessamir sidled toward me. "I feel it too. Whatever happens, I'm here."

I wanted to laugh with relief and weep for our collective losses, to break down, to rage at the gods, the Soulless, and our bleak future. Instead, I swallowed and looked up to meet her gaze, determined to follow through on my previous words, despite their naïve bravado.

"As am I. We'll get through this together."

She forced a tight smile that failed to reach her eyes. "I pray you're right."

I prayed I was too. Gods, I *wanted* to be there for her, to protect her, but we were both mired in the same hopeless situation. The best I could offer was to remain by her side as long as I was able. It wasn't enough, would never be enough, but it was all I had.

At the head of the column, a pair of Murkor broke away to approach the tower. It took me a moment to realize there was a door embedded in the glossy black exterior, nearly indistinguishable from the surrounding walls. As they disappeared inside, I spied another group of Murkor approaching from the direction of their camp. We were outnumbered as it was—why were more needed?

Tessamir nudged my side with her elbow and nodded in the newcomers' direction. "I don't like the look of this."

"Nor do I."

I struggled briefly against the bonds securing my wrists, but they had not loosened during the journey. One of the nearby soldiers noticed my futile action and turned his hooded countenance in my direction with a growl. His hand strayed to the hilt of his short sword as I expelled a sigh and grew still. I felt his eyes on me for several long seconds before he mercifully turned away.

"It would have been a sound idea if there weren't twice as many of them as there are of us," Tessamir whispered. "We may not have figured out how to escape the Murkor, but perhaps there will be an opportunity here. We simply must watch and wait."

I nodded. "If they don't plan to kill us, then there may be hope."

I kept my tone light, but I possessed none of the optimism present in my words. The future I imagined was bleak, and I was unable to shake off the dread that had taken root in my gut.

The Murkor from the camp arrived at our location before the others reappeared in the tower's open door. They bolstered the ranks of their brethren to outnumber us nearly four to one. I began to sense this wasn't an execution as I'd feared, but something far more horrific.

The doors to the tower were pushed open to their maximum by the Murkor who had entered previously, then held firmly in place. A trio of soldiers surrounded the woman at the head of the column; one stood on either side, and the third followed behind. She was taken inside as another trio encircled the next captive in line. He, too, was ushered inside.

Several minutes passed before the Murkor exited without the prisoners. They spoke with some of the others, then surrounded the next pair of captives and began to herd them toward the tower's gaping maw. More Murkor joined in the process, and soon, I found myself standing at the head of the column with Tessamir.

I peered through the door as we waited, hoping to glimpse one of the others who had entered before. There was a broad room within, illuminated by an unnaturally flat light, but I spied no one inside beyond another contingent of Murkor. Wherever the others had been taken was beyond my sight.

I braced myself as another group of Murkor appeared in the room and strode toward us. They swarmed Tessamir and I, and led me inside first. The soldier bringing up the rear jabbed something hard into my spine, forcing me forward relentlessly as his counterparts grasped my elbows between them roughly.

I was provided only moments to take in the tower's foyer. It was an unadorned, circular room carved from the same obsidian as the building's exterior. The eerie illumination emanated from the dark walls themselves; I didn't know much about magic, but I assumed this was a form of it. The base of a broad staircase rose from the floor on my right, while a closed door loomed on the curved wall on my left. Directly ahead was the entrance to another room, which I immediately realized was our destination.

A murmur of panicked voices drifted toward me from within. My Murkor escort prodded me forward and through the doors wordlessly. Inside was row upon row of wooden chairs, set to face a raised dais at the far end. The other captives had been led here, their wrists and ankles secured firmly to the chairs. Beneath each chair was a coiled mass of gray and green.

My eyes were drawn to the figures on the dais as I was marched toward the next available seat. A woman sat in a throne-like seat in the center, three colored orbs on the floor around her. The orbs glowed faintly as oily swirls danced across their surface. She rested her grayish hands lightly on the arms of the chair as her crimson eyes swept the room. Her expression was a mixture of haughty boredom and disdain.

The tall man at her side was no stranger to me. He was the same man responsible for the destruction of Stone Hill's southern gate and my fall from the nearby wall, the same man who had overseen Camden's execution. His angular jaw was set in a firm line as he watched us positioned inside. Though his face betrayed no emotion, there was a tightness around his eyes that indicated concern—or perhaps fear.

I suppressed a shudder as I wondered what would cause one of the Soulless to experience fear. What did they have planned?

I was pushed toward a seat midway along a row near the center of the room. One Murkor held my shoulders firmly in place as another secured my ankles to the chair legs. I resisted and was rewarded with a firm strike to my skull from the rear guard. I winced and glowered at him as the others cut the bonds on my wrists and yanked my arms forward.

I grunted as my right shoulder protested the motion, but the Murkor ignored my discomfort. Within moments, my wrists were tied to the chair's arms, and the Murkor moved away to make room for the next group. Tessamir was seated beside me and treated in an identical fashion.

Her blue eyes were wild with panic as they met mine, her face ashen. She remained silent until her Murkor handlers moved away, then a low moan escaped her lips.

"Tess, we'll get through this," I whispered.

"Why are there snakes? I *hate* snakes."

I frowned in confusion, then allowed my eyes to drift across the row of seats in front of us. The green and gray coils beneath each chair remained motionless, but on closer inspection, I understood the source of her fear. They weren't thick coils of rope or fabric. They were snakes; enormous constrictors wound tightly around themselves to form the scaly piles I'd assumed were harmless at first glance. The snake directly in front of me had buried its head between the coils of its body and appeared to be asleep, though it was impossible to know for certain. Each was as big around as my torso.

I gripped the arms of my chair so tightly my knuckles turned white. Panic threatened to overwhelm me, but I knew I must remain calm for Tessamir's sake. I dug my nails into the wood and clenched my jaw, unable to look away from the reptile beneath the chair in front of me. When I located my voice, it was strained.

"I don't know."

I shook my head and forced myself to turn away from the creature that I was certain would easily devour any one of us if given the opportunity. Instead, I turned toward Tessamir. Her eyes were locked on the nearest snake, wide and unblinking.

"Tess, look at me."

She swallowed, and with a monumental effort, turned to face me.

"Whatever is about to ensue, we'll survive it together."

She nodded, glanced at the nearest serpent, and shuddered visibly. "You'd best not be lying to me, Owen Greenwaters, or I'll see to it

Aeon allows me to haunt you for eternity. Why does it have to be fucking *snakes*?"

I wished I had an answer to her question, some means of assurance that we'd survive this ordeal—whatever it proved to be—unscathed. As the room continued to fill, the woman on the dais reached toward the glowing orbs, a cold smirk twisting her features. Her expression filled me with a greater dread than all the serpents combined.

Clearly, she had planned this moment for some time and was savoring our discomfort with every breath she drew. The man at her side did not move. They spoke briefly after a time, then I heard the doors at the rear of the room close.

We were bound, trapped, and at the whims of the Soulless. With a malevolent smile, the woman stretched her hands toward the orbs. A crackle of magical energy cascaded through the room and my body stiffened of its own accord.

Revulsion swept through me as I understood her intent. It was too late for any of us, but we hadn't been led here to die.

We were here to be *changed*. Irrevocably, horrifically changed.

17

A CREATURE OF NIGHTMARE

Fucking gods, *the pain…*

I'd known pain in my time, but nothing compared to this. Nothing would *ever* compare to this.

Magic swirled and billowed through the air, its piercing tendrils igniting a firestorm across my skin. It plunged beneath the surface, boiled the blood in my veins, shredded tendons, pulverized bone. I felt as though every fiber and fragment of my being was being rent and warped beyond repair.

My ears rang with the clamor of a thousand human voices shrieking in agony before they were drowned out by the thunderous pulse of my own tortured heartbeat. It stuttered and faltered. It nearly failed.

Gods, I wished it had. My torment would have been over.

I think I screamed, a visceral and animalistic reaction to the Soulless' twisted magic as it continued to ravage my body. I squeezed my eyes shut and roared until my throat was raw, but the onslaught continued.

If this didn't kill me, it would drive me to madness. No sane person could hope to withstand pain of this magnitude without losing the battle. And I was losing—we all were.

I was only dimly aware of Tessamir on my right and a man I didn't know on my left. The agony that coursed through my being was all-encompassing, absolute. I soon forgot they existed.

I prayed to Aeon for release. I begged Flariel to remove the cinders from my arteries, to alleviate the molten fire my blood had become. I sought Ukase's divine judgment and pleaded with him to seek revenge on the Soulless for all that they'd done. I asked Karmada to grace us with the fortune of deliverance—even if it meant death.

The gods did nothing. The pain intensified.

Something wrapped around my right leg and wound toward my torso. I was aware of its weight pressing against my body, but little else. I now understand it was the snake that had been feigning sleep beneath my chair, but at the time, my mind refused to grasp the enormity of what was occurring. The sheer agony of the Soulless' magic was too much to bear.

My consciousness flickered. For a moment, I believed Aeon had heard my previous pleas and I'd be freed of the anguish of my present existence. Then a fresh wave of pain flowed through my body, and I knew I'd been wrong to hope. Aeon would not come. We'd been forsaken, cast off as fodder for the Soulless' schemes.

I writhed in my bonds, the pain so intense I was no longer aware of the cords around my wrists and ankles, though I knew they must have cut into my flesh. My back arched, seemingly of its own accord, and I felt the vertebrae twist and snap. Tendons and ligaments stretched to breaking. Something deep inside my gut was torn free.

The back of my skull hit the back of the chair as my body continued to bend backwards. I couldn't stop the action if I'd tried; it was the work of the woman's foul magic. More bones snapped. I screamed anew.

My eyes flew open, though my vision was blurred by tears. I couldn't turn my head. It was held firmly in place by the invisible energy that coursed through the room, and my view was of the room's smooth obsidian ceiling. Black spots danced through my vision, and I prayed for a respite. If the gods wouldn't grant me death, perhaps they'd be merciful and allow me to fall unconscious.

Heat seared across my abdomen, intense and bright, as though I'd been cut in two by a superheated blade. I rolled my eyes in an attempt to see what had occurred, but without the use of my neck muscles, I could not. Later, I'd be grateful that I'd been unable to witness the horror the Soulless had unleashed upon us.

The heat reached unbearable levels. Sweat ran in rivulets from my brow, and my clothing clung to me in a sticky mass of damp fibers. I gasped for air between agonized screams, then panicked as I realized I could no longer feel my legs.

It wasn't an absence of pain. I was aware of every torturous second I spent strapped in that chair, and the pain had become my constant companion. My legs were *no longer there.*

Fucking gods, would this nightmare never end? I was at my breaking point, my sanity fleeting. Perhaps I'd hallucinated the sensation as my mind was broken under the continuous torture. It was the only scenario that made sense in my pain-riddled world.

My bones began to snap back into alignment, but the process was more agonizing than when Rej'vennar had reset my arm. The heat in my abdomen began to fade, and slowly, my pulse calmed as my blood cooled and the magic subsided. I remained rigidly in place, my face tilted toward the ceiling, even as the pain mercifully drained away.

I felt something thin and supple coil around my throat, and then *her* voice filled my mind.

You are bound to the Nameless god, and to us, his chosen servants. You are compelled to obey. Sit up.

I clenched my jaw and resisted. My body sat up as she commanded, though I'd refused to comply.

Shit. What manner of hell had I found myself in?

I turned my head to look toward the dais. The woman lounged on her throne, the glowing orbs around her. A weary, yet satisfied smirk played across her lips as she surveyed the room.

You will not speak unless asked a direct question. You will allow the Murkor to escort you to their camp, where you will act on the commander's orders.

To the man at her side, she said, "They are the Serpentus. They will obey our commands without question. Perfect soldiers."

Panic clawed at the remnants of my sanity. What in Aeon's hells were Serpentus? What had she—?

I made the mistake of looking away from the dais, my gaze falling to where my knees should have been. I hadn't imagined losing my legs. Fucking gods, I prayed I was in the grip of a delusion because the alternative was unthinkable. My mind refused to accept what my eyes perceived.

No. No, no, no, *no*…

I stared at the lower half of my body. It *was* mine, though it shouldn't have been. A ragged sob escaped my throat, unbidden. This shouldn't have happened. It was impossible. It was…

It wasn't the first time magic of this nature had been used against humanity. Before the pain began, I'd understood in a flash of clarity what the woman intended. I'd known what was about to happen, yet witnessing the result was a level of horror I simply couldn't fathom.

I'd been fused with that gods-damned snake. Just below my navel, my flesh transitioned to rough gray scales interspersed with a sinuous pattern of emerald green. The lower half of my body was serpentine. She'd performed the same magic that had created the Scorpion Men in ancient times, and we were now…*this*.

Fuck.

I risked a glance toward Tessamir and noted with a heavy heart that she'd suffered the same fate. No doubt we all had.

I opened my mouth to ask how she fared, but my throat constricted painfully and no sound issued forth. I swung my gaze toward the dais as fury replaced the terror, burning it away. The woman had commanded me not to speak, and my body obeyed her, though my mind did not.

She'd enslaved us with her magic. I was a fucking prisoner in my own ravaged and mutated body, as if being melded to a gods-damned *snake* wasn't enough. And she possessed the audacity to perch on her throne and *smirk*.

I silently vowed that if given the opportunity, I would kill her.

As my wrists were untied, I shot another heated glare toward the dais. Gods, I wanted to lash out at the woman, at the Murkor who had come to "free" me, at everyone and everything in my field of view. Raw hatred for the Soulless coursed through me as my body simply followed the hooded soldier along the row of chairs toward the room's exit.

I'd been commanded to follow their orders and could do nothing but comply. If I'd possessed the ability to strike at him, I would have. The spectacle would have forced the Soulless to intervene, and I'd be walking—no, *slithering*—toward Aeon's gates. The magical compulsion that controlled my actions wouldn't allow for it, and my fury grew.

As we moved toward the tower's exit, I grudgingly took stock of my personal situation. My wrists had been chafed raw as I'd writhed and struggled in my bonds, but I bore no other signs of physical injury. The true damage had been done to my psyche, and that was irreparable.

I wasn't certain if my new form of locomotion was intuitive or if my body was merely responding to the Soulless' orders, but the movement of my lower half seemed natural. I was repulsed by the thought; the sheer *wrongness* of what I'd become was impossible to ignore. Death would have been preferable to this living hell.

It wasn't until we reached the tower's exit that I realized what had been nagging at the back of my thoughts. I'd been focused on myself so thoroughly that I'd failed to pay attention to my Murkor escort and his seemingly diminutive stature. I was significantly taller than he was, but it wasn't only him. Every Murkor I passed stood no more than chest-high. The transformation had made me larger.

My thoughts flitted to the Scorpion Men once more. My encounters with them had been brief, but I'd always been stunned by their size. The same terrible magic had been performed on us; it made sense that we'd have grown in stature to match them. Based on the woman's comment, the Soulless wanted to use us as soldiers and it served to reason she believed their side required warriors equal to the enemy in size and strength. And given the monstrosities we'd become, we'd no doubt appear equally formidable.

Outside, it was dusk. The ordeal within the tower had begun well before noon. I'd been trapped in a singular moment of unending torment, oblivious to the passage of time, while the Soulless reshaped me into the creature I now was.

She'd called us Serpentus. It was an apt name, but one I was loath to accept. I couldn't stomach the use of her term for our kind. It was a betrayal of who we'd been and everything we'd stood for. *Creature* was sufficient, as was *monster*. Anything was better than *Serpentus*.

The Murkor I followed turned to peer over his shoulder briefly once we were a short distance from the tower. "We go…camp," he said in broken common. "You understand?"

"Yes," I replied in Murkor, my tongue briefly freed from the magic's influence. He'd asked me a question—I was allowed to respond.

"You know Murkor?" he asked in his own language, his tone a mixture of delight and surprise.

"Yes."

"This makes my task easier. The common tongue is *velan'sta.* Do all the prisoners understand as you do?"

"No."

An irritated growl issued from beneath his hood. "Disappointing."

There were a dozen questions I wanted to ask him, but the magic didn't permit it. Instead, I was forced to continue in silence until he spoke again several minutes later.

"Tents have been set up for you. The commander will address your people once all have been gathered." He paused to glance behind us, toward the tower, then continued in a lower tone. "What they've done to your people is unforgivable. We mourn for you."

I clenched my jaw and averted my gaze as rage boiled in my veins. The Murkor had taken us to the tower; they were complicit in the Soulless' schemes. Even if they'd been ignorant of that woman's true intent, they'd still led us willingly to the tower when ordered. They could have prevented this atrocity, but instead, they'd done nothing.

After weeks spent in their caverns, I'd come to believe their promises of protection from death. Grudgingly, I admitted they'd upheld their word, but at what cost? How many of us would pointlessly die in the Soulless' war, conscripted as were to do their bidding? We were incapable of refusing their demands.

She'd called us perfect soldiers, but we were nothing more than fucking puppets, pulled along by magical strings. And the Murkor had helped bring us to this fate.

My hatred simmered beneath the surface, yearning to be released. They'd taken everything from me, and they would pay once I was freed. *If* I was freed.

"We share your anger," he went on, oblivious to the fact that he was as much a target of my rage as the Soulless. "Were you a soldier before the war?"

"Yes," I growled but could not elaborate further.

"So few of your kind were. Many have said they were merchants, bakers, craftsmen…"

I tuned him out as he continued to prattle on about the lives we'd once enjoyed. He'd never understand the enormity of our devastation. We hadn't simply lost our homes or loved ones; we'd lost our *humanity*, and with it, our sense of self.

Fury enveloped me, and I embraced it, welcomed it. It was all I had left to live for.

If the Soulless had hoped to create monsters, they'd succeeded with me. I'd become a being of rage, a creature of nightmare, and one day I would have my revenge.

18

WORDS UNSAID

It wasn't until after we'd reached the Murkor camp that I realized I could see.

The sun had set some time before, the moon was yet to rise, and there were only a scant handful of torches and campfires lit throughout the camp. Yet I could see as clearly as I did in daylight.

I frowned as I wracked my brain for information but came up with nothing. I was unable to voice my questions to the Murkor soldier who led the way, though I doubted he'd know why I suddenly possessed superior night vision. Perhaps it was an artifact leftover from the snake I'd been fused with, or an addition the Soulless had made to enhance our role in their army. Whatever the cause, it was another unsettling item to add to the list of attributes that marked me as inhuman.

I was taken to a large pavilion along the southern perimeter of the camp. Others of my kind were there, but no one spoke. We couldn't, but a gathering without a word uttered in greeting was eerie. Heads turned at my arrival, and eyes followed my progress as I sought a familiar face. Where was Tessamir? She'd been led away before I had.

"You may wait here," the soldier said. "The commander will arrive later to speak with you."

I nodded and moved further into the pavilion. Some of the others wept silently, others appeared depressed or despondent, and a handful wore murderous glares. A few nodded as I passed; at least we'd been granted that shred of freedom.

We all appeared haggard, the toll of the day's events etched in our faces, in the ragged state of our garments, and in the haunted state of our eyes. The stench of blood, sweat, and feces clung to our group like a noxious perfume. The only item any of us sported that appeared untarnished was the leather bands that encircled our necks, a sign of our forced conscription.

I searched the pavilion for Tessamir, threading through clusters of other captives and peering into its shadowed corners. After several minutes, I located her. She was huddled near the rear wall as she hugged her arms around herself. Her lower body was coiled tightly. Even from a distance, I spied the glisten of tears on her face.

My heart stuttered and my throat constricted as I realized I wouldn't be able to draw her into my arms to provide the comfort she desperately sought. I'd been ordered to wait, nothing more. My body would obey no matter how much I struggled to overcome the magical compulsion that bound me.

I made my way to her and waited for her to take notice while I attempted to devise a thread of logic that would allow me to move a hand, an arm, *anything* that might provide her with reassurance. Nothing came, and I remained silent at her side.

After some time, she drew a shuddering breath and looked up. Her eyes widened and her mouth opened, but like me, she was unable to speak. She blinked away a fresh set of tears, then uncoiled her lower half to stand erect.

I lifted my eyebrows in mild surprise. She stood nearly as tall as I did. Before, she'd been less than shoulder-high in comparison.

A dozen emotions crossed her features as her eyes—the same midnight blue as before—took in my form. Anguish, relief, horror, rage… The same as I experienced, and more. After a time, she closed her eyes, drew a steadying breath, then edged closer. When she opened them once more, she managed a tremulous smile that failed to staunch her sorrow.

I nodded once, acknowledging her grief, her pain. I'd promised her we'd survive together, but fucking gods, I'd never imagined our lives would become *this*. It was hell being so damned close, yet unable to lift a finger or whisper a word.

I don't know how long we remained there, locked in one another's gazes, a handspan away yet worlds apart. Time passed, and eventually the Murkor commander arrived with a small contingent of soldiers in his wake. Almost as one, we turned to listen to his words, compelled by the Soulless' iron will. He spoke in fluent common, his voice strong, bolstered by years spent issuing commands.

"I have spoken to Kama, the Soulless who oversees the army. You are to support our forces as we prepare our next strike on the Five Kingdoms. Your…homeland." His voice cracked with unexpected emotion, but he shook his head and pressed on. "Kama has indicated you will obey my orders. I must ask you to follow the Arms Master's as well. Jal'den is my second-in-command."

He gestured to a tall Murkor on his left, who nodded once.

"The Arms Master will see to it you are properly outfitted. Given the nature of your servitude, I am obligated to state this." The commander's hood dipped forward, as though the act pained him. "When dawn breaks each day, you may return here to sleep. You will be expected to report to your various duties at sundown. Those duties will be assigned in the hours to come. Likewise, should you need to relieve yourselves, the latrines have been dug past the northern perimeter. You do not need permission to attend bodily functions. When you have finished, return here or to your assigned duties."

Several dozen people broke away at his words and departed the pavilion for the northern section of camp. I'd go later; I wasn't in any mindset to learn how the process worked with my new biology. And I wanted to hear what more the commander had to say before he departed.

He waited until the others disappeared outside before continuing in a weary tone. "We'll begin the process of outfitting now. The Arms Master or one of the others will speak with each of you to learn what weapons may suit you best." Once finished, he was gone.

I glanced at Tessamir. She stared at the pavilion's rough floor as tears welled in her eyes. She'd once regaled me with the story of how she'd taken to Daesan's streets during the recent battle to defend her tavern, but she hadn't lasted long in the fray.

Gods-damn it, I'd never been so helpless.

I sent a silent prayer to Blademon while I awaited my turn with the Murkor outfitters. The god of war had landed us in this mess; perhaps he'd see fit to save us as well. I rarely wasted my breath—or my internal musings—on him, but tonight, I'd make an exception. If the legends were true, he'd once taken pity on the Scorpion Men and spared them from death in the Soulless' first war. I hoped he'd deign to do the same for us.

Blademon was a fickle god, as likely to lend aid as to do nothing as events unfolded. He never chose sides in mortal conflicts, but would influence events to maximize his entertainment. It was often said he'd personally train a pair of warriors, knowing they'd fight on opposing sides, simply to watch their inevitable and bloody confrontation.

But we'd been ignored by the war god's siblings. Blademon was the only one left we could turn to.

The Murkor made their way through the room, spending only a few moments with each of us before moving on to the next. Even with six working through our collective masses, it was well after midnight before the Arms Master approached.

"What is your name and former profession?"

I'd heard the question repeated countless times and had been expecting it. "Owen Greenwaters. Knight."

The Arms Master paused and tilted his hood thoughtfully to one side. "A knight? You are the first we've encountered."

Panic welled within me. Where was Petric? He should have been here, unless he'd perished during our ordeal in the tower. My eyes darted through the dark pavilion, but I could not locate the older man. *Shit.* And where was Senna?

"Should there be another?" he asked.

"Yes."

I wanted to elaborate, to tell him their names and that more than one knight was missing from our number, but I could not. My frustration mounted as my inability to communicate became ever more apparent.

He held up his hands, sensing the change in my demeanor. "Calm down. I'm aware how gods-damned difficult it is for you to speak, and I don't like what they've done to you. None of us do, though I doubt you'll believe it." He shook his head. "What is the other knight's name?"

"Petric and Senna."

"There are two?"

"*Yes*," I replied through clenched teeth. Gods, this was aggravating.

He motioned to one of the others, who had just finished a round of questions with a nearby man. They spoke quietly in Murkor, unaware I knew their language.

"There are two knights—or there *were*, before the fucking Soulless worked their magic," the Arms Master spat. "Find them. They'll be the best warriors of this lot, and if we hope to survive this war, we'll need them. I suspect the Serpentus will need them as well, as a boost to morale."

The other soldier nodded. "I'll search for them, sir."

The Arms Master turned back toward me. "What weaponry did you specialize in?"

"War hammers."

He paused and was silent for several moments. "Two?"

"Yes."

"That's unusual, but I know you're unable to lie."

I scowled at him, allowing all of my frustration to seep into my expression. Who was he to question my expertise in arms? From the timber of his voice, he was young, perhaps in his early twenties. I had at least a decade's more experience—and due to my recent change, a longer reach and larger stature. If I wasn't compelled to obey, I'd teach him a lesson none of the Murkor would soon forget. I would have relished having an outlet for my simmering anger.

He shifted his weight and released a sigh. "I wouldn't like to prove myself if I were in your situation either. Look."

He reached over his shoulder to grasp the hilt of the broadsword strapped across his back. He drew the weapon, then held it in one hand while he pointed to an engraving on the steel midway down its length. It was a scorpion, carved in ornate detail. I recognized the mark and silently cursed the god it belonged to as a meddlesome bastard.

"This blade was gifted to me by Blademon himself. I know weaponry, Owen Greenwaters, and what I said is true. Your choice is unusual."

I stared a challenge at him as he sheathed his blade. He may have been chosen by the war god, but I would stand by my decision. And gods-damn it, I liked my hammers. They were familiar, deadly, and versatile.

"Our smiths may not be able to accommodate your request," he continued after a few moments. "My people don't engage in mounted combat. We have no horses. A war hammer is less useful from the ground. Is there a secondary weapon you might wield?"

My glare intensified. "Yes."

He made a sound of frustration. "Fucking gods, I should know not to phrase my words that way by now," he muttered in Murkor. In common, he said, "What other weapons are you proficient in?"

"Mace, club, short sword."

"Do you prefer to wield two weapons at once?"

"Yes."

"I'll do my best to find you a pair of proper war hammers, but I can make no promises," he said. "Our smiths' experience with them is limited, and we're short on supplies. I hope you understand."

Grudgingly, I nodded.

"Good. You'll be assigned to perimeter patrol beginning tomorrow evening. Until then, rest if you can."

I was exhausted by the time dawn began to tint the sky. It had been a full two days since I'd last slept, and the transformation I'd undergone had sapped much of my energy. I'd stubbornly refused to sleep until Tessamir settled in, and our orders had indicated we'd sleep through the day. I'd cherish the small freedoms we were provided in any form they took.

We visited the latrines once she was finished with her round of questioning. The process was awkward and disgusting. Everything exited the same orifice near the end of my tail—fucking gods, it was unnerving to acknowledge I had a *tail*. I quickly realized it was easiest to face away from the trench and allow the end of my tail to overhang the edge while my biological processes finished.

I was certain my face was several shades of crimson darker than its norm as we departed for the pavilion once more. Gods, it was humiliating.

We returned to the area we'd departed from but didn't immediately rest as many of the others did. Our gazes locked, and I wished with every fiber of my being that I could overcome the magical shackles that chained my tongue. There were so many things I wanted to say to her, so many things I should have said previously, but I'd foolishly internalized my thoughts and desires. Now, I could say nothing, do nothing without our overlords' permission.

I should have told her how much I truly cared, that I'd imagined a life with her after the war. I should have told her I thought she was beautiful. I still believed she was; her human half was unchanged, though I was unused to seeing such sorrow etched in her features. I'd been a coward, afraid to make a solid connection with her for fear of losing her entirely.

Now, I could only stare and hope my eyes conveyed everything my lips could not. I'd left too many damned words unsaid… And we both suffered for it.

The sky was beginning to lighten when she dropped her gaze and curled up. She rested her forearms atop her coiled lower body, then lay her head atop them. Her dark hair cascaded over her face, shielding her from my view.

I settled in a similar fashion nearby, but tilted my head in her direction.

Not long after, I drifted to sleep. The last image I had was the woman who had captured my heart, the one I could not hold or comfort.

19

A MEAGER GIFT

Only a handful of our people had been selected for perimeter patrol. We were all former soldiers of some form, but I was the only knight. I'd yet to locate Petric or Senna and doubted I would. They were likely with Aeon, at peace, immune to the horrors we'd been forced to endure.

The Arms Master, Jal'den, came to the pavilion at dusk to collect us for duty. I recognized only two faces amongst our group, though I'd never learned their names. Both had been in Stone Hill when it fell. Most of the others bore the dark hair and pale complexion that marked them as Deluchan. I assumed they'd been captured in Daesan with Tessamir.

Tessamir had been assigned to assist the camp cooks until we were ordered into the field. Her experience as a barkeep had determined her role, and I knew she'd excel even if she hadn't been compelled to obey. The look she gave me in parting spoke volumes; heartbreak and fear coupled with a profound longing. She wasn't certain she'd see me again.

I offered her my best expression of reassurance, though I knew she saw through the stoic façade. I turned away, drawn by the Murkor's orders, and focused on my fury instead. It would sustain me in her absence.

Jal'den led us into the camp, then took a winding route through the tents toward the southern perimeter. A cluster of soldiers awaited us, and we were each paired with a Murkor for the nightly patrol. Jal'den chose me to accompany him.

I was mildly surprised by the decision. Didn't the Arms Master have better things to do than work patrol? It seemed a task better suited for soldiers beneath his station.

We moved in silence for some time, following a dusty track worn into the cracked earth by myriad footsteps. I glowered into the darkness at the realization that I'd never leave prints of that nature in my wake again. Gods-damn the Soulless.

"I felt obligated to speak with you privately," Jal'den said as we rounded a curve toward the camp's eastern side. "I have news I believe you ought to hear."

I peered at the shadow beneath his hood and wished I could glean something of his expression with my newly superior vision. It seemed even a serpent's sight had its limitations.

"After we interviewed all of your people, we did not find anyone by the name of Petric or Senna. I'm sorry."

I nodded and looked away. It was as I'd feared. Both must have perished in the tower, and I was the only knight remaining. The Balotican survivors would undoubtedly look to me for guidance if we were ever freed. I'd never been a true leader and didn't have an inkling of where to begin. If the past few months were any indication, I was inept. A failure. I had no business leading our kind.

And Petric had been a friend, one of the few men I'd been able to count on for advice. His loss tore a ragged hole through the shredded remains of my soul.

"There were nearly one hundred dead in the tower," Jal'den went on, heedless of my silent grief. "I have not been inside myself, but some of my people were tasked to help clean up. What you underwent was brutal. I will never forgive the Matriarch for agreeing to bring you here."

I turned to study him once more, stunned by the vehemence in his tone. I'd anticipated the Murkor would back their leader's decision, but perhaps I'd been mistaken. The furious, hate-filled part of me didn't want to believe him, but the dwindling, rational side of me did.

My internal conflict must have been evident in my features, for he said, "My people are in a difficult situation, one that even I am not privy to the details of, but what was done to you is gods-damned unforgivable. It's an atrocity unheard of since the first Great War." He clenched one hand into a fist and struck his other palm forcefully. "If we survive this, I'll make certain your people receive justice. As one warrior to another, you have my word."

He offered his hand, but I was unable to shake it. I clenched my jaw in frustration and nodded.

He groaned. "Gods, I'm sorry. Did you want to take my hand?"

"Yes."

"Then do so."

My arm moved of its own volition, but he'd given me the choice, and for that, I was grateful. We shook, and when he stepped away, he pointed toward the camp's center.

"I must speak with the commander. Continue your patrol. At midnight, someone will arrive to relieve you for a time. Go to the cookfires and take a meal, then resume your duty. I'll return to speak with you again—but not this night."

I nodded and began to move away, following the same course along the camp's perimeter, while he strode purposefully into the maze of tents. I was left alone with my tangled thoughts, my conflicted feelings regarding the Murkor and their role in the war, and my profound regrets. My body obeyed its commands, despite the hunger gnawing at my gut. I completed three solitary circuits of the camp, my mind adrift in a tumultuous sea of rage and despair.

As I began my fourth circuit, a purple flash of light drew my attention. A plume of color arced across the southern sky from the direction of the chasm, the color only vaguely differentiated from the background of stars. I frowned, perplexed by the sight, and wondered if it was one of the countless flares I'd once helped Aj'ana create. The light wasn't natural, nor did it appear magical, but an alchemical concoction made sense.

Moments after I'd taken notice of the flare, my Murkor replacement arrived. He muttered his commands in broken common, and I once again wished I could state I spoke their tongue. But I could not and was forced to listen to him needlessly struggle through the unfamiliar words. My body followed his orders without hesitation, and I was drawn toward the camp's heart and the promise of a meal.

The mess tents were erected in a U-shape not far from the commander's tent. Several dozen Murkor were stationed inside, ready to serve their brethren and my kind as we arrived. Amongst them were a trio of Serpentus.

Fucking gods, I hated that term, but what else was I to call the creatures we'd become?

I spied Tessamir, dutifully ladling the contents of an iron cookpot into dented mugs. Her back was toward me, but I'd recognize her thick mane of dark hair anywhere. I approached the nearest Murkor, who handed me a pair of mugs and nodded toward the battered tables at the heart of the mess area.

I peered into the mugs as I crossed to an open space amongst the other soldiers. One contained a chunky stew filled with the now-familiar mushrooms the Murkor seemed to favor. The other held clean water. I placed them on the rough tabletop and glanced at the hooded figures surrounding me. A few nodded in greeting, but none spoke to me. They continued their conversation in Murkor; they discussed the upcoming training exercises the Arms Master had planned and wondered aloud if any of my kind would be joining them.

I listened while I ate. It was an invaluable means of obtaining information—they spoke freely, unaware that I understood their words. I learned the commander's name was Aran'daj, the Arms Master was well-liked and respected by the soldiers, and the exercises were scheduled to begin the next night. One spoke of their craftsmen and complained of the sudden increase in their workload with the addition of my people to their ranks, but it was clear the commander was as good as his word. We'd be provided with armor and weapons.

Once finished with my meal, I rose and returned to the perimeter to complete my patrol. The night was cold, but the constant movement kept me warm enough. The thin gray tunic I wore, a remnant of my time in the caverns, did little to stave off the chill. It was soiled and tattered, the seams split at my shoulders and elbows, but it was the only garment I had—unless I counted the gods-damned collar I was forced to wear.

I hoped the armor the Murkor were crafting would fit my frame better. And perhaps if I was lucky, it would be warmer too… But I could no longer count on luck to see me through life. Karmada had turned her fickle attentions elsewhere, as I'd long feared she would.

When I returned to our pavilion with the dawn, I sought Tessamir's presence. We couldn't speak, but I'd do everything in my power to ensure she understood how much I truly cared. She was near the rear of the structure, in what I'd come to consider "our" space, coiled in a manner that would have broken her spine prior to our transformation. Her eyes were closed, but they snapped open when she heard me approach.

I offered what I hoped was a genuine smile. A glimmer shone in her eyes as she returned the gesture, and my heart leapt at the glimpse of her former, happier self. It was fleeting, but an image I'd hold dear.

Gods, she was still beautiful, despite everything we'd been forced to endure.

I settled next to her and watched as her eyes grew heavy and her breathing slowed. Soon after, I succumbed to my own exhaustion and drifted into a mercifully dreamless sleep.

We were roused well before sundown. Jal'den arrived with a contingent of brown-clad craftsmen, and several wagons were maneuvered into position just outside the pavilion's exit. The Arms Master's posture was slumped and he lacked the energy of the previous evening. The other Murkor were likewise subdued. Something must have occurred during our mandated sleep, but the snatches of conversation that drifted toward my location were too muted to understand.

Jal'den took up a position near the exit, drew a breath, then began to speak. "As the…*former* commander promised, we've procured arms and armor for you. Form into a line. We'll issue what's been allocated to you."

His dark hood swiveled as we began to move, then stopped as he spied me. "Owen, you'll come with me."

I nodded and adjusted my route to comply. He led me outside to a position equidistant between the supply wagons. I squinted in the harsh glare of the sun, no longer accustomed to its brilliance.

"Whether you accept it or not, you're the highest-ranking soldier amongst your kind. As one commander to another, I owe it to you to oversee this process." He released a ragged sigh and seemed to deflate.

"The Soulless executed Aran'daj at noon. As his second, I'm now in charge."

I narrowed my eyes in question.

"They claimed he committed treason against them. I… We lost nearly a thousand soldiers during the night. Aran'daj knew of their plan. They've defected, due in part because of what was done to you." He fell silent for a moment, then whispered in Murkor, "Gods-damn it, I wish I were with them."

A pair of craftsmen approached, and he straightened. One carried a thick leather jacket and bracers, while the other held a pair of war hammers and a belt. They were larger than the pair I'd lost in Stone Hill, but would suit my new stature well. I glanced at Jal'den curiously.

"Take off your tunic and try on the armor," he said.

I did as instructed with a grim smile. The armor fit surprisingly well, given that I hadn't been measured, and the bracers were comfortable against my forearms. I nodded once in approval.

"The others will receive similar garb," Jal'den said as the first craftsmen scurried away. "You'll do the army no good if you aren't properly protected." He pointed to the hammers. "Those took some explaining to our smiths, but I think I've described them properly. I'm likely the only Murkor who could have done so. They're yours to wield in the battles to come. Take them. Carry them with you until they're needed."

I took the belt and strapped it on. It was strange wearing a belt without trousers or greaves to run it through, but cinched tightly enough, it remained in place. It covered the transition between flesh and scale, a dividing line between man and beast. I shoved the thought aside and picked up the hammers.

They were heavy, forged of the black metal the Murkor preferred, and perfectly balanced in my hands. The hafts were stout, with leather wrapping around the grips. Each head sported a squared-off blunt end that would crush bones with proper leverage and force. I possessed the leverage, and I doubted it would take long for me to regain my former strength. My arm hadn't ached at all since the transformation. The back end of each hammer was fashioned into a single, wicked spike. I knew at a glance it would pierce steel plate.

I slid the weapons into the loops on either side of my belt and gave Jal'den another nod. He'd designed them well.

"Yours were the only weapons the smiths were tasked to make," Jal'den said. "We have swords, daggers, and axes by the hundreds. Most are standard steel, confiscated during the battles across the mountains."

I frowned in question.

He looked down. "You may be enslaved to the bastards in the tower, but I will do everything I can to ensure your people are treated fairly in this camp. You are their leader. As such, I believe you should have the best weapons we can offer. That black metal is forged with scorpion venom. It's as deadly as their sting." He paused to study me for a time. "There are snakes in the desert south of here that carry venom in their fangs, but I don't believe you were…forged? with the same variety. Are you venomous?"

"I don't know."

I hadn't considered the possibility, and like Jal'den, I didn't know what sort of serpent we'd been fused with. I ran my tongue along the back side of my teeth, but they felt unchanged. I certainly didn't have fangs.

Jal'den shrugged. "I suppose it doesn't matter. Treat the black metal with caution. Don't cut yourself on the spikes."

When I nodded, he turned toward the entrance of the pavilion and the line of Murkor craftsmen with their goods. "Let's begin. I'd like everyone outfitted before sundown," he called in Murkor. To me, he said, "You will observe. When we're finished, I will accompany you on patrol for a time."

I sensed there was more he wished to say, but we lacked the necessary privacy at present. I'd welcome his company, if even for a short time. He was willing to understand our predicament, our torment, and I grudgingly believed he was sincere in his desire to help. We needed the Murkor if we were to survive, despite the treachery of their leader, and I knew I should be thankful for every courtesy Jal'den provided. It was just so gods-damned difficult to *trust* his people after all we'd been through.

If Petric had been present, he would have advised me to give the young commander an opportunity to prove himself. Petric had been a more tolerant man, more forgiving, and I owed it to his memory to try acting the same. I hoped he'd found solace in Aeon's realm.

It took the team of Murkor several hours to outfit all of my people, but they were industrious and efficient. I learned there were three other pavilions like the one I frequented reserved for us, and in total, just under nine hundred surviving Serpentus. Given the nature of our servitude, I doubted even half would survive the remainder of the war. We'd been created for the singular purpose of fighting the Soulless' battles, and I didn't believe our overlords would consider our welfare in the slightest. We were fodder for the enemies' blades, nothing more.

The sun had set by the time the task was finished and my people were outfitted for war. Jal'den motioned for me to follow him as the craftsmen began to push their wagons away. We made our way to the southern perimeter and began the night's patrol, but he didn't speak until we were well away from anyone else.

"I knew of Aran'daj's plan prior to last night. It was my wish to join the others, but I've been ordered to remain here. My people need a leader who will see to their welfare where the Soulless will not, and the Kal has decided it must be me." His tone was laden with exhaustion, his posture slumped as he trudged along. "You must wonder why I've decided to tell you this."

I nodded.

"We are both victims of circumstance, Owen. I was chosen by Blademon due to my skill with a blade. I didn't ask to become Arms Master, and I certainly didn't expect to be fighting in a gods-damned war when I sought to become a soldier. We'd been at peace for generations." He shook his head and turned to gaze longingly toward the distant mountains in the west. "I suspect it is the same for you. And you are the last soldier of rank amongst your people. As such, you must lead them, whether you wish to or not."

I scowled into the growing darkness. He wasn't wrong, but I also wasn't cut out to be a leader. Who would willingly follow a man who had chosen a life on the road over a family and a home? I'd never been good with people, was terrible at recalling names most of the time, and if my interactions with Tessamir were any indication, I was fucking rubbish with matters of the heart. I was a man of squandered opportunity and misfortune, a man with a lifetime of grief he couldn't relinquish, and that grief, that *fear*, had created a coward.

No, I wasn't meant to lead. I was meant to fight and die on the battlefield, and the mantle would pass on to someone more qualified.

"Do you know of *ujar'havel*?" Jal'den asked, his tone wistful.

"Yes."

"My partner leads the rebels. He was taken to the tower months ago to learn the ways of magic. He was always a key piece of the Kal's plot, but hadn't decided when to make his move. Do you know what prompted him into action?"

I shook my head.

"It was your people. When he realized the gods-damned atrocity that had been committed against you, he refused to remain here any longer. He signaled the others, and they fled into the night."

I recalled the purple flare, nearly indistinguishable from the midnight sky. It had been a call to action, a summons many of the Murkor had long awaited.

Jal'den deflated further. "I've always been nearby to protect him. Now, he is alone, running from the Soulless and preparing those who went with him to…to fight us." He released an agonized groan and muttered in Murkor. "Fucking gods, it should never have come to this. Why have the gods forsaken us?"

The question loosened my tongue, and I replied in Murkor. "I don't have an answer, but I feel the same."

His hood whipped around to face me. "You speak our language?"

"Yes."

He chuckled. "I wish I'd known this sooner, but I never asked… Who else amongst the Serpentus knows the Murkor language?"

"I don't know. I may be the only one, though Tess has picked up some."

"Who is Tess? Is she important to you?"

Prompted by the magic that bound me, I couldn't mask my true feelings when asked directly. "She's the woman I seek when I return each morning. She's a former barkeep, a friend, and someone I love. Yes, she is important to me."

"She is not your partner? Your wife?"

I shook my head. "No."

"But you wish for it?"

"Yes."

My face flushed with shame. She should have been the first to hear, not the Murkor commander, but the compulsion that drove my answers didn't allow for hedging or half-truths.

"Does she know how you feel?"

"I don't know." I didn't understand his interest in our relationship, but I was in no position to alter the course of our conversation.

"She deserves to know for certain," Jal'den stated after a moment's pause. "I give you this order. When you see her next, you must tell her you love her."

I nodded in assent, though I could not hide my bewilderment.

He chuckled at my reaction. "I may be young, but I understand love…and loss. Perhaps my command is a meager gift, but you deserve better than this gods-damned fate."

I wanted to express my gratitude, to convey the hope his order provided, but my voice was mute. Tessamir would know my true feelings, and no matter the outcome, it was a small measure of peace to calm the maelstrom of my soul.

When I returned to the pavilion at dawn, Tessamir was in our usual space. When I'd been granted my meal breaks during the night, I hadn't spied her in the mess tents and hadn't yet completed the commander's oddly sentimental orders. As I took my place beside her, my stomach twisted itself into knots only a serpentine body was capable of.

When her eyes met mine, I blurted, "Tess, I love you."

She blinked, stunned, then narrowed her eyes in question while her expression told me she sought more. *Needed* more. The yearning painted across her features was heartbreaking.

But I'd completed the order and could say nothing more. I offered her an uncertain smile, yet couldn't mask the disappointment I experienced with my inability to elaborate. There was so much I wanted to say. So much she deserved to hear.

A slow, sorrowful smile crept across her lips, and her eyes remained fixed on mine. I believed she understood I was incapable of saying anything further, but I couldn't be certain. If we survived to see an end to our captivity, I'd share the details of Jal'den's orders with her.

He'd called it a meager gift, but to me, it was profound. I prayed she felt the same.

Even if she did not, I was comforted, knowing she was aware of my feelings at long last. I'd been a gods-damned fool, but at least I'd been provided an opportunity to remedy this particular mistake.

Her eyes fluttered closed after a time. I smiled as I drifted into sleep, my heart marginally at peace for the first time since we'd departed the caverns.

She knew. Nothing else truly mattered.

20

A NEW HELL

When I awoke, I was greeted with a smile from Tessamir. She was coiled in the same position she'd been in when I drifted off, her head resting on her forearms, tilted toward me. The smile held a warmth and strength I hadn't seen from her since we entered the tower. I flashed a brief grin, and her smile widened.

By the gods, Jal'den had been right. My heart soared.

Our brief moment was shattered as a pair of Murkor appeared in the pavilion's entrance, their shadows stretched long in the last rays of the setting sun. I stretched and unwound my body from its tight spiral; it was time to begin my night's work. Tessamir and I shared a final glance as I adjusted my belt, then I departed for the latrines. Once finished, I went to the mess tents for a portable meal—tonight, the Murkor provided a soft, flat bread stuffed with fried onions and mushrooms.

I was becoming accustomed to the routines of the camp, my newfound duties, and my altered biology. I remained bitter at our conscription and my inability to speak when I wished to, but the Murkor had accepted us and treated us well enough. I'd have heated words for their leaders one day, but I no longer blamed their whole species. I'd been blind in my fury when I arrived from the tower, but time and Jal'den's actions had tempered my rage toward his people.

I ate as I made my way to the perimeter to report for my next patrol. I was even growing used to the Murkors' penchant for mushrooms… Or perhaps the unusual lightness in my mood was making them a bit more palatable.

I was paired with an older Murkor for the night, who introduced himself as Dav'len. He was garbed in the soldier's customary black, but wore a set of dark ring mail as well. A battle axe hung from his left hip; it sported a wicked half-moon blade on one end and a sharp spike on the other.

He nodded at my hammers as we set off. "Shen'daj made your weapons," he said in Murkor. "He made mine as well. He's a good smith. One of our best."

I nodded.

"The commander said you know our tongue. Is it true?"

"Yes."

He chuckled humorlessly. "I wish we could have a proper conversation. Fucking Soulless."

With every waking moment, I wished the same, but the magic that bound me was unyielding.

We circled the camp in silence for a time, following the western perimeter south toward the gaping maw of the nearby chasm. Even in darkness, it was visible, a black scar on the shadowed landscape. A light wind blew across the parched earth, stirring dust into the air, but it was warmer than it had been on previous nights.

I surveyed the nearby camp as we passed. It was a hive of activity every night as Murkor, following their natural nocturnal cycles, went about the myriad tasks required to keep the army functioning. My kind moved amongst them, and I wondered if we'd become truly nocturnal as well. I'd assumed our time in the caverns had forced us to adjust, and the transition to life in the camp was merely an extension of it… Yet it felt natural since our transformation, whereas it had not before.

We'd never know the true extent of our changes until we were freed of the Soulless' influence, and I wasn't certain I'd live to see that day. Perhaps none of us would.

My gaze drifted from the camp to the dark silhouette of the tower beyond. Lights glimmered in some of the windows at this early hour, a poignant reminder of the Shadow Council's presence and the watchful eyes of their devious masters.

In that moment, I prayed not for my freedom, but for the tower's utter destruction. The Soulless had been responsible for countless atrocities throughout the centuries; the creation of the Serpentus was only the latest in their long list of unforgivable crimes. The Tower of Obsidian was a symbol of their work, an icon celebrating the horror they'd unleashed. I longed to watch it crumble and burn, razed beyond recognition just as Jennavere had been. As Stone Hill had been.

The wind stilled as our circuit brought us nearer to the chasm, and Dav'len paused, his hooded head tilted to one side.

"Wait," he whispered. "Something feels amiss."

I stopped at his command, though I would have even if free. I sensed it too. The world seemed to be holding its breath, awaiting a momentous event that had yet to be unveiled.

I strained my ears, but heard little beyond the distant susurration of voices in the nearby camp and the clang of hammers on steel. I looked south, but the chasm remained unchanged, dark and foreboding.

A blaze of light illuminated the sky overhead, and for an instant, the landscape was lit in harsh contrast, nearly blinding in its brilliance. Another flash arced across my field of view as a fireball of celestial proportions plummeted toward the earth somewhere far to the east. Another and another crossed the sky. I'd witnessed falling stars before, but these were orders of magnitude larger than the paltry flares I'd seen in the past. Plumes of smoke and fire trailed in their wake.

"Gods," Dav'len breathed, his face tipped skyward.

I glanced at him and was startled to find the light was bright enough to reveal the blue face beneath his hood. He had strikingly human features, and like his hands, his face was painted in a swirl of silvery tattoos. His eyes were pale, almost colorless. I recognized his likeness from my infrequent visits to the temples of my childhood—the Murkor were Ukase's people. I hadn't realized the god was a patron deity until now.

Dav'len shook himself as the sky's fiery display ended as abruptly as it had begun. He rubbed his eyes with one hand and muttered a string of curses.

"Murkor eyes aren't designed for staring into bright lights," he growled. "I need time to adjust. Gods-damn it, that was stupid." He shook his head again. "Can you see?"

Blue after-images streaked my vision, but I could make out the darkened landscape well enough. "Yes."

"Good. If I'm still blind in a few minutes, I may need your help to reach the alchemists' tents." He sat down heavily on the ground and sighed. "I'm told they have a cure for blindness."

I stood sentinel while he continued to massage his eyes. After a time, he rose unsteadily to his feet with a groan.

"I'm not—"

His words were swallowed by a deafening crack. In the same instant, the ground shifted and tilted precariously beneath us. I coiled my lower body on instinct, anchoring myself in place while the world continued to heave. Dav'len stumbled and careened into my side. He grasped my arm and clung to it as though it were a lifeline.

"What in Aeon's hells is happening?" Panic laced his tone as his fingernails dug painfully into my forearm.

"An earthquake."

I was no stranger to quakes. The Crystal Isles of Balotica, my childhood home, experienced them on occasion, though none compared to the strength of this one. It was fortunate we were on the camp's perimeter, away from the temporary structures that were rapidly tumbling down on their present occupants' heads. My gaze flicked toward the tower, and my heart stuttered as I watched it sway.

Fucking gods, if it fell toward us, we'd be flattened before an evacuation could be signaled. And without an order, I could do nothing but remain in place, helpless in the face of my doom. Gods-damn the Soulless and their infernal magic.

Shouts rang throughout the camp as Murkor and Serpentus alike milled about and began to right toppled tents and wagons. Above the din of voices, the cracking sound continued. The earth vibrated in response beneath my scales.

"What is that?" Dav'len hissed.

"I don't know."

He swiveled his head to face the chasm. "It comes from there."

I turned to follow his gaze, and a fresh wave of panic gripped my heart. A tear had formed in the chasm's side, rending a new fissure through the desolate landscape. The jagged crack was tracing its way toward our location, and I could do nothing but stare.

I clenched my jaw, furious that I was forbidden to act.

"What is it?" Dav'len asked in an urgent tone.

Relief bled through my rage as my tongue was loosened. "The chasm widens in this direction."

"Shit. Take us out of here! North! Go north!"

I scooped him roughly into my arms and raced along the camp's perimeter toward the northern end and what I hoped was safety. Behind us, the crack continued its path toward our location. The sound of the earth splitting became a roar that drowned out the noise from the camp entirely, and I pressed forward ever faster.

Thank the gods he'd managed to state the damned order before we fell needlessly into the depths.

Abruptly, silence descended and the land stilled. A heaviness filled the air for several moments before shouts and curses erupted from the camp.

"You can stop now," Dav'len said, his voice shaky. "Put me down. I think you've saved both our lives tonight."

I nodded and complied.

"My eyesight seems to be coming back on its own. It's just as well. The alchemists will be busy with others tonight and I'd hate to be a bother." He paused to peer toward the chasm. "The rift seems to have stopped, doesn't it?"

"Yes."

"How far were we from the edge?"

I studied the route we'd taken. "Not far. Paces away."

He growled beneath his hood. "I have a mind to tear that damned contraption from your neck, our orders be damned."

I narrowed my eyes in question, though I believed I understood. The collars weren't simply a symbol of our forced subservience, they were the mechanism responsible for it. Fury clouded my vision. The Murkor *were* complicit in at least a portion of our captivity. Despite the repeated assurances they wished to help, they'd lied to us, used us…

If I'd been free, I would have lashed out. My hands ached to take up the hammers that hung from my belt and let loose the caged beast the Soulless had created. Dav'len was fortunate I could do nothing.

He held up his hands in supplication. "You aren't supposed to know it's the collars responsible for their control. Shit, *I'm* not supposed to know either, but I overheard the former commander speaking with the Soulless. That tall one with the hooked nose. He threatened to reduce our camp and our people to ashes if we set you free, and I believed him." He crossed his arms and looked away. "We can't combat their magic. We've seen what they're capable of, as have you."

I glared at him in response.

"Would you rather I free you and condemn my entire species to death, or do nothing and cling to the hope that we may yet live?"

I closed my eyes and attempted to infuse calm through my being. The rage would not abate, but I understood the difficulty in his decision. "Hope is the better option," I said through clenched teeth.

"I thought you were a reasonable sort," he replied. "I haven't spoken of what I know to anyone, and it's best we keep it that way. You will not speak a word of this conversation, even if questioned by another."

I wasn't certain if his command would hold up if I were ordered to speak by one of the Soulless, but I nodded in assent.

"Good. Follow me. I'd like to look at the new branch of the chasm."

As we began to retrace our previous path, I was unexpectedly overwhelmed by a deep sense of unease. An essence seeped into my mind from afar, hate-filled and vengeful. I intuited that its control was absolute; if it ordered me or one of the others to act, there would be no resistance on our part. It overshadowed the Soulless' hold on my actions and stained my soul with its mere presence.

A cold, emotionless voice echoed through my skull. *She has outdone herself this time. You are a fine gift, the jewels of my army. Continue as you were—for now.*

The presence dissipated but did not disappear. Fucking gods, what was this new hell? And if we'd been created as a gift, who was the recipient?

A chill rippled through my core. I knew the answer.

There was only one being the Soulless answered to, one god they deemed worthy of their twisted devotion.

We'd been gifted to the Nameless god.

21

WANING HOPE

His malevolent presence was a constant from that moment forward, a sinister shadow looming in the back of my mind. He didn't speak again as he'd done when he first wrested control of our lives from the Soulless. I'd begun to cling to the faint hope that my life wouldn't become any worse, despite the Nameless god's unwanted influence in it.

I'd never been so damned wrong. He'd merely been biding his time.

I had just settled down alongside Tessamir for the day when his first summons came. His command rang through my skull, and despite my fatigue, I was compelled to obey.

You will present yourself at the entrance to the tower. I have a task you are particularly suited for.

His words stirred a loathing in my gut so powerful I nearly vomited. I drew a breath and shook my head as my body rose and began to move toward the pavilion's exit. Tessamir eyed me in question, and I offered her an uncertain frown. I masked my fear to the best of my ability; she didn't need to waste her allotted rest worried over my welfare.

I would face the Nameless god and complete whatever dire undertaking he'd selected me for, then return silently to her side. Perhaps one day she would learn the details of my assignment, but not this day.

I squinted in the morning light as I threaded my way through the camp. Most of the Murkor were settling in to sleep, and few soldiers moved about the maze of canvas. Those who did peered at me curiously, but did nothing to hinder my progress. They understood I acted on orders from the tower.

There were no other Serpentus visible in the camp. It seemed I'd been singled out, though I could not fathom why. We'd been rendered equal in our captivity, each capable of the same tasks, the same feats... The same atrocities, if commanded. Why had he chosen me?

Unease rippled through my gut as I moved beyond the camp's perimeter. The tower loomed some distance ahead, its base lost in the heat shimmer reflecting off the parched ground. As I neared, a wooden platform coalesced from within the haze. A woman knelt upon it, her hands and ankles bound, her face tear-stained and hair unkempt. Her dress was of fine quality, but it was rumpled and soiled, torn at the hem and sleeves. I suspected she was a member of the Shadow Council.

As I studied her, *he* materialized beside the platform. He towered over even my enhanced height, his skin pallid and gray in the manner of the Soulless. Baleful, yellow eyes locked on mine, and a cold smile crossed his lips. He wore a ruggedly handsome face, short dark hair, and an outfit of black leather. I could sense his power, his threat, even without the compulsion that drove me. He was the Nameless god, the god of death—and he'd summoned me to become his instrument.

I attempted to resist his dark pull. I fought with every ounce of strength I possessed as panic swelled within, but the collar's magic was absolute. My body continued forward. I was a mere passenger in my malformed shell, and my body would do his bidding.

He smirked knowingly at my approach. "The commander indicated you are one of the most skilled warriors amongst your kind. A former knight, and now my plaything." He chuckled darkly, the sound rumbling through the air like distant thunder. "You can stop your futile attempts at resistance, Owen Greenwaters. They will not avail you. You are *mine*."

I shouldn't have been shocked that he knew my name—he was a *god*, after all—but his mention of it terrified me. He knew what I was, what I had been. He knew me as intimately as I knew myself. Fucking gods, why would none of his siblings intervene to spare me? To spare *us?*

He pointed one gray finger toward the woman on the platform. "She has conspired against me. You will show her the error of her ways, my fallen knight. Show no mercy as you kill her."

The hammers were in my hands in an instant, even as I screamed internally to refuse his commands. I'd welcome death if it meant I'd avoid spilling innocent blood.

My body darted toward the platform, swifter than I'd realized possible, my hammers poised to strike. I railed against my invisible bonds. The Nameless god laughed, and his siblings failed to appear.

A glimmering blue barrier erupted around the woman as my hammers whirled toward her head. My strikes hit true but were repelled by the magic she'd summoned.

The Nameless god *tsked.* "It was a brave attempt to save yourself, dear Shara, but I cannot allow you to live."

The blue barrier dissolved at his words while Shara began to scream. My body reacted to the opening. I spun the hammers in my hands and drove one spike into her heart, while the second buried itself in her neck. I wrenched them free as she gasped and gurgled, her scream cut short.

I wanted to vomit.

I spun the hammers again and struck the flat ends against her skull. She convulsed once, then fell still. Blood and brain matter leaked from the final impact sites, while more blood poured from the puncture wounds. I loomed over her, my weapons held high as I watched the life fade from her eyes.

Gore had never turned my stomach, but the act I'd just committed caused bile to rise in my throat. I'd murdered her under the command of the Nameless god, and I'd been helpless to alter my actions. Aeon's hells would have been preferable to this.

The Nameless god laughed, delighted by the outcome. "Ah, your people will serve my purposes well. She shall be rewarded."

I had no doubt the *she* he referred to was the woman responsible for the horror our lives had become. And he was *pleased.*

I swallowed another wave of nausea.

"I've seen enough for one day. You may return to your duties."

He disappeared in a brilliant flash as I turned to leave the gruesome scene of my crime. The woman's sightless eyes stared skyward, her body left to the scavengers in my wake. I dropped the bloody hammers through the loops on my belt, repulsed that the fine weapons had been desecrated by the Nameless god's foul commands. I managed to control the roiling of my gut long enough to reach the midway point between the tower and the camp, then I turned aside and heaved, expelling the contents of my stomach in violent fashion.

I'd followed the path to knighthood to help others, to defend those who could not defend themselves. In an instant, the Nameless god had decimated all I stood for and made me his unwilling, monstrous pawn.

Tessamir was asleep when I returned to the pavilion, as were all the others. I settled myself near her and considered what I would tell her about the morning's events—if I lived to speak freely one day. What would she think when she learned of what I'd been forced to do? I knew any one of us could have been singled out, that I had the sour luck to be chosen first, but my skin crawled at the memory of the woman's terrified expression as I struck her down.

I felt vile. Ruined. *Used.*

I closed my eyes as my mind continued to whirl. I shouldn't have been capable of sleep in my present state, but our standing orders to rest during the daylight hours overrode my internal maelstrom. I slept dreamlessly, yet another thing that shouldn't have been possible. My sleep should have been riddled with guilt-induced nightmares.

The lack of dreams was a byproduct of our enforced routine, and I counted it as a small blessing. I could rest without the image of the woman's bloody corpse haunting my every moment, though she'd return when I awakened once more. It didn't matter that she'd been a member of the Shadow Council—she'd been helpless, unarmed, defenseless.

If the Nameless god hoped to break my mind as his minion had broken my body, I feared he knew precisely how to go about the process. Repeated performances like the one from this morning would certainly drive me to the brink if I continued to dwell on them. How in Aeon's hells would I survive a determined onslaught by the *Nameless god?* Was there any way to protect myself, chained to his will as I was?

When I woke the next evening, I had received no epiphanies, no answers to my desperate questions. But Tessamir was there, her gaze locked on mine, and the simple fact that I wasn't truly alone eased my conscience. Questions sparkled in her eyes.

I grimaced and shot a pointed glance at the bloody hammers hanging from my belt. The weapons needed to be cleaned, but I couldn't properly maintain them without a gods-damned order. And I needed to be rid of the evidence of the morning's crime, for my sanity's sake.

When I looked up once more, Tessamir's expression was pensive. It was clear she understood something of what had transpired, or at the very least, she harbored suspicions. Gods, I wished I could speak—but what would I say? I was riddled with guilt and sickened by shame.

Our silent conversation was interrupted by the arrival of several brown-clad Murkor at the pavilion's entrance. I was spared further scrutiny when they summoned Tessamir, along with several dozen others, to accompany them. The rest of us were commanded to go about our usual duties before the craftsmen departed with those they'd chosen as assistants.

I followed my dictated routine while my thoughts continued to tumble and whirl. If I allowed myself to succumb to the despair that threatened, I'd lose the last scraps of humanity I retained. Yet it was so gods-damned difficult to remain optimistic in the face of the Nameless god's reappearance and our roles as his enforcers, his minions.

I'd never been a pious man and had often jested about the other gods' influence over my life, but now I regretted every moment I'd spent cursing Karmada, shunning Blademon, and outright ignoring many of the others. If I'd been more diligent in my faith, would I have been spared this torturous existence?

Perhaps it was for this reason Petric had been taken by Aeon while I remained. I'd never heard *him* curse the gods, even in jest. He'd been spared the torment I now endured. This near-silent hell was my penance for a lifetime spent goading the gods with my off-hand remarks and my cynicism.

Would further pleas sway their opinion of me? Would they take pity on our plight and eventually release us from their brother's hold?

Doubt plagued my every breath, but I clung desperately to the waning hope they'd intervene. The alternative was unthinkable.

That night, I began the first of what would become many wordless litanies sent to the gods who seemed to have forsaken us. It was all I had left at my disposal—even my rage was useless when faced with the Nameless' dire commands.

I prayed to Karmada for a reversal in our fortunes, to Ukase to reach a divine verdict and oust the Soulless from their dark thrones. I asked the elementals to combine their might and strike down the black tower that loomed on the horizon, the beacon of our suffering. I sought Blademon's warmongering—perhaps his battle prowess would be sufficient to break our bonds and set us free. I pled with Solsticia to revoke the Soulless' magic, to undo the horrors that had been inflicted on our bodies and souls. I called for Minora to speed up time to a point where we were no longer slaves to her brother's horrific designs and for Aeon to take pity on us when we reached the Underworld.

The only god I omitted from my prayers was the Nameless. He was undeserving of my time.

I received no answers, but I didn't expect them. If I had learned anything during the course of my life, it was that the gods acted only when they were convinced of one's needs.

And I'd be damned if I forfeited my only chance at freedom. I'd continue to pray, continue to hope that they'd arrive one day to put an end to our suffering. Even if that end meant death.

It had only been a few scant weeks ago that I'd been unprepared to face my demise, but everything had changed. If the gods condemned us to die, I'd embrace their decision.

Death was preferable to a life unwillingly bound to the Nameless' whims.

22

CONTROL

Days bled into weeks. The nights grew marginally warmer, and my patrols remained relatively uneventful, broken only by the occasional summons to the tower. The Nameless god had singled me out as his preferred executioner, and while I continued to struggle against the compulsion that drove my actions, it was fruitless.

My attempts to refuse his demands were met with grim amusement. His hold was absolute, while the fragile grip I retained on my sanity began to crumble. I couldn't withstand his taunts and demands much longer without devolving into the creature of nightmare I'd once threatened to become.

I hadn't truly meant those words when they'd entered my mind. I'd been consumed with rage at the Soulless, the Murkor, the gods... But as I neared the brink and was continually confronted with the Nameless' smirks and bloody commands, I realized my threats had been hollow. My reality had become far bleaker than I'd imagined possible.

Fucking gods, I needed a respite, a release from my unending misery, but the Nameless god refused to end my life. He was the god of death, yet he denied it to me—to *us*, as a people. He gained a sadistic pleasure from our suffering and his control over it.

Few of my visits to the tower were as quiet as the first had been. Often, the Nameless stood alongside the platform with the dark-haired Soulless woman responsible for our grotesque transformation. They watched impassively as I threaded my way through a throng of mages toward the bound victim of their god's wrath.

It was clear he'd claimed her as his favorite. His gaze lingered on her, hungry and possessive, while she seemed to thrive under his dark scrutiny. Sometimes my actions were dictated by the Nameless alone, but at others, he encouraged her to take control. Her savagery was unparalleled, and I was the instrument of her merciless and unbridled rage. I learned her name was Dranamir—she was the same woman who had threatened to kill the captives taken from Stone Hill.

Gods-damn her, I wished she would have. It would have been better than what we'd become.

After my first summons, I realized I could close my eyes while my body followed its unspoken orders. I was aware of my movements, could hear the gasps and shouts of the crowds, but I wasn't forced to bear witness to the carnage that ensued. I'd return to camp spattered with gore while the Nameless god's dry laughter rang in my ears.

My consolations were few. Since the Nameless had singled me out for the task, none of the others were forced to endure the same level of mental anguish I bore. Jal'den understood what occurred and often met me at the camp's perimeter upon my return. He'd order me to clean up and ensure my weapons were cared for before my scheduled rest, then accompany me as I complied. I sensed sympathy from him, and he often cursed his inability to remedy my plight. Though our conversations were one-sided, I'd begun to consider him an ally, if not a friend.

If we lived to see freedom, perhaps we'd find a place with the Murkor—though the Matriarch and their Kal would need to convince me of their intentions first. I'd lost my ability to trust them after everything we'd been through. Their betrayal of our people stung bitterly.

The days began to blur as time stretched interminably toward a future as grim as the present. I could see no end to our captivity and began to lose my tenuous hold on the hope that had once been my only source of true comfort. We were doomed to a life of servitude, shackled to the Nameless god.

I despaired. The prayers I offered to the other gods became pleading rants that seemingly went unheard.

Death was the only way out, and we were denied even that.

One of Jal'den's officers roused us early one afternoon, his gruff voice edged with fear. A distant roar could be heard outside, though I couldn't place its source. Something had changed, and based on the Murkor's tone, it wasn't for the better.

"Don your armor and weapons immediately. Report to the eastern perimeter without delay," he barked. "The commander will speak with you there."

Collectively, we followed the orders. I could sense nothing of the Soulless or the Nameless god as I departed the pavilion at Tessamir's side. The past weeks hadn't been kind to her—the strain of our situation had etched worry lines into the fine skin near the corners of her eyes, and the light that had once illuminated them was extinguished. She was but a shell of the woman I'd met in the caverns, though I supposed I hadn't fared any better. I yearned for the ability to gather her into my arms and promise I'd see her safely to the end—whatever end that proved to be.

The source of the clamor we'd heard within the pavilion was revealed as we reached the camp's perimeter and our view was no longer obstructed by canvas walls. An army sprawled across the parched plains, distant enough to be indistinct, yet near enough I recognized it as the force it was. Dust swirled through their ranks, obscuring details; they were on the march, the sound of thousands of footsteps accompanied by drums and shouts.

Murkor streamed around us and began to form ranks at Jal'den's behest. The young commander strode purposefully through the chaos, outwardly unperturbed by the prospect of battle. The tall Soulless I'd encountered from Stone Hill's tower moved in his wake, his crimson eyes calculating as he surveyed our gathering forces.

The Soulless paused as his eyes settled on our group, then he broke away from Jal'den to address us directly. "The Serpentus will disperse throughout the Murkor forces. You will reinforce each regiment with your numbers, and will obey the captain of the unit you're assigned to." He pointed a gray finger at me. "Executioner, you will accompany the commander. I'll not lose a second so soon. It is your duty to ensure his safety."

Behind the Soulless, Jal'den shook his head, but remained silent. Any protest he made would be ignored, and the Soulless' orders would override his own. I moved toward him without prompting as the rest of my people departed in a dozen different directions. Seemingly satisfied, the Soulless strode away.

"Gods-damn it," Jal'den swore once we were alone. "I don't require a fucking body guard, and you don't need to be in the thick of the fighting, which is where I plan to be."

I disagreed. The heart of the battle was exactly where I wanted to be. The odds of death would be the highest there, and I was eager to meet Aeon. A sword to the gut or an axe to the throat meant freedom.

"I believe I understand what runs through your mind," Jal'den continued after a moment. "I don't like it, Owen, and I won't fucking stand for it. You will not sacrifice yourself tonight, nor at any time to come. You will fight valiantly as you were trained, and when this is over, I'll see you freed."

I shot him a murderous glare. He'd ruined my plans, and I wasn't certain he'd be granted the opportunity to uphold his promise. What did he stand to gain? I'd watched him spar with the other Murkor from afar, and he certainly didn't require my protection. He was a whirlwind of black armor, his broadsword a deadly silver arc when aimed at his foes.

Fucking gods, I craved release from this hell. What didn't he understand?

Jal'den tilted his head, and I imagined he returned my glare. "It's for your own damned good. You'll thank me one day."

When I narrowed my eyes into slits, he growled a string of curses in Murkor. "I'd command you to do as the others have, but I suspect Kama's orders supersede my own." He turned on his heel and marched toward the head of the formation.

As I followed him, I noted the opposing army had moved nearer. Several figures towered over the rest, but I didn't immediately register their significance. Instead, I focused on their numbers; by my estimates, we were evenly matched. I assumed wizards were present to counter the Shadow Council and the Soulless, but I could not make out individuals from our present distance.

Jal'den gestured to the column forming on our left. "This is my unit. I may be commander in name, but Kama will give the order to attack." His tone was laden with displeasure.

We reached the front lines as the sun began to sink below the horizon. Several dozen Murkor soldiers greeted Jal'den with nods and salutes. One passed him a spyglass. He peered through it, then expelled a frustrated sigh.

"It's as we assumed," he said. "The gods have taken up arms against the Nameless. This will be a bloody fight." He thrust the spyglass toward me. "Look for yourself, Owen."

I lifted the instrument to my eye while I wondered why he'd grant me this courtesy. Knowing what we faced meant nothing while I remained a slave to the Nameless god's will. He'd send us to our slaughter if it meant he bested his siblings. Our welfare was inconsequential.

I scanned the ranks of the opposing army as they marched toward our location. Thousands were gathered; humans, hooded Murkor, Scorpion Men… And the gods themselves. Blademon strode ahead of the rest, clad in black armor the same color as the carapace that covered his lower half. His eyes burned with an otherworldly light as he surveyed the field. The others were scattered through the ranks. I spied Ukase with the Murkor defectors, his blue face bared for all to see. A swirl of flame marked Flariel's location near the rear.

I shifted my view to study those farthest from the front lines. Many were without armor; I suspected they were wizards or healers. Armistral marched with them, his golden wings catching the fading rays of the sun. Not far from his position was Solsticia, the patron goddess of humanity whose purview was over magic.

Rage flared in my core at the sight. Solsticia was our protector, yet she'd been absent while we were tortured and transformed. She'd allowed the Soulless' magic to bind us. She should have stepped in, should have spared us this wretched fate, yet she'd done nothing. Her apathy had cost us *everything*.

"Owen, return the spyglass."

Jal'den's voice cut through the haze of my anger. I handed the instrument back and forced my jaw to relax. I'd clenched my teeth so hard they ached.

He issued orders to his officers, but I didn't listen to his words. My gaze was fixed on the distant point where Solsticia walked amongst the wizards. I could no longer see her, but I hoped she sensed my fury. If any god should have stepped in to spare us from our present fate, it was her.

The officers dispersed, and Jal'den gripped my elbow. "What did you see?" he asked in a low tone. "Your rage is fucking terrifying."

A humorless chuckle escaped my lips. "I saw the gods. I saw Solsticia."

"Your fight isn't with her. Not yet," he said firmly. "But I believe I understand. She is—*was*—your people's guardian."

I glowered and managed a terse nod. His perceptiveness continued to surprise me.

I followed him as he spoke with the soldiers assigned to his unit. I scanned the faces of the Serpentus we passed and was relieved to find Tessamir amongst them. When our eyes met, she nodded once. Despite her gesture of reassurance, fear was evident in the tightness of her expression and the set of her jaw. I'd be near enough during the battle to assist her, though I wasn't certain how far I could push the bounds of our magical tethers if it came to it.

After ensuring his unit was in order, Jal'den beckoned to me. "I must have a few final words with Kama before we engage the foe."

We made our way toward the rear of the soldiers' ranks, where a contingent of violet-clad Murkor beat a cadence on their drums. Kama barked orders, and the rhythm of the beat changed subtly in response.

"Wait here," Jal'den said. "He'll order you to do so, even if I do not."

As he began to stride toward the Soulless, my body followed. He growled beneath his hood, but fell silent before we reached Kama's location.

The Soulless studied us for a moment before he pointed toward the rear of Jal'den's column. "Wait there, Serpentus. Our words are not meant for your ears."

As I moved to obey, Jal'den crossed his arms. "I ordered him to remain behind, but it seems your commands override mine."

"Their binding was designed that way," I heard Kama reply. He lowered his voice before he continued, and the remainder of their conversation was lost beneath the beat of the drums and the clamor of the gathering armies.

I scanned the throngs as they organized into proper lines, spurred on by the drummers. I didn't understand the intricacies of the slight shifts in the cadence, but the Murkor soldiers moved according to the beat's wordless commands. I lifted my gaze toward the opposing army, but found the dust kicked up by their passage had been enveloped in the gathering twilight. I could no longer make out their ranks, but I could sense the tension their proximity elicited in our own forces.

Jal'den returned several minutes later and motioned that I follow him. "We are to await a signal from the Nameless god before we begin the assault. Owen…" His voice broke, and he shook his head.

I peered at him sharply.

Jal'den drew a breath and squared his shoulders. "Owen, Kama believes the Nameless god intends to take direct control of your people during the battle. Fucking gods, I'm sorry. I wish there was something I could do to prevent it."

I clenched my jaw. There *was* something he could do, but I'd suspected for some time he wasn't aware the collars were the mechanism of the Soulless' control over us. And I was unable to tell him, rendered mute by their gods-damned orders. I allowed fury to fill me. It was the only way I knew to survive.

"I'm so fucking sorry," he said again. "Should I tell the others?"

I considered his question a moment before I hissed, "Yes."

They deserved to know what was in store, to be granted time to prepare themselves for the god's foul intrusion into their minds. I'd endured his control in the past, but most of the others had been spared. Tessamir had been spared. No longer.

"Then we'll warn them. Come."

23

THE COMMANDER'S PROMISE

I'd made a grave mistake.

The expression on each Serpentus face as Jal'den relayed the news would haunt me through eternity. Some glared murderously, some were shaken to their core, others were left clinging to the precipice of sanity. Few shed tears; most of my people were beyond weeping over their fates.

I was riddled with guilt. Perhaps it would have been better if they weren't aware of the next horror we'd be forced to endure, but I'd never know. I'd made my decision, for good or ill, and my people knew the truth of our situation. I was certain many hated me, but I believed knowing what was in store was better than not. They had time to prepare; how much, I couldn't say, but it was something. Wasn't it?

Fucking gods, this was why I'd never aspired to a position of leadership. Some would applaud my decision were they allowed to, while others would condemn it and curse my name for the rest of their days. I would never please everyone. Gods-damn it, I yearned for the simple days I'd spent roaming the Balotican countryside at the king's behest. I hadn't been forced to make decisions like this. I'd had little responsibility and the world to explore. No longer.

As Jal'den finished speaking with the final group of Serpentus, I followed him as he retraced his steps to the central column and his unit. It was past midnight, and the opposing army had yet to strike. The Nameless god had not reappeared, nor had he seized control of our actions. Tension was palpable in the air, a heavy vibration broken by the clamor of soldiers preparing for war.

"It may not seem so to you, but I believe you did the right thing," Jal'den said somberly as we moved. "If they learned you knew and hadn't informed them prior, many would hate you for it."

I clenched my jaw in frustration and focused on the darkness beyond our front lines. I'd be forced to fight the combined forces of the Scorpion Men and the Five Kingdoms in a few hours' time, perhaps even people I'd recognize. The weight of that knowledge, coupled with Jal'den's assurances, only served to sour my stomach. He might believe I'd acted for the best, but it certainly didn't feel that way.

I hoped one of the gods on the far side of the field would take pity on us and set us free—one way or another.

When we reached Jal'den's column, he said, "I doubt we will strike before the dawn. Rest while you can."

I wanted to remain awake to spite him, but the command had been given and my body obeyed. My thoughts continued to whirl as I coiled up and closed my eyes. Under normal circumstances, sleep would have proven elusive, but it claimed me within moments. Normalcy had long abandoned my life of unwilling servitude.

I was jolted awake several hours later as his first command echoed in my skull. *Rise, Serpentus, and prepare yourselves for battle!*

I rose to my full height and peered through the pre-dawn light at the nearby Murkor. Jal'den turned his hood toward me, his head tilted in question at my abrupt movement. I loosened the hammers at my belt and hefted them into my hands, while simultaneously pleading with my eyes. He possessed the power to end my torment. Gods, I wished he would.

Jal'den strode toward my location but maintained a wary distance. "Does he command you?"

"Yes," I hissed through clenched teeth.

"I'm so fucking sorry it has come to this." He hung his head and turned away, forlorn.

I wanted to rage, to scream at the indignity we'd been saddled with, the unfairness of it all. I wanted to break my magical shackles and take the fight to the Nameless god directly, regardless of the outcome. I wanted to charge recklessly forward into the ranks of waiting enemies with the hope I'd be skewered on a spear or shot down by a rain of arrows.

I could do none of those things. Instead, I awaited the next command, poised for combat, hammers in hand.

Observe as I ascend to glory.

I turned to face the chasm south of our location as insidious laughter ricocheted from its obsidian walls. The Nameless god materialized at its rim and faced the opposing army, a smirk on his face. A pair of enormous swords were strapped to his back, but he made no move to reach for them. Clad in black armor akin to Blademon's, he crossed his arms.

"Welcome, my brothers and sisters. It's been far too long since last we spoke." His voice rolled across the cracked plains, sonorous and sure.

I grimaced and struggled futilely against his hold. Fucking gods, I would have done *anything* to be free in that moment.

Blademon skittered forward to stand at the forefront of his army, a dangerous light in his eyes. "Choose your words carefully, brother, for they may be your last."

The Nameless bellowed a laugh. "Arrogant as ever, I see." He gestured toward our army, comprised of conscripted Murkor and enslaved Serpentus, while the insufferable smirk returned to his face. "I've gathered my pets, just as you've gathered yours. Shall we dance?"

A heartbeat later, brilliant plumes of magic streaked across the sky, sizzling and crackling as it shot through the air toward our foes. Internally, I recoiled. I had no defenses against magic, and we'd be facing wizards.

The Nameless god drew his swords and grinned at his siblings. "This will be fun."

His next command lanced through my mind an instant later. *Follow the Murkor into battle. Fight each opponent fiercely and without mercy. Stop for no one and nothing.*

The Serpentus began to press forward, and I with them. Jal'den understood what had occurred, and within moments, the Murkor marched to join our charge. Jal'den lengthened his stride to keep pace with me while unsheathing his broadsword.

"I hate this as much as you do," he growled. "I'd never raise my blade against Sal'zar if I'd been given a say in the matter. But I wasn't, and I must. I doubt my words can override the Nameless' commands, but I will do my best to remain with you through the fight."

I nodded once, though I wished he'd spend his energy on Tessamir. She wasn't a warrior, and this was no place for her. But I could say nothing without prompting, and the time for discussion was past. The other army was moving to meet our charge head-on, while the gods appeared at the chasm's lip to face their wayward brother.

Jal'den lifted the sword above his head, a signal to the other Murkor. "Brace yourselves!"

Arrows began to whistle between us. I was keenly aware of my vulnerability to the projectiles; leather armor allowed for freedom of movement, but was easily penetrated. The arrows were few however, and were easily dodged in my serpentine form, an unexpected boon.

I focused on the onrush of enemies as we drew ever nearer to one another. Most of the soldiers directly in line with our unit wore the black and gray of Kamshat. The howling wolf that adorned many breastplates and the mahogany tones of their skin was further proof of their origins. In the distance, a contingent of cavalry swung toward the army's northern flank. I could not make out their standards or colors, but I assumed they were Santinian. My homeland lacked the horses required to gather in such numbers.

Magical energy continued to lance across the sky, blinding in its brilliance. At times, it outshone the newly risen sun.

The clamor as the armies collided was deafening. Weapons clashed, armor was rent, soldiers roared, cursed, and screamed. My hammers made swift and bloody work of my first opponent, though I strained against the compulsion that drove me forward.

My struggle was fruitless, as I'd known it would be. The Nameless god was in complete control.

An upwelling of rage and despair flowed through me as I struck down another Kamshati. These people should have been my allies, yet I was relegated to the role of monstrous slaughterer at the Nameless' behest, an observer trapped in my own gods-damned skin.

Nearby, Jal'den was a dark whirlwind, his broadsword a deadly scythe as it cut down each foe. He was cold and efficient; I sensed he took no joy from the deaths attributed to his blade.

My next opponent was not felled as easily as his predecessors. He was a tall, brutish man with a hooked nose visible beneath his helm. He wielded a heavy mace and a shield nearly as large as he was, and wore a set of plate mail that was already spattered with gore. His dark eyes glinted as he shouldered past several others on his way to face me, while he beat the mace against his shield menacingly. The man was clearly seeking to prove himself against a formidable opponent, and I fit the description.

Resigned to a fight I didn't want to engage in, I darted forward. A grim smile split the big Kamshati's features, and he adjusted his shield to deflect my first pair of blows. The shield was solidly constructed of a hard wood, perhaps oak, and it would take more force than I could muster to sunder it. I needed to maneuver behind or beneath it if my next strikes were to be effective.

As I lunged to one side, the mace swung toward my head. I raised my left hammer in time to block the intended blow, then swung my right toward his exposed wrist. It wouldn't be a fatal blow, but perhaps I could injure his dominant arm. I wouldn't attack with the spiked ends of my hammers unless I had no other option—poison was a horrendous way to die.

The Kamshati yanked his mace away before my hammer hit its mark, then shoved me backward with his shield. The blow would have caused a human to stumble and perhaps fall, but my unfortunate physiology had the benefit of stability. I kept my balance and ducked under his next swing. I was faster and had a longer reach, and then there was the matter of my lower half…

The thought entered my mind unbidden. I understood its source as belonging to the foul being waging his own battle against the gods along the distant chasm's ledge, and I knew I'd be unable to fight the compulsion that followed. Repulsed by what I was about to do, I darted forward to close the gap between us.

The Kamshati was slow to adjust his heavy shield as I veered toward his right. His mace swung at my head. I'd anticipated the move and hunched low, able to maintain my momentum due to the sinuous nature of my lower half. While he worked to recover from the errant swing, I lunged. In an eyeblink, I'd wound my lower half around his torso and began to squeeze.

He gasped as the mace fell from his hand. His eyes bulged beneath his helm, and for the first time since our fight had begun, true fear shone in his eyes. I intensified my grip and held my hammers aloft, prepared to strike him dead should I fail to incapacitate him. His armor crumpled as I applied even more pressure.

"Gods," he wheezed. "I beg of you… Let me… go…"

I closed my eyes, ashamed and horrified, but unable to grant him the mercy he deserved. My orders had been explicit and unyielding.

"Please…"

I squeezed tighter in response. Ribs cracked audibly. Tears leaked from my closed eyes. This was wrong on every level, and I was helpless to stop it.

He gasped for air. His lungs, crushed beneath the heavy steel plate that was now his tomb, failed to draw it in. He would die even if I released him, but I held the power to give him a swift end rather than watch him suffer.

I spun my right hammer and aimed the spiked end at his helm. If I could have spoken, I would have apologized profusely. I didn't want this. He didn't deserve this.

The hammer met his helm with a crunch. The spike penetrated the steel as I'd expected it would, and an instant later, he fell limp in my scaly embrace. I wrenched the weapon free and uncoiled my body as I prepared to face the next foe.

The Kamshati's lifeless eyes stared skyward, his body crushed to a pulp beneath the mangled mass that had once been his armor. And I was responsible for the carnage.

Fucking gods, I truly had become a monster.

It was nearing noon when Jal'den signaled our group to return to camp while the reserves in the rear took our places at the front. Mercifully, my body followed his commands. I needed a rest, food and water, perhaps an hour's worth of sleep. It seemed the Nameless god understood our mortal requirements and would abide by them for the present. I didn't delude myself into believing it would last.

I sported a few bruises, but no serious injuries. My armor was spattered with the blood of the opposition—I refused to think of them as the enemy—and sweat dripped from my brow. Not all of my people fared as well.

Brown-clad Murkor met us at the camp's perimeter with cups of water and dented tins of stew. Jal'den issued the order to eat and rest before he disappeared into the crowd. A group of alchemists descended on our location as we ate and began tending to the most severe wounds. Tessamir coiled up at my side, sporting a laceration on her forehead, though she appeared otherwise unharmed.

The relief in my expression must have been evident, for she managed a weary smile. Her eyes betrayed her inner turmoil, a mirror of my own. Gods, I hoped she lived to see the end of this war. I'd rebuild her tavern and turn my hammers toward a new purpose if it meant I could see her smile without such unspoken pain.

Jal'den returned as I finished eating and drew me aside while one of the alchemists cleaned the gash on Tessamir's forehead.

"She is the one?" he asked once we were beyond her hearing range.

"Yes."

"I will have her fight at my side from here on," he promised. "I will protect her in your stead. It's the least I can do."

I tried and failed to express the depth of my gratitude with my eyes alone.

He clapped me on the shoulder. "Go to her. Rest. We'll be summoned to the front again before nightfall."

24

KARMADA'S ROTTEN LUCK

Late afternoon brought with it a surge from the opposing army. I was near the front once more, not far from Jal'den's location, while Tessamir battled between us. A wave of reinforcements pushed toward us; most were Scorpion Men, though many humans were dispersed amongst them. To the north, the Santinian cavalry was driving a wedge into our flank as bursts of fire cut through our lines, moving in the direction of the tower. Magic continued to blaze across the darkening sky. Caught between the twin assaults and the chasm, we were slowly driven back.

As night fell, I found myself face-to-face with a pair of Scorpion Men as tall as I was, but broader in shoulder and far more muscular. Each sported a set of sturdy plate mail on their human halves, and they moved with a speed and agility I'd never realized was possible. I knew it was a losing battle before I engaged. Their training at arms was superior to my own, and their venomous stingers had a remarkable reach. Yet the Nameless' compulsion propelled me endlessly forward.

There was no malice in my opponents' eyes as they closed in for the attack. One wore a sympathetic frown, while the other appeared pained. They understood my situation, but knew they'd be forced to defend themselves just as I was forced to attack. Their unspoken pity only made my internal anguish more pronounced.

I spun the hammers in my hands as I approached. The spike end would be more useful to me in this fight, and they were immune to the metal's effects. As I darted forward, the Nameless god released a wordless bellow of rage. The sound rolled across the battlefield, momentarily drowning out the clash of weapons and the shouts of mortals.

One of my opponents paused to glance toward the chasm. It was the opening I required.

I altered my trajectory and closed the remaining distance between us while he remained distracted. I landed one solid blow to the gap between his breastplate and rerebrace. He howled in pain as I wrenched the hammer free and ducked beneath his companion's retaliatory strike. She wielded a sword and shield, and while I'd managed to avoid her blade, I'd failed to anticipate a follow-up by her shield.

It struck my right side with enough force to knock the air from my lungs. I gasped for breath as I slithered backward and assessed the pair again. Despite the injury to his shoulder, the man had recovered. He bore down on me with a poleaxe. I darted to one side, narrowly missing his blow, only to be faced with the woman's blade. I raised my right hammer in time to parry her strike, but I would soon be pinned between them with little room to maneuver.

I'd moved precisely as they'd planned, and soon, I'd be faced with my inevitable end.

I ground my teeth and continued to fight. I dodged and deflected blows more often than I landed strikes of my own. Time and again, the woman's shield rammed into my bruised side. I maintained my balance, but I was rapidly weakening. The man's poleaxe whirled in a deadly silver arc that I managed to divert at the last moment, while the woman's shield crashed into my side once more.

I grimaced as several ribs cracked. I was unable to keep pace with them as my injuries mounted, and I wasn't permitted to retreat. Each ragged breath I drew was searing agony. I was certain I was going to die.

Then another blade entered the fray and drove the woman away. I risked a glance toward my savior and was unsurprised to find Jal'den.

"Owen," he called over his shoulder. "Return to camp and seek treatment! *Now!*"

Obediently, I disengaged and backed away from the fight. Three Murkor joined their commander in my stead. I scanned the press of bodies for Tessamir and located her not far from Jal'den. I prayed he'd keep her as safe as circumstance allowed while I sought the alchemists' healing touch.

I slid the gore-spattered hammers into the loops on my belt once I was sufficiently away from the action. My right side throbbed incessantly, and the pain I experienced with each breath did not abate. I began to suspect my ribs weren't merely cracked, but broken.

The alchemists and their assistants had been set up near our camp's eastern perimeter. It wasn't a short distance from the front lines, but Jal'den's order urged my body forward. It was the first time I didn't curse the collar's hold over my actions. It forced me to move on despite my injuries and fatigue, when it was likely I wouldn't have if my will had been in command.

As I made my way past the ranks of soldiers awaiting their turn at the front, I took a moment to take in the fight between the gods at the chasm's rim. The Nameless' obsidian blades glinted in the twilight as they arced toward his siblings. A gout of flame erupted near his feet. He danced backward, a sneer twisting his lips as the flame was followed by a charge from Blademon. The war god's sword was met by the Nameless' twin blades, and the pair began a silent struggle of wills.

I turned away as I began to pass through the campsite. Murkor raced between tents, the army, and the tower to the east. I could see nothing of the alchemists, but there was some commotion amongst the Shadow Council where they were set up between the army's camp and the tower.

As I drew nearer, I noted two of the Soulless were at the center of the uproar. Kama knelt amidst a ring of mages, the left side of his body a mass of burned and blistered flesh. He clutched his left arm to his chest. Dranamir stood impassively to one side, her gaze fixed on the Nameless god's location.

If I hadn't been so exhausted, I would have smirked at the injured Soulless as I passed. His pain was nothing compared to what my people had endured at their hands.

A flash of green drew my attention to the tower's entrance as an alchemist darted inside. They had moved their make-shift infirmary indoors. My body followed the Murkor, though my mind clamored against it. The tower was the last gods-damned place I wanted to be.

Inside, the foyer was littered with piles of soiled bandages, empty vials, and various urns in need of washing. The stench of blood and death was nearly overpowering. The alchemist I'd followed inside ignored the mess and disappeared through the open doors of the same room we'd been taken to for our transformation.

I fought against the compulsion to no avail. Within moments, I'd entered the space behind the alchemist.

The room had been transformed into a field hospital. Beds and tables formed rows the length of the room, while Murkor and a handful of mages worked amongst them. Most of the beds and tables were occupied by the wounded, many sporting injuries far more severe than my broken ribs. I paused within the threshold as a harried alchemist with an armload of bloody bandages moved toward me.

"I'll see to you in a moment," she said brusquely in common.

I remained where I was until she returned moments later. "Who sent you?" she asked.

"Jal'den."

"*Oh.*" She glanced over one shoulder, then beckoned for me to follow. "You're the Serpentus leader. I didn't recognize you beneath the gore."

I was led to an open space at the foot of the dais. Dranamir's throne sat in its center, unoccupied, though my mind replayed the images of her perched there, surrounded by glowing magical orbs. I clenched my jaw and stared at the throne, unable to avert my gaze as I relived the hours of torture I'd so recently endured.

A hand gripped mine firmly and squeezed. "Where are you hurt?" The alchemist's voice mercifully broke through my bleak reverie. I tore my gaze from the throne to face her. "My ribs."

"Remove your armor. I'll patch you up as well as I can."

I grimaced as I began to unbuckle my belt and blood-spattered jacket. My battered ribs and sore muscles protested each movement. I looked down at my torso as I pulled my jacket off; my right side was a mass of blue and purple bruises.

The alchemist ran her fingers along my ribs, then nodded to herself as I winced from the pressure. "Two are certainly broken, perhaps a third. I will bind them, but afterwards, you must return to your unit."

I nodded my understanding.

"Good. Lift your arms and remain still."

I scanned the room while she worked. Most of the wounded were Murkor, but a few of my people were amongst them. I recognized some faces from our time in the army's camp, but I didn't know their names. That the Murkor considered me their leader when I'd scarcely been afforded an opportunity to learn who they were was gods-damned ironic.

"Move your torso a bit. Are the bindings comfortable?" she asked when she was finished.

I twisted experimentally. The pain remained, but it wasn't as sharp as it had been, and the bindings didn't hinder my movement. "Yes."

"Good. Don your armor, then return to your unit."

She strode away as I began to comply, her attention already fixed on the next wounded soldier. I wished I could thank her for her time, but I suspected she intuited my gratitude. I was equally grateful to depart the room, the scene of my people's irrevocable change.

When I exited the tower, a brilliant white light blazed from the direction of the chasm. I squinted, nearly blinded by the display that would have outshone the noonday sun, and moved toward the camp. An eerie hush fell over the landscape as soldiers from both sides paused in their fight to gape at the spectacle.

The light dissipated after several minutes as thunder rumbled overhead. In the distance, the cadence of the Murkor drums abruptly changed while the opposition issued signals of their own. Both armies were sounding the retreat.

Rain began to fall and a howling wind arose, causing the cold droplets to lash at my exposed skin. Lightning arced across the sky to strike the ground at the Nameless god's feet. The earth shifted and groaned in response.

Our forces were gathered in loose ranks as I reached the western edge of the camp. The storm made it difficult to make out individuals, but my orders guided my path. I searched the sodden hoods and rain-streaked faces of Jal'den's unit, seeking a sign of Tessamir or the young commander.

I located him first. He was huddled a short distance away from the column with his captains, his form marked by the steel broadsword across his back.

I wound my way through the lines while panic began to grip my core. Where was Tessamir? She should have been here. It took me several minutes to realize most of the other Serpentus from our unit were missing as well.

What in Aeon's hells had occurred while I was in the tower? Where were the others?

Fucking gods, I didn't want to face the prospect of life without Tessamir. If she was gone, I no longer had any reason to live. I couldn't return to Balotica if freed—not in my loathsome new form. The shame and humiliation would be too great, and I couldn't stomach the piteous stares I knew I'd receive from my countrymen.

I'd opened my heart to Tessamir when I'd never done so for another woman. If she was dead, the Soulless had succeeded in taking everything I had left. Tears stung my eyes, and I allowed them to fall. The raging storm, the embodiment of Maelstrom's divine fury, masked my grief from the others.

I squeezed my eyes shut as my soul threatened to splinter. This anguish, this unspeakable *pain,* was the very reason I'd feared growing too close to anyone. It would consume me and leave me hollow, a shell of the man I'd once been. The Nameless god himself could stride through our ranks, striking anyone unfortunate enough to cross his path, and I wouldn't care.

Shouts of alarm invaded my bleak thoughts, and gradually, I opened my eyes. Brilliant flares of magic streaked across the battlefield as the storm continued to rage overhead, but the dueling mages weren't in their customary positions. Bursts of violent light erupted from a silhouette at the center of the empty field to be countered by streams of blinding luminescence by another nearer the opposition's front lines.

I rose to my full height to witness the unfolding spectacle above the heads of the Murkor. The motion caught Jal'den's attention, and he appeared at my side moments later.

"We'll remain here until they're finished," he said in a low tone. "Some of the soldiers report Dranamir slaughtered dozens of *our* people as she prepared for this new offensive. The mage she faces was on the wall at Delucha. He's fucking powerful."

I nodded absently. I didn't care who the mages were. My only concern was Tessamir's whereabouts. I scanned our regiment again but failed to locate her.

"He freed many of your people as we called the retreat," Jal'den continued. "She's with them now, Owen. She's safe."

I turned to stare at him, uncomprehending.

"He broke through the Nameless' control," he said evenly. "I wasn't watching closely enough to see how, but he did it. Most of the Serpentus in my unit are gone. You would have been with them if I hadn't sent you to the alchemists."

I was at once relieved and frustrated. Tessamir was safe, freed of the vile compulsion that continued to grip my mind, but Jal'den didn't understand the mechanism was the gods-damned collar encircling my throat. And I had no way of informing him.

The mages continued to battle for some time, their attacks illuminating the night in lurid shades of red and bursts of white, blue, and green. Jal'den departed to speak with others while I continued to watch the ethereal display. After a time, a column of white fire raked across the battlefield.

As I blinked away the after-images, the Nameless god released a furious roar unlike anything I'd heard previously. The sound was laden with rage and laced with soul-rending anguish, a wordless expression of raw emotion only a god could muster.

He did not issue new commands to the Serpentus who remained under his control, but seemed to redouble his attacks against his siblings. The battlefield fell eerily silent in the wake of his outburst.

I didn't need further confirmation that his Soulless was dead. Dranamir, the woman who had stolen my humanity and usurped my freedom, was dead. The mage had stolen my opportunity for revenge, but he'd given me something meaningful in return.

Hope burned in my heart for the first time in weeks. Tessamir was free, and our tormentor had been killed.

Now, I merely needed to keep myself alive long enough to rejoin her.

We reformed our ranks with the dawn. In the light of the new day, the damage the gods' fury and the mages' battle had wrought upon the landscape became clear. The dry earth was muddied, scorch marks marred its surface, and another new fissure had opened where the magical duel had occurred. The gods continued their onslaught against the Nameless, but he showed no signs of weakening.

Jal'den stood a few paces ahead of my location, his right hand lifted to shield his eyes further from the rising sun. With his left, he held a spyglass in place while he surveyed the opposition's ranks. After a few moments, he handed the glass to the nearest captain and nodded once.

"My column will face the group *there*." He pointed to another column almost directly across the battlefield from ours.

"You choose to fight the rogue soldiers?" another of his captains asked, mild surprise in his tone.

Jal'den crossed his arms. "Yes. When it's your turn to use the glass, look at the figure who leads them. He is not Murkor, but he *is* my counterpart. I promised him a rematch, and I intend to give him one."

Nods and murmurs of understanding greeted his pronouncement. I didn't know what he spoke of, but it was clear the Murkor did. They continued to discuss which of the opposition's units each captain would face when the sound of hilts striking shields echoed across the battlefield. It seemed Jal'den's counterpart had issued marching orders. Within moments, the other army began to move.

Jal'den swore. "Return to your units. We've run out of gods-damned time."

As they scurried away, he barked commands to a runner who departed swiftly to relay the news to the drummers at our rear.

"Owen, come here."

I moved to stand beside him and lifted an eyebrow in question.

"We will face the rogue Murkor. I cannot override the Nameless' commands to you, but if you have any control over your actions, please don't kill any of the alchemists we might encounter." His voice was strained, thick with emotion. When I nodded, he continued in a stronger tone. "I will face their leader myself. He is one of Blademon's people and was chosen by the war god just as I was. It is our destiny to fight once more. Do not stand in my way."

I resisted the urge to roll my eyes. I was no match for Jal'den, let alone his mysterious counterpart. Unless the Nameless god compelled me to interfere in their fight, I'd occupy my hammers with another foe.

The drummers began to beat their marching cadence, and Jal'den unsheathed his sword. I moved forward in time with his strides and drew the hammers from my belt. My injured ribs protested the movement, but the binding made the pain tolerable. It was going to be another long, blood-drenched day.

At least Tessamir was safely away from the conflict. The knowledge that she was free and receiving what aid the other army could provide bolstered my spirits. She was the sole bright spot in my otherwise bleak future.

When we were within bowshot of the opposing army, Jal'den signaled our archers, then sent a wave of shield-bearing Murkor ahead. Arrows pelted their advance, but most crossed the distance relatively unscathed. The opposing force used a similar tactic. While the archers prepared to fire again, Jal'den motioned for the second wave to charge.

"The axe-wielding Scorpion Man is mine," he growled over his shoulder a moment before we entered the fray.

Most of the Murkor we faced wore the black of the soldier's caste, though I spied a few green hoods farther back in their ranks. I would uphold Jal'den's request if I was able, though I had little control over who I attacked or the savagery I employed while doing so. After all he'd done to help my people, it would devastate me if I knowingly harmed his partner.

Jal'den's target was a short distance away. Flanked on two sides by Murkor, his axe flashed in the sun as it struck a black-clad soldier down. Beside him was a creature half his height, covered in striped orange fur beneath oiled leather armor. A feline face akin to Aeon's snarled a warning as a pair of daggers sliced through the air. I didn't know what manner of creature it was, but the resemblance to the Underworld's guardian was unmistakable.

I kept pace with Jal'den as we cut our way toward the pair. I'd challenge the feline while he busied himself with the Scorpion Man.

A Murkor blocked my path and growled a warning which I was compelled to ignore. I swung my right hammer toward his head and my left at his sword arm. He parried the right and ducked to avoid the left. I brought my left hammer back in a reverse arc. The spiked end tore through the Murkor's hood and lodged in the side of his neck. He stiffened, and I wrenched my weapons free. He crumpled and fell.

I moved on, silently grieving his demise as I darted toward the dagger-wielding feline. Jal'den cut down another Murkor, then braced himself for his next opponent. The Scorpion Man conferred with the feline warrior briefly, then focused on Jal'den. The feline motioned to the two Murkor behind him, and the trio converged on my location.

The feline had proven quick with his daggers, but I didn't consider him the greatest threat of the group. At half my height, he was at a disadvantage. One Murkor was tall and wiry; he wore ring mail and carried a short sword and shield. The other was shorter but bulged with muscle. He brandished a two-handed mace. The heavy weapon would be difficult to parry with a single hammer. I prepared to go on the defensive.

The mace-wielding Murkor moved to flank my left side. I turned slightly to face him, while keeping the others within my field of view. I flicked a glance in Jal'den's direction and knew I'd receive no intervention from him this time. He was holding his own against his counterpart, but they were equally matched. Nearby soldiers had moved away from the pair, creating an eddy within the battle.

When I looked back to the Murkor, their feline companion had disappeared. I narrowed my eyes and braced myself as they charged.

The mace-wielder swung first, as I'd anticipated he would. I met his strike with both hammers and grunted as the impact sent a jolt of pain through my ribs. He shifted the mace slightly in an attempt to lock my weapons in place. I wrenched them back before he succeeded, but failed to block the swordsman's attack. His shield rammed into my injured side with enough force to drive the air from my lungs.

I hissed from the pain and swung my hammers recklessly toward him. He danced nimbly away with a humorless chuckle.

The other Murkor used my momentary distraction and pressed his advantage. The mace arced toward my left shoulder, but I managed to lean away from his swing. I loathed my new form and what it symbolized, but my spine was far more flexible than it had once been.

As I rose to my full height once more, I felt claws dig into my armor from the rear. I bucked and hissed as I tried to dislodge my newest opponent, but they held firm.

"Gods-damn it, hold still," a voice snarled near my ear. "I'm trying to help you here."

The words went unheeded as I continued to struggle. The two Murkor glanced at one another, and the mace-wielder shrugged. The swordsman shouted a warning to his companion, who clung stubbornly to my back, then charged again.

I braced myself and swung my left hammer wildly over my shoulder. My assailant growled as it struck, but remained firmly in place. The Murkor's shield struck my right arm in the same instant. I grimaced as my arm was rendered numb from the blow.

Cold steel slid against the back of my neck as the mace wielder swung again. I lifted my hammers to block the strike just as I felt the collar fall away.

I froze, stunned. The compulsion to fight was gone.

The orange-furred feline leapt to the ground, rubbing his left shoulder while I stared wide-eyed at the Murkor mace hurtling toward my skull. I managed to raise my left hammer enough to deflect the blow slightly, but the weapon still found its mark. It struck the side of my head with a crunch and I crumpled to the ground.

As consciousness fled, I cursed Karmada's rotten luck and foul sense of humor. I should have known I'd taste freedom for a heartbeat alone before I'd find myself standing before Aeon's jeweled gates.

25

SURVIVORS

"Gods, he's heavy."

The words drifted toward me on a current of pain. I groaned but could not force my eyes open. Hands gripped my shoulders, and an arm wrapped around the lower half of my tail. My head felt as though it had split open. Perhaps it had.

"If you'd pulled your strike as the captain ordered, we wouldn't be lugging him across the battlefield."

It took me several moments to realize the pair spoke in Murkor, and it was likely they were the same soldiers I'd been fighting before I fell.

The hands on my shoulders shifted, and the movement sent a blinding lance of pain through my skull, rendering me senseless once more.

When I awakened the next time, I was lying flat on my back. A pair of hands clasped my left palm in a light grip. My head throbbed in time with my heartbeat, my right side ached, and the end of my tail felt as though it had been stomped on. I opened my eyes a sliver and winced at the muted light.

"Owen?"

Through the haze of discomfort, her voice broke through like a ray of sunlight at the end of a storm. "Tess?"

The hands squeezed mine in reassurance. "I'm here. Lay still. I need to tell the wizards you're awake."

"Hmm."

I didn't have the strength to muster any further response, but she was alive, safe as Jal'den had promised. *Free.*

Gods, I'd never fully appreciated my life prior to our months-long captivity. To be granted the choice to make my own way in the world… I'd squandered so many years running from my misguided fears that I'd failed to appreciate what I had. What I *could have* had. It had taken an atrocity of the greatest magnitude before I realized my error.

I would not repeat it. I would seize each day as though it were my last and make the most of the life I had—such as it was. I could never return to Balotica or the knighthood, but I could make a life with Tessamir. Where we'd go and what we'd do was a matter for another day, but we now had the freedom to *choose.*

I smiled as I heard the rasp of her scales against the ground upon her return. Her hands grasped mine and gave a gentle squeeze.

"Radosan is on his way. He's the leader of the Greens. The healers," she added for my benefit. "The wizards have been doing their best to heal your injuries when they aren't pulled away for those with more serious wounds. Your head wound was concerning, but since you've awakened, I'll take it as a sign you're recovering."

My smile widened, but I didn't open my eyes. "It's good to hear your voice."

"I've been speaking to you for nearly a week. I'm merely pleased you're awake to hear it."

"A week?"

I lifted my right hand toward my head. My fingers were met with strips of cloth, wound around my scalp. The mace had struck me more fiercely than I'd realized.

"Almost. It has been five days. You're lucky to be alive," she replied in a tremulous tone. "There were times when I thought I'd lost you, and I…" Her voice broke and dissolved into a strangled sob.

I mustered what little strength I possessed and squeezed her hand. "But you didn't. I'm here."

She sniffled and was silent for a time. "Do you recall the last words you said to me?"

I began to nod, but agony blazed through my skull. I clenched my jaw in an attempt to fight off the accompanying wave of nausea. Once it passed, I said, "I remember, and I'll say it again. I love you, Tess."

She leaned her forehead against my shoulder and held my hand tighter. "Without those words, I would have given up. I would have fought recklessly as that Nameless bastard pushed me to do. I would have died seeking the release from the hell our world has become because I had nothing left to live for. But your words… They gave me reason, hope. I couldn't imagine leaving you alone to suffer through this life. I wanted to be here for you, to be strong for you as you've so often done for me."

Hot tears fell from her eyes and spattered on my bare shoulder. I cracked my eyes open a sliver to take in the mass of dark hair that obscured her face.

"And you are, Tess."

"Gods-damn it, I wish I'd met you years ago." She lifted her face to peer into my eyes. "If I had, there would have been no smith in my life, and certainly no thieving bastard."

"I doubt you'd have wasted your time on me fifteen years ago," I replied with a weary grin. "I'm not the same man I was then."

She snorted. "None of us are. It doesn't change the fact that I love you too."

"That isn't what I meant—"

"I know, but it's the truth we must face. Jal'den's partner has been spreading a rumor that you're our leader, you know."

I closed my eyes and suppressed a sigh. It would only make my ribs hurt to release it.

"And how does Jal'den's partner know of me?" I asked. "I'm aware he was in the tower when we were taken there, but how does he know of *me?*"

She laughed softly. "Jal'den is here too. He's a prisoner of the Scorpion Men, but he's alive and has been allowed to speak with his partner."

"Then his fight with their leader didn't go as he hoped."

"If you mean Vardak, he isn't their leader, though he was chosen by Blademon." Tessamir squeezed my hand again. "Radosan is here. We'll speak more after he's finished with you."

I opened my eyes a fraction as the wizard knelt at my right side. He was middle-aged, with the typical light skin and dark hair of a Deluchan. A thin scar marred one side of his face, and dark rings encircled his green eyes. Even in my present state, I could see the man was exhausted.

"It's a pleasure to finally meet you properly." He offered a tired smile. "I'm Radosan, a healer by trade. You've been unconscious for several days."

"Tess told me as much."

"It seems you haven't suffered any short-term memory loss," he said with a nod. "That's good. How does your head feel?"

"Like a Murkor struck it full-force with a mace."

Radosan's smile faltered. "Maryn told me what happened when they freed you. It was unfortunate."

I allowed my eyes to drift closed. "I didn't make it easy for them. I'm alive, and the fucking Soulless no longer have control. They saved me. I can't blame them for what occurred."

"Are you tired, Owen?"

I began to shake my head and stopped as nausea threatened once more. "No. The light makes the headache worse. Moving does too."

"Hmm." His tone indicated worry, and I cracked one eye open in response. "Coreyaless has a remedy for concussive symptoms. I'll ask her to see you once she's free." He managed another tired smile. "My magic is spent at present, but there is too much work to be done before I can rest. Most of my order fares similarly. Until Coreyaless arrives, try to remain still."

"Thank you," I mumbled as he rose to depart.

Once he was gone, Tessamir said, "Do you need anything, Owen? Water or something to eat?"

My stomach had threatened to empty itself twice since I'd awakened. I didn't believe I could handle food, but I was thirsty. "Water sounds wonderful."

She released my hand. "I'll return soon."

Moments after she left, a different woman took her place at my side. "Radosan believes you have a concussion. I'd be surprised if you didn't, given the state your head was in when you arrived."

I chuckled weakly. "You must be Coreyaless."

"Yes. And you're Owen Greenwaters, the Serpentus commander. Now that we've met, I need you to sit up. My remedy comes in tea form."

I grimaced. "Every time I move my head, I feel the urge to vomit."

"Then it's fortunate I've brought an empty urn along for that very purpose."

Cool hands touched my shoulders. I opened my eyes to find a tall woman kneeling at my side. She appeared human at first glance, though her features were sharper than the average, and her hair was the palest shade of blonde I'd ever seen. When she sat back on her heels, I noted the pink and white moth-like wings sprouting from between her shoulder blades. I gaped at her. Airess were creatures of myth, yet she knelt at my side.

"I'll help you rise," she said, then moved the urn into position between us. "The tea will mitigate the worst of your symptoms, but first, you must drink it."

I allowed her to help me into what passed for sitting in my new form. The pounding in my skull intensified as I righted my torso and coiled my lower body beneath it. I groaned, then heaved into the urn as the pain overwhelmed my senses. I wasn't certain I'd manage to keep her tea down, no matter how beneficial it proved to be.

"I'd hoped you'd be beyond this stage after five days asleep," she said in a gentler tone. "Here."

She held a cup to my lips. The liquid was tepid and smelled astringent. I grimaced as I swallowed the first bitter mouthful. "Fucking gods, what's in this?"

"Herbs. Nothing in it will harm you. Drink."

She pressed the cup to my mouth, and I drained it in a few gulps. It seemed better than prolonging the experience. Gods, her brew was foul.

Tessamir arrived as I finished and coiled up facing me. She held a flagon aloft for Coreyaless' inspection. "Is he allowed water?"

"Yes. I suspect he'll be grateful for it at present." She shot me a smirk before returning her attention to Tessamir. "When the cooks bring food, ensure he eats. Broth or thin soup will be best until his stomach settles. Anything more will be wasted."

"I'm right here," I grumbled.

Coreyaless laughed. "And I'm familiar with the ability of my patients to properly listen. They often don't."

I scowled and rested my arms atop the serpentine coils of my lower body, then laid my head atop them, angled in Tessamir's direction. The brief interactions I'd had since awakening had left me fatigued, and I lacked the energy to argue.

"Let him sleep," I heard Coreyaless say as I closed my eyes. "It will help speed his recovery, but make certain you wake him to eat."

"I will," she promised.

I listened as Coreyaless rose and strode away to tend her next patient. Tessamir's hand touched my elbow, and I forced my eyes open.

"I'll be here, Owen. Sleep."

I managed a smile and allowed my eyes to close once more. As much as I detested what we'd become, in that moment, I was strangely content.

A feather-light touch on my arm roused me. I blinked several times as my eyes struggled to focus on Tessamir's face.

"Did the food arrive?" I asked around a yawn.

She shook her head. It was then I noted the fear in her expression, the concern in her eyes. "Not yet. Something is happening outside. I didn't want to leave without telling you."

I lifted my head and rubbed my eyes. The headache was gone. Not muted or subdued, but completely gone. I flashed a grin. "I'll come with you."

She fixed me with a knowing stare. "I don't believe it's a good idea. You should stay here."

"I've never been one to make sound decisions," I replied with a smirk. "There's no sense in starting now."

She groaned. "If I've learned anything about you, it's that your stubbornness is nearly legendary. If you insist on joining me, I won't stop you, but once we learn what is happening, we're returning here."

I nodded and was pleased to realize the motion didn't unsettle my stomach or cause additional pain. The gods-damned tea was a work of magic, despite its foul taste. Even my battered ribs didn't protest as I unwound my body and followed her.

I looked around our surroundings for the first time. We were in a large canvas pavilion. Dozens of mats covered the floor, most occupied by wounded or ill people of a vast variety. There were other Serpentus, humans, Murkor, a few Scorpion Men… Many appeared asleep, but some were simply too weak or injured to do more than lie down and watch our progress toward the exit.

A crowd was gathered outside the pavilion, their attention drawn toward the black tower looming in the east. A semi-transparent, shimmering dome encased the tower from its apex to its base. I stared, unable to make sense of the scene. Was it magic? And if so, whose?

Figures swarmed toward the dome's base. I narrowed my eyes, but from our present distance, they were little more than silhouettes. They moved rapidly and disappeared inside the tower moments later. As I watched, the dome seemed to solidify; the tower remained visible beneath it but became hazy and indistinct.

I scanned the crowd, hoping someone held a spyglass and had seen who the figures were. Most were bandaged like myself, fellow patients drawn outside by their curiosity. None possessed a spyglass.

Radosan exited a nearby pavilion moments later to peer toward the tower, then shook his head as he faced our group.

"None of you should be out here," he said wearily. "Go back inside and rest. You'll undo all the work we've done to heal your injuries."

Tessamir gripped my elbow. "We'll learn what happened soon enough."

"I—"

My words were cut off as a low rumble rent the air. I ducked and covered my ears on instinct, as did many others, but we needn't have feared an attack. The dome flickered, then collapsed upon itself, its magic spent.

Moments later, the ground quaked beneath us. Tessamir drew her arm around my waist and held firm. As the tremors passed, a deafening crack sounded. I gaped as I watched the tower, the symbol of the Nameless god's power and the Soulless' foul reign, begin to crumble and fall. Tessamir's grip tightened, and she leaned into my bandaged side. I ignored the discomfort and pulled her closer as we watched the stronghold of our former captors and overseers destroyed.

"It's over," she breathed. "Our nightmare is finally over."

I nodded. "We've seen worse than Aeon's hell and survived, Tess. Now, we can look to our future. Our *people's* future."

26

THE ROOT OF THE MESS

I'd been awake but feigning sleep for some time before Tessamir shook my left shoulder. "Owen, you have visitors."

My headache had returned with newfound fury during the night, and the mere notion of opening my eyes was loathsome. "Is it important?" I mumbled into my arms.

She laughed softly. "The Warleader of the Scorpion Men is here, as is Coreyaless."

I cracked one eye open a sliver. "Unless she brings more of her foul tea, I don't want to see her."

A concerned frown etched her brow. "Your headache returned, didn't it?"

"Mmm."

She rose and moved away. I heard her whisper to the visitors for a time, then she returned. "She's gone to fetch the tea, but Makta would like to speak with you for a moment."

"Fine."

I forced myself upright with a grimace. The pavilion spun when I opened my eyes, but slowly resolved into a steady image after several moments. My stomach lurched, but I managed to keep its contents down. Fucking gods, I'd never experienced a head injury like this. I prayed Coreyaless' tea, combined with the wizards' magic, would make it heal soon.

The Warleader was seated near the end of my mat. She was younger than I'd anticipated, perhaps in her late twenties, with muscular arms I associated with the smithing trade. Her chestnut-colored hair was bound in a thick braid, her brown eyes searching.

She studied me for a moment, then said, "My name is Makta. I'm the interim Warleader for my people until the conclave can be summoned to select my uncle's proper successor. That isn't why I've come. I've been hoping to speak with you since you arrived, but the healers wouldn't allow you any visitors."

I pointed at my bandaged head. "I wasn't in any state to see you before today. I'm Owen, and I believe you've already met Tess."

Makta's lips quirked into a smile. "I have. When I mentioned I may have a proposal for your people, she insisted I speak with you. She refused to speak on your behalf."

I lifted my eyebrows in question, and Tessamir shrugged. "You were a knight, and the Murkor placed you in a position to lead us, even before we were freed. Protest all you like, but I don't believe any of us will contest your position."

I frowned. "*I* contest it."

"Your vote doesn't count," she replied with a smirk.

I groaned and focused my attention on Makta. "What is your proposal?"

Coreyaless appeared then, bearing a steaming mug of her vile tea. I accepted it from her and took a sip. It was too hot to down it as I'd done the previous afternoon, but the heat obscured the flavor enough I didn't want to gag.

"I'd like to offer your people sanctuary in the Stronghold." Makta crossed her arms and leaned back, her expression uncertain.

It was a tantalizing offer, but I wasn't comfortable agreeing to the arrangement without speaking to some of the others first. It was past time I learned most of their names, and if they chose to defer to me as Tessamir alluded they would, I wanted to hear their opinions. We'd suffered enough indignities while bound to the Soulless; I wouldn't add another to the tally.

"I'd like to speak with my people before I commit to this," I replied evenly. "They deserve to have a voice in our future."

A flicker of a smile returned to her face. "I'd expect nothing less. I'll return at sundown with Vardak. As Blademon's chosen and Emra's general, his word carries more weight than mine, and he has agreed to back my decision. Regardless, it's past time the two of you met."

As Makta rose to her feet, Coreyaless pointed a finger at me. "You will remain here. The others can come to you."

"And the other wounded?" I demanded.

"I can speak with them," Tessamir cut in. "Owen, you asked for more tea. After all the griping you did last night about its taste, your head must be in sorry shape this morning."

I glowered and looked away. "It is. You didn't seem keen on speaking to Makta in my place, Tess. Why the change of heart?"

"You're seeking opinions," she replied with a laugh. "I can collect opinions in your stead. I'm not making a life-altering decision for anyone."

I sipped at the tea while I considered my response. "Did you truly believe I'd choose for all of us without seeking approval or advice?"

She shrugged. "I didn't know. I wanted to believe you'd act as you have, but I couldn't be certain. Not after everything we've endured."

She'd feared our ordeal had fundamentally changed me. It had, but not in the manner she'd been concerned with. It had led me to embrace those who came into my life, to make friends, to find *love*, for our time on this world was fleeting. And despite our monstrous new forms, I planned to live for every moment I was given.

"Tess, I may look like shit, but I won't act like it."

Relieved laughter bubbled from her lips. "You said it, Owen. Not me."

Countless conversations filled my day. I spoke with dozens of other Serpentus, and with few exceptions, most were amenable to Makta's offer. I did my best to commit each name to memory, but succeeded in recalling only a few. Names had always been a struggle, and my unyielding headache did little to help the matter.

Coreyealess brought tea twice more while I met with the others, and by midafternoon, the pain had dimmed to a dull but persistent roar. When Tessamir returned not long before sunset, I was weary, yet pleased with the day's work. I was confident in my decision to accept

Makta's offer, and I'd learned much about the leadership of the camp as well.

"You're in better spirits," she said as she handed me a wrapped parcel and sat down at my side.

"What's this?"

"A bacon sandwich. I spoke to Coreyaless outside. She thought you could use something with a bit of substance."

I grinned. How long had it been since I'd last had real meat? Months had passed since my capture in Stone Hill, and the Murkor preferred fish from their subterranean lake and mushrooms to pork or beef. I unwrapped the paper package and bit into it. The bread was a day past stale, but the cheese was sharp and the bacon crisp. I closed my eyes and savored the first bite—and the second.

"She's been by a few times since you left," I said after a moment. "Gods, I've missed food like this."

Tessamir snickered. "I noticed."

"If I never eat another mushroom again, I'll be fine with it."

She tipped her head back and laughed. "Mushrooms aren't so bad. Or are you still upset you've been eating fungus?"

I chuckled. "I'd forgotten about that conversation."

"I haven't." She paused to stare up at the canvas ceiling, momentarily lost in thought. "It seems a lifetime ago. And my greatest concern was the possibility of brewing ale."

"Tess…"

She shook her head and turned to face me. "I'm still coming to terms with who and what I am now. I used to fear snakes, Owen. Now, I'm cursed to *be* one. And some of the things I was forced to do…"

"You can't blame yourself for those actions—it wasn't *you* acting, it was *them*."

She closed her eyes and drew a breath. "I know, but the guilt weighs heavily on my soul. After speaking with the others, I believe most of us feel the same. Some have no desire to continue living. I understand, yet at the same time, it feels wrong." She heaved a sigh. "Makta's offer has brought them hope. No one I spoke to was opposed to the idea, and I was asked more than once to thank you for seeking their opinions."

"It was the right thing to do," I said with a shrug, then grimaced.

"Your ribs?"

I nodded. "The headache is better, but if I move the wrong way, my ribs remind me I'm far from recovered."

"I suspect Coreyaless will have a remedy for those as well. I'll pay her another visit while you speak with Makta." She nodded toward the entrance, where the Warleader was ducking inside. "You can say with confidence our people will accept their offer."

"Tess?" I asked as she turned away.

"Yes?"

"Will you bring me another sandwich?"

She laughed. "I should have expected as much. Yes, I'll bring you another sandwich, but don't become used to this."

I grinned at her retreating form, savoring the brief moment of lighthearted banter before I'd be forced into a more serious discussion. Makta was making her way toward me with another of her people in tow. He was a head taller than she was, and I recognized him from his fight with Jal'den. He was Blademon's chosen. Without a helm to obscure some of his features, I realized he was younger than I'd assumed, but the recent battle had taken its toll. He appeared as exhausted as the healers who worked amongst the other wounded nearby.

Makta led him to my mat. "Owen, this is Vardak."

I straightened and offered my hand. "It's a pleasure to finally meet Emra's general and Blademon's other chosen."

We shook, and he said, "You are the leader of your people?"

I snorted, unwilling to accept the title yet. "Leader is too strong a word for what I am. I am—I *was* a knight. One of only a handful captured and taken to the Murkor caverns. I… I don't believe the others survived this war."

I knew I was the only one left, but it was difficult to admit Petric and Senna had both met their end in the tower.

Vardak dropped his gaze. "I'm sorry."

I shrugged, then grimaced at the motion. "Gods, I hope I heal soon. But back to the matter at hand—as the only person of rank left to us, the others have begun deferring to me. We don't know what the future might hold for us, and who am I to decide what path we ought to take? I'm still struggling to come to terms with what she did to us.

It was not enough to strip our humanity. We were made slaves as well. So many good people were killed needlessly, simply because we were unable to resist the demands of the Nameless god and the Soulless."

I hadn't planned to say half of what spilled from my lips, but knowing they understood what we'd been through had freed my tongue.

Vardak folded his legs beneath him and sat. "Your tale is akin to our ancestors'. Makta and I have spoken, and I believe we can help—if you and the rest of your people are amenable, that is."

I smiled. Our decision had already been made, but I'd hear what more he had to say.

"I'm listening."

He glanced at Makta, who motioned for him to continue. He frowned briefly, then said, "Our people can offer refuge. When we return to the Stronghold, the Serpentus are welcome to join us. It may take time to secure lodgings for all of your people, but I'm confident our elders will make certain it's done."

My smile widened. "Thank you both. I'll speak with the others. It is a far better solution than anything I've come up with so far. And as you've said, our peoples share a similar history. We are kin, of a sort."

Vardak nodded, while Makta said, "I will send word to the Stronghold of your decision once it has been made. No matter what your people choose, know that we will be allies."

I chuckled. "We've come to a decision, Makta. I meant I'd speak with them again, now that I know it's been finalized. Most of my people are in favor of your offer. The few who aren't are free to go where they wish, but the rest… We will join you at the Stronghold."

Makta glanced at Vardak. "I'll send a runner with the news to the Stronghold tonight. I've much to prepare before our…*guests* arrive." She inclined her head toward me. "I'm pleased you've accepted our offer, Owen. If anyone can help your people find their place, we can."

Vardak remained seated and stared silently after Makta as she made her way to the exit. His expression betrayed little emotion, but when he turned to face me, he appeared pensive.

"She was against telling your people of our visitors," he said after a moment's pause. "I can't fault her hesitation, but I believe you deserve to know."

I narrowed my eyes. I could think of only one reason why Makta wouldn't wish us to know who was traveling to her camp—the remaining Serpentus would be furious with their presence. With the Soulless gone, that left only one possibility. The Murkor leaders were on their way.

"If it's who I think it is, she was right to keep it a secret," I hissed. "They sent us to the tower. They were complicit in *this!*" I gestured toward my lower half, nearly blind in my sudden rage.

Vardak held up his hands in a futile gesture meant to calm my fury. "Ukase has agreed to oversee our discussion with them. We don't know their full story—nor do you. They may have had no other choice."

"Did they know what the Soulless planned to do?" I demanded, my voice rising to a near shout. "Fucking gods, I don't care what the healers say about my present condition. I'll have justice for my gods-damned people!"

Heads turned to stare at us from throughout the pavilion. I didn't care who overheard my outburst. I was livid, and I would not be swayed.

"Which is why Ukase has agreed to oversee the meeting," Vardak replied in an even tone. "Let the gods sort this out. Their brother was the root of this damned mess, after all."

I looked at him sharply. "Was?"

He nodded. "The Nameless god is dead. I don't fully understand what occurred in the tower before it fell, but a powerful mage entered and struck a fatal blow to him. Aeon confirmed it later. The Nameless will spend his eternity doing penance in Aeon's realm."

I looked down as a flood of emotions consumed me. Shock at the notion a god could be *killed*, relief that he'd never return to repeat his atrocities, disappointment that I'd been unable to seek revenge on any of my tormentors, and a strange sense of peace that our long ordeal was truly at an end.

I drew a breath and winced in pain as I expelled it. As much as I wanted revenge, perhaps Vardak's point was valid. Ukase was better equipped to handle the Murkor, and my recent outburst was proof that my temper would only get in the way.

"Fine. I won't interfere in the discussion." I crossed my arms. "The others won't like this, but I'll do my best to assure them Ukase's judgment will be fair."

"I'll increase the number of guards I've assigned to escort them as well," Vardak replied. "You can't oversee the actions of all your people in your present state."

I snorted. "Did I mention that I hope I'm healed soon? I'm restless." I glanced behind him as Tessamir appeared, bearing another paper-wrapped parcel and a steaming mug. "And I'm sick of that gods-damned tea."

Vardak was still laughing as Tessamir settled herself at my side. "I have no fond memories of Coreyaless' brew, but it works wonders, doesn't it?"

27

SECURING THE FUTURE

When the Murkor leaders arrived, the camp erupted in a flurry of activity. A dozen Scorpion Men had been assigned to oversee their safety; my people weren't the only ones displeased by their arrival, though we had more reason than most to distrust them. I swallowed my rage and focused on seeing to the Serpentus' needs.

Most had nothing but the leather armor the Murkor had given them. Few had kept their weapons after being freed, instead, they donated them to soldiers who had lost theirs during the fight. I kept my hammers, though I prayed I'd never be forced to use them in battle again. They'd been a gift, and one I was reluctant to part with. I was no longer a knight of Balotica, but I would always be a soldier.

We were reliant on the charity of others until we could establish ourselves properly. It was frustrating, a wound to my pride, but I would not allow my people to starve due to my ego—and I required a diversion from the Murkor leaders' presence. With Coreyaless' grudging acceptance, I paid a visit to the camp's quartermaster to seek supplies. Tessamir was insistent that I not go alone, despite my protests otherwise, and eventually, my resolve crumbled.

She was damned persuasive when she chose to be, and I was helpless against her charms. She knew it too.

"I'll ask Aren to accompany you," she said once the matter was settled. "He's young and inquisitive, and one of the few who came away from the battle nearly unscathed."

I frowned. I knew the name but could not recall the face of its owner.

She laughed. "You'll remember him when he arrives. I also believe he needs a distraction," she said in a lower tone. "I've heard he's been tailing the Matriarch's guards since they arrived yesterday. Think of it as an opportunity to set an example for our people."

Reluctantly, I nodded. "You're right."

"I usually am."

She flashed a grin and my pulse quickened in response. Gods, she was beautiful when she smiled.

A half-hour later, Tessamir had helped me into my armor, buckling it in place atop the bandages. Someone had taken the time to clean it while I was unconscious. I suspected Tessamir had done it herself, though she refused to admit it. I left my belt and hammers on my mat, and headed toward the exit as Aren entered, escorted by a pair of humans in full armor.

As Tessamir had said, I recognized him. He wasn't yet twenty, and was lanky even by Serpentus standards. A mop of unruly blond hair fell over his forehead to obscure one of his green eyes. He wore the leather armor he'd been given in the Murkor camp, a thin belt, and a sheepish grin. When I'd spoken with him previously, I'd pegged him as a mischief-maker, and he'd confirmed it by confessing he'd pulled a few minor pranks on some of the others.

Neither of his escorts appeared pleased with him, and I groaned internally. What had the boy done now?

"It's good you have a task for this one," one of the soldiers said wryly, while the other nudged Aren roughly in the back. "We caught him stealing mushrooms from the Murkor mess tent."

"Mushrooms?" I asked incredulously.

Aren offered a weak grin. "I've grown rather fond of them, and I was hungry."

I snorted. "You should have asked. Thieving isn't necessary."

"Yes, Ser." He looked down, clearly chagrined. "Why did you send for me? Am I to be punished?"

I suppressed a laugh and motioned for the two soldiers that they were free to go. "No. I'm still recovering from my injuries, and the healers demand I have an escort when I leave. Tess suggested you'd be up for the task."

He brightened and looked up. "Me, Ser? But I'm nobody. I'm a farmer. Or I was. I was with my father delivering squash and potatoes to Stone Hill when the gates were locked. I'm no guard."

I chuckled and pointed toward the door. "I don't believe I'll need guarding today, but I may need your help returning if I grow too tired." I pointed at the bandage that wound around my head. "I can say with certainty that head wounds are the worst."

"So, I'm to act as your assistant, Ser?"

"Yes, and call me Owen. I'm not fit to be a knight any longer."

"I disagree, Ser…Owen. I watched you fight sometimes. You're better than any of us."

I paused once outside of the pavilion and shaded my eyes from the sun. I scanned the sprawling camp; the convergence of four armies, the wizards, Drakkon, and the Murkor leaders had created a temporary city of canvas and leather that rivaled Stone Hill in size. I didn't know where to begin my search for the quartermaster.

"Combat ability isn't the only requirement for a knight," I replied somberly. "I'll never ride a horse again. Half of my training has gone to waste." I sighed. "Do you know where we can find the quartermaster?"

"Do you mean Danness, Ser? He's Emra's quartermaster. There's also Dav'rim, with the rogue Murkor, or Kennik with the Scorpion Men."

"I don't know. I suppose any of them may be willing to help." I frowned. I hadn't considered there would be more than one quartermaster to speak with, but perhaps it was another opportunity. "Let's begin with the first one you mentioned. Danness."

Aren grinned. "He's Airess, like the healer. I didn't believe they were *real*, Ser. And—"

"It's Owen," I cut in.

"—Danness introduced me to Emra herself. She wielded the Fireblade!"

His enthusiasm was unparalleled, and his optimism refreshing. I laughed, then winced as my ribs protested—but the mild discomfort was worth seeing one of my people so filled with life despite everything we'd been through.

"It seems you've met every celebrity in this camp, Aren."

His eyes widened, and he shook his head. "Oh, no, Ser. I haven't met any of the wizards, and I don't plan to. I want nothing to do with magic."

I smirked. "If the legends of the Fireblade are true, Emra is a mage."

He blanched. "I didn't realize… She's a soldier, and the Fireblade is… Well, it's a sword, and I thought—"

I stopped and turned to face him, then placed my hands atop his shoulders. "Listen to me, Aren. Not all mages are evil. The Soulless certainly were, and many of their followers as well. But the wizards have helped heal many of our people's worst injuries. You've met Emra, and it was a mage who freed many of us during the battle. I don't claim to understand magic, but I suspect it's not so different than a standard weapon. The intent behind it is what matters."

He nodded. "I think I understand, but I still don't like it."

"I don't believe many of us do," I replied. "Come. We have at least one quartermaster to visit today."

"Yes, Ser."

"It's Owen."

He shook his head. "I am—*was*—Balotican, just as you were, Ser. To me, you will always be a knight. My father taught me to show respect to your kind, and I will always do so. I owe it to his memory."

I winced. "I'm sorry. I should have asked after his welfare when you mentioned he was with you at Stone Hill."

Aren shrugged. "It doesn't matter. That Soulless bitch killed him when he stood in front of me. She'd have killed me too if not for the Murkor." A pained expression crossed his face, and he turned to peer in the direction of the Matriarch's camp on the outskirts. "They saved our lives, then sent us to the tower anyway. Why?"

"I'd like an explanation myself," I replied. "They're to speak with Ukase tonight. We'll learn more afterward."

"You won't be there, Ser?"

I shook my head. "Vardak doesn't believe it's wise, and my temper only reaffirmed his decision, I'm afraid."

"Hmm."

I lifted an eyebrow in question. "What's wrong?"

"My father always said knights were thoughtful and never quick to anger."

A bitter laugh escaped my lips. "Your father never met me. And after the tower, it has been gods-damned difficult to rein in my fury."

"I feel the same. I know I've been causing trouble around the camp, but I don't know what else to *do*."

His unsteady tone drew my attention. His lower lip trembled, and his eyes shone with unshed tears that he struggled to contain. As tall as he was, I'd forgotten he was little more than a boy—and a terrified one at that.

"No one blames you, Aren. We're all coping with what we've become and all we've lost, but I will do my best to see us thrive one day."

He blinked, and several tears spilled down his cheeks. "We can't go back home."

"No, but we can create a new one," I replied.

"Will we go to the Stronghold? Was that the decision?" When I nodded, he smiled through his tears. "The Scorpion Men understand us. I'm glad we're going with them."

"As am I. Not everyone will choose that path, but they are free to do as they will. I won't force the decision upon them."

He spun abruptly and threw his arms around me in a fierce hug. I gasped at the pressure he exerted on my injured ribs, but didn't push him away. He needed this moment and the comfort it brought. After a time, he released his hold and moved backwards.

"I'm sorry, Ser. I just—"

I held up one hand. "Don't apologize, Aren. Never be ashamed of your grief."

He wiped his eyes and nodded once. "I'm glad you're our leader, Ser. I'll try to do better around camp. For you."

He turned away while I grappled for words. Had I truly made such an impact during our brief interactions? And what would Tessamir say when she learned of it? I smiled as I imagined her reaction. I believed she'd be pleased.

Perhaps I truly could become the leader our people required, despite my initial misgivings.

Aren pointed in the direction of an open-sided tent ringed by wagons and carts. "Danness will be there, Ser. May I go to the mess tent while you speak to him?"

I chuckled. "Yes, but queue up like a respectable adult. Don't steal any mushrooms."

He grinned. "I won't, Ser. I'll return soon."

I watched him go, amused and amazed by his youthful resilience. He'd lost more than I had by that age, yet he handled it far better than I'd managed to. He was a symbol of hope for our future, and I'd do my damnedest to ensure he succeeded—no matter what he chose to do in life.

I returned my attention to the quartermaster's tent and spied movement amongst the crates and barrels within. I paused at the threshold and waited while the winged man continued to rummage through an open crate. He paused now and then to make brief notes in a ledger that lay atop another crate at his side.

I cleared my throat to draw his attention. He glanced over one narrow shoulder and smiled. "I'll be with you in a moment."

Like Coreyaless, he sported pale blond hair and sharp features, but his eyes were coal-dark, and his wings were varied shades of green. He returned to his work for a time while I sat down to rest. The journey from the healers' pavilion had taken more energy than I'd realized.

He made a final note in his ledger, then strode toward me. "I hope my partner has cleared your visit, else I'll never hear the end of it later." He flashed a grin and extended his hand. "I'm Danness."

I straightened and accepted his hand. "Owen. And yes, Coreyaless has allowed me to pay you a visit."

"She's fiercely protective of her patients. Sometimes overly so, but don't tell her I said that."

We shared a laugh, then he said, "I've been expecting you. Coreyaless has told me much about you, and I assumed you'd come seeking aid for your people. I'm happy to provide what I can, but our resources are tight. I must ensure there's enough food for our return across the mountains."

"I understand."

"Then let's discuss your options, shall we?"

By the time I returned to the pavilion late in the afternoon, I was exhausted, and my headache had returned. I leaned heavily on Aren's arm for support, which elicited concern from Tessamir and a pointed admonishment from Coreyaless, who departed immediately to brew more of her foul tea. The discomfort was a minor inconvenience; I'd secured enough supplies for our people to make the journey to the Stronghold.

"Tess, I'm fine," I insisted as she fretted over my condition. "I'm tired, but I'm fine."

"You don't look 'fine,' Owen." She crossed her arms with a shake of her head. "I hope your adventure today was worth it."

I grinned. "It was."

Her expression softened, then she graced me with a smile. "Tell me."

I leaned my arms atop the coil of my lower body and leaned toward her. "Danness can provide garments and armor for some. He can't spare enough for everyone, but it's better than nothing. Kennik assured me he has enough food and water to accommodate our people during our journey to the Stronghold. That was my greatest concern," I admitted in a lower tone.

"And Aren kept himself out of trouble?" she asked.

I chuckled and told her of our initial conversation. "I believe he'll do as I ask, Tess. He's a good sort."

She shifted closer and drew an arm around my shoulders. "I wasn't certain you'd have the patience for him, but I'm glad you found it. He needs something to aspire to and someone to guide him. I'm not saying you're that person," she said evenly when I began to protest, "but he may *choose* you for that role. As I see it, it'd be good for you both."

I shot her my best skeptical frown. "I doubt I'm cut out to be a mentor."

She laughed and drew closer while my pulse accelerated. I could smell the faint scent of woodsmoke in her hair.

"I disagree." Her gaze flitted across the pavilion. "You didn't happen to ask any of the quartermasters about tents, did you?"

"I did. Kennik claims he has that covered as well."

She snickered. "Good, because as soon as your ribs are healed, I expect to have some time with you. *Alone.*"

I lifted an eyebrow and grinned. "Then you'll have it, and anything else your heart desires."

She leaned her head against my shoulder with a laugh. "Be careful what you wish for, Owen. I'm past the point of shameless flirting."

I leaned my head against hers. "As am I, Tess. As am I."

28

HEALING

I was nudged awake by Tessamir's elbow, her preferred means of drawing my consciousness from the depths of sleep. I felt as though I'd only just closed my eyes and I wasn't prepared to face the morning yet. But her elbow was sharp against my good side, and she was persistent.

"What is it?" I mumbled without lifting my head from where it rested on my forearms.

"You have a visitor."

I groaned but didn't look up. "Who?"

When she didn't immediately answer, I turned my head and opened one eye to peer at her. Her gaze was fixed on the pavilion's entrance, her expression wary.

"Tess?"

Finally, she turned toward me and released a sigh. "It's the Murkor commander."

I pushed myself upright to look for myself, then waved him toward us. Tessamir glowered at my apparent welcome.

"Jal'den wasn't at fault for the gods-damned war, Tess. It'll be nice to have a real conversation with him, one in which I can speak when and how I wish."

"His people—"

"I suspect it's why he's here," I said, cutting her off before Jal'den was within earshot. "Please hear him out. He's the one who allowed me to share my feelings with you."

She nodded once, and much of the fire faded from her eyes. "I suppose it can't hurt to listen."

"Thank you."

Jal'den made his way toward us and seated himself on the floor a few paces away. "It's good to finally see you, Owen. How do you fare?"

I smirked. "Well enough. The healers don't like to let me out of their sight yet, but each day is better than the last." I paused to nod in Tessamir's direction. "This is Tessamir. I owe you a debt for keeping her safe."

Tessamir crossed her arms and stared at him impassively. "We've met. It will take time to earn my trust. You may have granted Owen a favor or two while we were captives of the Soulless, but you worked for them. I am not as forgiving as my partner."

My heart stuttered at her declaration. I gaped at her, at a loss for words, until Jal'den cleared his throat. I forced my attention back to the Murkor seated before us.

"I understand your position," he replied evenly. "I also understand the drive to protect those you love. I did not come here to attempt an apology—nothing I say will ever be sufficient to express my sorrow over what occurred in the tower."

"Then why are you here?" she demanded.

"To bring news. Ukase was here last night to oversee negotiations between the various factions within my people's ranks. The reason behind the Matriach's actions—and the Kal's—was explained. I don't believe even Aran'daj was privy to the whole truth." He dropped his head and seemed to deflate. "Their position was difficult. The Soulless would have killed her if she refused to obey, and without her, our people would have been lost to the chaos of their schemes. They'd promised genocide if she didn't comply with their orders. We all know they would have followed through."

I clenched my jaw and looked away. If I'd been forced to choose between my people and a group of prisoners from a foreign land, I would have chosen my people. It didn't make our reality any less painful—we'd been nothing more than a bargaining chip as the

Murkor leaders battled for their people's survival—but I understood on a fundamental level. Like humans, Murkor were compelled to protect their own.

"Do you believe she'd speak with me?" I asked thoughtfully after a time.

Jal'den shrugged. "I don't know, but I will ask. She fears your people, Owen."

"And rightly so," I replied. "They've agreed to defer to me, but I'm in no state to monitor everyone even if I wanted to. Most blame her for what was done to us. We're fucking furious, Jal'den. We didn't simply lose friends and loved ones to the ravages of war. We lost our gods-damned *humanity*. Your people will never fully understand what we've been through." I paused to draw a calming breath and counted to five before I released it. "If you arrange a meeting, I promise I won't harm her or your Kal. Makta or Emra can oversee the discussion if it will ease her mind, but I need to hear the story from *her*."

Tessamir gripped my hand in a silent show of support.

He nodded. "I'll do what I can to arrange the meeting."

"Thank you."

He rose to leave, when Tessamir said, "Is it true your partner led the rogue Murkor?"

Jal'den chuckled. "Yes. It's likely you've seen him with the wounded. He's an alchemist. A healer."

"I have, and I've spoken with him once or twice. He's a kind soul, though I'm not certain I can say the same for you. I still don't fully trust you, but perhaps you're not a complete bastard if you've tied your future to his." She didn't smile, but a glint of mischief sparkled in her eyes.

He shrugged uncomfortably. "I was never your enemy."

"That remains to be seen," she replied. "We look forward to speaking with your Matriarch."

Jal'den nodded and strode away, his pace uncharacteristically swift.

I snickered. "Gods, Tess, he's terrified of you. I didn't believe it was possible to instill that level of fear in one of Blademon's chosen."

She flashed a grin. "I was simply making a point. It has been too long since I was given the freedom to make a man squirm. But when we visit the Matriarch, I promise I won't interfere."

"We?" I lifted my eyebrows and matched her grin.

"Of course. We're partners, Owen. In life, in love, in crime... Whatever label you wish to apply."

I reached my hand toward her, and when she didn't back away, I caressed the side of her face. "I don't know what I did to deserve you. And fucking gods, what I wouldn't give for my own tent right now."

She laughed. "Keep it in your scales for now. You need to finish healing first."

Heat rose into my cheeks, and I glanced down at the serpentine half of my body, my eyes drawn to the cluster of slightly darker gray scales a handspan below my navel. My manhood remained safely retracted behind them; there was no visible indication of the arousal I currently experienced.

Her hand touched the side of my face. "I'm well aware of how your body operates now. Some of our people are married. While you were with Aren yesterday, I may have asked some of the women for...advice."

My eyebrows rose in surprise. "Then they've...?"

She tilted her head back and laughed. "Yes. According to Rosalin and Wenda, sex is more pleasurable than it was before. But I will not be responsible for undoing all the work the healers have done for you. We'll wait—for now."

I groaned in mock agony. "I'm not sure how long I can hold out."

"Be patient. I'll make certain it's worth the wait."

"I'll hold you to your word."

She grinned. "And I'll keep it."

Radosan arrived mid-morning to assess my condition. I hadn't seen him but in passing since I'd awakened in the pavilion several days past, but he appeared rested and moved with an energy he'd been lacking previously.

"Your skull hasn't healed as fast as I'd hoped," he said after he'd unwound the bandage from my head. "I can fuse the bones back into place now that I'm certain there hasn't been any damage to your brain, but I must ask your permission first." He glanced between me and Tessamir. "My healing requires magic."

I appreciated his thoughtfulness and was certain some of my people would have balked at the offer. Aren had made it clear he wanted nothing to do with magic of any kind, but I'd spoken with wizards on occasion during my tenure as a knight. I trusted their order, and I trusted him.

"As Tess can attest, I'm restless. Anything you can do to speed my recovery is appreciated. My people need me, and I'm useless when confined in here."

Tessamir nodded and grasped my hand, threading her fingers through mine. When I glanced at her, her expression was pained.

"What's wrong?"

"Your wound looks worse now that it's scabbed over."

Radosan nodded. "It is healing, but slowly. I only seek to increase its pace."

"If it means I won't have to choke down any more of that gods-damned tea, you have my leave."

My words elicited a brief laugh from Tessamir, though they didn't eliminate the concern in her gaze as Radosan placed his hands lightly on my head. A prickle of energy danced across my scalp, accompanied by a soothing sensation. I relaxed in response and allowed my eyes to drift closed, at ease. His healing magic was markedly different than the agonizing knives of dark power that had reshaped me in the tower. It was almost pleasant.

I felt a light pressure as my skull knitted itself back together and a tingle as the remainder of the wound sealed itself. The dull ache that I'd come to associate with being awake and conscious faded into nothingness.

"Remarkable," Tessamir breathed.

I opened my eyes as Radosan stepped back and Tessamir touched the space where his hands had been. Her fingertips brushed through my hair and explored my scalp.

"I would have offered this sooner, but there were others—"

I lifted my free hand and smiled. "My wounds weren't as severe as some, and the wizards were exhausted. I understand." I glanced down at my torso. "But now that you're rested, is there any chance you can mend my ribs too?"

He chuckled. "Of course."

Tessamir reached around me to assist the wizard in unwinding the remainder of my bandages. I grinned when she glanced at my face; her proximity was intoxicating, and once I was healed…

Radosan cleared his throat, and I realized I'd been staring. Tessamir smirked and began to pick up the soiled bandages, while the wizard's magic flowed through me a second time. My face flushed, and I was certain it was several shades beyond crimson.

"I'll take these to be cleaned," she said with a laugh as she turned away.

Radosan spent only a few moments on my damaged ribs. I watched as the bruised flesh slowly receded and was replaced by healthy tissue. When he dropped his hands, I drew a deep breath and exhaled experimentally. There was no longer any pain.

"Gods, you're a miracle worker."

He smiled. "I help where and when I'm able, nothing more. You may tire easily for a few days still. While I've healed your wounds, my magic requires some of your body's energy to work. It's an imperfect system, I'm afraid."

I reached for my armor and marveled when I twisted without a flare of pain. "Nevertheless, I'm grateful. You've allowed me to begin work. There's much to be done before we leave for the Stronghold."

I pulled on my armor, offered my hand to him, and we shook. "Some of my people may not trust the wizards," I said, "but I consider you an ally, if not a friend. Thank you for all you've done."

He nodded, but his smile was laced with sadness. "I wish we could have done more, but there is no way to reverse the Soulless' magic. I sought Solsticia's input myself, and she confirmed the change is permanent. I'm sorry."

I looked down, disappointed, though his words came as no surprise. A few days ago, I would have been furious with the news, but I'd watched from a distance as my people began to accept their newfound place in our world. We had a temporary home with the Scorpion Men, our freedom, and one another. We were survivors, and I believed we'd one day thrive.

"We have a future, thanks to everyone in this camp," I said after a moment. "That's more than I could have said two weeks ago."

"If there is anything the Council of Auras can do for your people, all you need do is ask." He moved to depart, then added, "That includes after we've gone our separate ways, Owen. We will answer your call, no matter how much time may pass."

I thanked him again, then focused my attention on buckling my belt in place. Tessamir returned as I slipped my hammers into its loops. She paused to appraise my appearance as I moved toward her location near the exit.

"You almost look yourself again," she said when I drew near. She reached up to touch the side of my face with a knowing smile. "Will you keep the beard?"

I chuckled. "Perhaps. I've grown used to it, and there's a certain woman in my life who once said it suits me."

"She sounds wise. It does, though it could use a trim."

"As does my hair," I replied, "but that's a matter for another time. There are other tasks I'd like to accomplish today."

"Such as?"

"I'd like to visit as many of our people as I can, then speak with Kennik." I flashed a grin. "He claimed he has tents to spare, and I'm free to move on from the healers."

"I'll accompany you. I'll even help you set up your tent."

"No, Tess. It'll be *ours*. Unless you've had a change of heart?" I teased.

She laughed and grasped my hand. "Never. Let's go."

29

A LIFE DEBT

"Ser? *Ser!*"

I groaned and resisted the urge to throw the nearest object at the tent's covered entrance. I recognized Aren's voice and prayed for his sake the matter was as urgent as his tone indicated. Tessamir laughed softly and pushed away from my side.

"You weren't asleep yet, Owen. Go see what the boy needs."

"If he'd arrived ten minutes ago, I would have ignored him." I reached for my discarded armor and pulled it on, while she did the same.

"Good. If you had paid him any heed ten minutes ago, you'd be sleeping beneath the stars tonight." She flashed a playful grin, radiant even in the darkness. "I must admit, Rosalin was right, and the wait was certainly worth it."

I grinned. "I'd be happy to—"

"Ser!" Aren hissed toward the tent's opening.

"Fucking gods," I growled as the euphoric mood I'd been enjoying dissolved. "This had better be important."

I noted Tessamir was dressed, then wrenched the tent flap open. "What in Aeon's hells do you need, Aren?"

He froze, his eyes wide with fear and surprise.

I expelled a long breath, counted to five, then attempted to speak in a calmer tone. The boy didn't understand what he'd nearly interrupted, and I didn't believe he'd come on an errand of mischief.

"Tess and I were occupied. Why are you here?"

His face reddened in the moonlight as he understood the implication. "I'm sorry, Ser. I didn't realize… I was asked to fetch you. The Murkor commander has been trying to locate you all evening."

I raked a hand through my hair. "I'll go to him. Where is he?"

"He's with Makta, Ser. In her command tent."

Tessamir emerged from the tent and handed me my belt. "If Jal'den seeks you, it must mean he's arranged a meeting with the Matriarch. I'm coming with you."

I nodded as I buckled it on. Without my hammers, the garment felt unnecessary, but clearly, Tessamir believed otherwise. I gestured for Aren to move ahead. "Lead the way."

He darted ahead, then cast a glance over his shoulder to ensure we followed. When his eyes met Tessamir's, his face reddened again, and he hastily looked away.

"You've scarred the poor boy for life." She snickered softly and tossed her head. "Subtlety isn't one of your strengths, is it?"

"Decidedly not. I ought to apologize."

She gestured toward Aren's retreating form with an amused smirk. I increased my pace, cursing myself for a fool. The fragile rapport I'd built with the boy was at risk of crumbling due to my gods-damned temper.

"Aren," I said as I caught up to him, "I should not have said what I did."

He flushed and averted his gaze. "I didn't mean to interrupt you, Ser, but Makta—"

"You were only following her orders, and I didn't tell anyone what I had planned with Tess. I'm not angry with you. I'm sorry it came across as such."

His blush deepened. "What was it like, Ser?" he whispered. "We aren't the same now, and I've been curious."

I cleared my throat, unprepared for the turn in the conversation and uncomfortable explaining it to the young man. Tessamir wasn't far away, and I was certain she was listening intently. By the gods, what should I say?

"Have you been intimate with a woman before?" I asked with an uncertain glance over my shoulder. Tessamir held one hand over her mouth while her shoulders shook in silent laughter. I should have known she'd find humor in the situation.

"Once, Ser, but my father didn't know." He fixed his gaze on the path ahead as we moved between tents. "My cousin took me to a brothel in Jennavere a few weeks before we traveled to Stone Hill. That was the only time."

I nodded, relieved. I wouldn't need to describe the entire process. Thank the gods.

"The basic act is largely the same," I replied. "It's simply a matter of alignment—"

"That's Makta's tent," Aren cut in. He pointed toward one of the largest tents, with a quartet of armed Scorpion Men stationed outside the entrance.

"Thank you. We'll speak later," I told him, elated I'd managed to avoid the remainder of our awkward discussion.

"Of course, Ser. Good night!" He waved and darted away.

I raked a hand through my hair as Tessamir made her way to my side. "A matter of alignment?" She laughed and wiped at her eyes. "Oh gods, your descriptions need some work."

I groaned. "I didn't expect him to ask me for details."

She moved to stand in front of me, then placed her hands on my shoulders. "You've clearly made an impression on him. He lost his father. It's only natural that he'd ask you. Who else does he have to turn to? You should be flattered."

Reluctantly, I nodded. She was right. "I'll try to remember that next time. Gods, I hope he doesn't bring up this subject again."

She laughed again. "You handled it well enough. Now that your face isn't red as a berry, we should go inside."

We were stopped at the entrance by the soldiers stationed there. They searched us for weapons, but I'd left my hammers behind in our tent. Tessamir had refused to carry anything more deadly than a sewing kit since the battle, and she'd arrived with her pockets empty. I raised my arms as the Scorpion Men searched my person and wondered if it was common practice when approaching the Warleader, or if others were inside the tent with her.

"Makta has been expecting you," one said with a wry grin. "You're free to go inside."

I nodded and followed Tessamir into the sprawling tent. Braziers burned in each corner, providing a dim reddish glow. Four red-clad Murkor stood in a line near the tent's center. I noted with a frown that they'd been permitted to keep their weapons. Beyond them, I spied Makta's tall form on one side, and Vardak's nearer the tent's rear. He was in conversation with a black-clad Murkor I suspected was Jal'den. His signature broadsword was nowhere to be seen, and without the weapon to mark his person, I wasn't certain it was him.

Two other Murkor were seated near Makta. One was clad in shimmering silver, the other in copper. I recognized the copper attire, the heavy chain draped across his shoulders, and the curved black saber at his hip—the Kal. I assumed the frail figure garbed in silver was the Matriarch.

I ground my teeth as a wave of anger threatened to consume me. I'd asked for this meeting, but seeing them prompted an unexpected flood of horrific memories to play through my mind. They'd sent us to the fucking tower, while they remained safe in their gods-damned caverns. My people had been forced to endure weeks of silent servitude, while the Murkor retained their relative freedoms.

I closed my eyes and clenched my fists, shaking as I struggled to contain my rage. My ears rang.

This had been a mistake. I wasn't prepared to face the Murkor leaders without seeking to crush the life out of their frail, aged forms. And I was Serpentus—I didn't require conventional weapons in order to kill. My *body* was a weapon.

Hands touched the sides of my face, gentle and cool. "Owen, look at me."

At the sound of Tessamir's voice, I forced my eyes open. Her face was a hair's breadth from my own, her brow etched with concern.

"Do we need to leave?" she whispered. "No one will fault you for it."

I stared into the fathomless depths of her blue eyes, my anchor in the tumultuous tides of rage that battered my psyche. I drew a deep breath, held it, then released it slowly while I focused on her. My fury began to subside as I continued to breathe.

Finally, I shook my head. "No. I can do this. I *need* to do this."

She dropped her hands from my face. "You're certain?"

"Yes, but stay near. I may need you to intervene."

She clasped my right hand in her left and squeezed. "I'll be here."

I focused on Makta as we moved past the red-clad Murkor guards. I didn't trust myself to look upon the Murkor leaders yet. I was too near the brink of losing control.

Vardak moved to stand between us and the Murkor leaders at a nod from the Warleader. I was grateful for his presence and trusted him to restrain me if I succumbed to my violent instincts. If anyone could stop an angry Serpentus, he could. Jal'den took up the open space between the Matriarch and Makta.

"Jal'den relayed your desire to hear the Murkors' version of events," Makta began. "Given your reaction to their presence, I believe it was wise you sought a mediator. I've asked Vardak to assist me."

"Thank you," I managed through my teeth, my voice rough from emotion.

"We have agreed to tell you what we shared with Ukase, Jal'den, Daj'ven, and Sal'zar," the Matriarch stated in a wavering tone. "The Kal acted without my knowledge for much of his schemes, but I was aware of your journey to the tower. I was the one who agreed to it."

Tessamir's hand tightened on mine, and I squeezed my eyes shut. To look upon the hooded countenance of the woman who had sentenced us to a fate worse than death was unthinkable—and unwise. Fucking gods, I wanted to lash out, to strike, to wrap my serpentine body around hers until her bones snapped and she breathed her last.

If not for Tessamir's calming presence, I would have.

"Our people were deceived by the Soulless," the Kal said after a moment. "After their return, the man known as Kama arrived at the caverns. He demanded an audience, but refused to enter our home. We did not understand what he was or why he sought us when the summons came, but he would not be denied a meeting. He killed one of our sentries as an example of what he would do to the rest of our people if we refused. I counseled he must have come from the mad wizard who stirred trouble near the chasm, but we didn't know the wizard was already dead."

When I didn't move or react to his words, Makta said, "Please, continue."

"I led the Matriarch through the caverns to its exit, where we met with Kama." The Kal sighed heavily. "He struck her with a magical illness, and informed us we would comply with his wishes or she would die. Any attempt on her part to subvert his orders would result in a weakening of her condition. She was in great pain the instant he acted, and remained so until his death. He promised the curse would transfer to her successor when she died to ensure our continued compliance. Without the Matriarch to guide our path, our people would have been lost."

"He ordered you to take us to the tower," I said. My anger was beginning to abate, but I was left hollow and sickened by his tale.

"Yes," the Matriarch confirmed. "The ailment I suffered was debilitating. If Kama's words were true, to deny him would have killed me. I did not know what he planned for your people, though I suspected you were slated for execution. I never imagined they'd do *this*."

I opened my eyes and risked a glance in her direction. Her gnarled blue hands covered her hooded face as she wept for her fate and ours.

"I decided to take a calculated risk long before you were taken to the tower," the Kal said as he drew one arm around her shoulders. "Kama's curse afflicted our Matriarch alone. He knew well how our society is organized, and didn't consider that I held enough power to act against him. Aran'daj, our former commander, was a part of my schemes, as were Jal'den and his partner. We learned what we could of the Soulless' plans, and when the time was right, Sal'zar led his faction away from the fighting. For his apparent betrayal, Aran'daj paid with his life."

"Sal'zar left when he learned what had been done to your people," Jal'den added. "I was forced to remain with the army and act the part of commander, though I would have preferred to be *anywhere* else." His head swiveled toward the Kal, and I imagined he glared.

"We have discussed my reasoning, Jal'den," the Kal replied evenly. "Now is not the time to rehash that conversation. We owe it to those we've wronged to focus on their part of the story."

The Matriarch leaned into the Kal's embrace. "I have no words to express the depth of my sorrow. What you have suffered makes my trials seem paltry in comparison. If I had known what they planned, I would never have followed Kama's orders. The Murkor people would have found a way to survive without me."

I didn't know what to say in response, and instead, I looked away.

"I believe you are sincere," Tessamir said quietly. "While a mere apology will never suffice to erase our pain, perhaps with time, our people will learn to manage it."

"I think it best if you keep an armed escort with you until you return home," I added. "I will share your story with the others, but I can't guarantee your safety. We bear too much rage, too much gods-damned *grief*. I could not trust myself alone with you—and there are others who will undoubtedly react more poorly to your presence than I did."

"I'm in agreement," Vardak replied as he crossed his arms. "I'll ensure we keep the Murkor separate from the Serpentus until your departure."

We spoke a bit more, then Tessamir and I bid them all a good night. With my rage spent, I was exhausted. I wanted nothing more than to return to our tent and lose myself in Tessamir's embrace while I slept.

She didn't know it, but she'd saved the Matriarch's life when she decided to accompany me. Without her, I was adrift; volatile and dangerous. Our people would have been condemned as true monsters if I'd acted on my dark impulses.

Thanks to her, they were not. Thanks to her, our place with the Scorpion Men was secure, and we'd have a future. From that moment forward, I would do anything she asked of me, no matter how mundane or difficult it proved to be. I owed her an unspoken life debt, and I would gladly repay it.

Gods, I loved that woman.

30

PARTNERS

Over the course of two months, we left the site of the Nameless god's final battle and the broken remains of the black tower behind to establish ourselves within the Stronghold. The Scorpion Men elders upheld Makta's promise to us, and we were welcomed unconditionally into their ancestral home. A conclave was scheduled to name the next Warleader. Her name was not put forth as a candidate, but Makta was commended for her interim role.

Tessamir and I were given quarters not far from the marketplace. It was a small space, but cozy, with a sitting room adjoined to a tiny kitchen, and two small private rooms on either side. I used one room for meetings with my people—I spent much of my days there as we determined a path for our future—and the other was our sleeping quarters. I looked forward to the evenings far more than I did the mornings.

For her part, Tessamir became friendly with several tavern owners and began to experiment with a new batch of ale once she'd proven herself a competent barkeep. While I was occupied with my duties as our people's leader, she poured drinks, made connections, and listened to every bit of gossip the Stronghold had to offer. She thrived in her new role, and the smiles I'd once craved from her returned to grace our private moments. She was happy, and though my role was trying, I was too.

I couldn't say the same for every Serpentus. On the night before the scheduled conclave, I was roused by an urgent knock on our door. I uncoiled myself from Tessamir as she thrust a shirt in my direction and stifled a yawn.

"I'll return when I can," I promised.

She rose to kiss me firmly. "I know. I hope you'll return before midmorning. I have news to share, and I was too distracted earlier to tell you."

I chuckled. "You always have news, Tess."

She grinned. "This is different. Now, go. Someone needs you, and I've already had you twice tonight."

I laughed and made my way toward the door. "You're still a shameless flirt."

"For you, always."

I opened the door to the outer corridor to find Aren. He was garbed in light plate mail and a leather belt. A mace hung at his hip, and a bow was slung across his back. He'd joined the guard as an overnight sentry within days of our arrival in the Stronghold. While his skill in archery was exceptional, his close-range combat skills required work, but he was willing to learn, and the Scorpion Men were willing to teach.

He saluted. It wasn't the first time he'd summoned me during his scheduled shift, but his expression gave me pause.

"What's wrong?" I asked as I exited my quarters and closed the door.

"There's a disturbance involving one of our people, Ser. It's…It's Carrelin."

I closed my eyes briefly and nodded. Carrelin had struggled to transition to our new way of life more than most, and I'd been summoned to her residence several times previously. She'd been nobility in Daesan, and our captivity during the war had splintered her delicate constitution almost beyond repair. She'd lived a life of opulence, wanting for nothing. Her wealth was now gone, her family dead, and she claimed to have no useful skills in which to establish herself in our new home. Her experience while under the compulsion of the Soulless had not been remarkably different than anyone else's, but she'd proven more fragile than most.

"I'll see to her," I replied somberly. "Go back to your post."

"Yes, Ser."

"And Aren?" I asked as he began to move away. He paused to glance over his shoulder. "Thank you. She'll thank you too, one day."

He shrugged. "I'm simply doing my duty, Ser."

"Nevertheless, you have my thanks."

The route from my quarters to Carrelin's wound through a section of the vast marketplace to a residential corridor near the forges at the Stronghold's heart. As late as it was, I encountered few people along the way, but as I neared Carrelin's, I was greeted by a trio of Serpentus soldiers clad similarly to Aren. Beyond them, I spied Ilen, one of the candidates for Warleader, and her husband, Vesik. Ilen peered into Carrelin's door, while her husband spoke with my people.

At my arrival, all but Ilen straightened and offered a salute. She was preoccupied with the woman inside the home.

"How does she fare?" I asked.

Vesik shook his head. "We've attempted to talk her down for some time. She slit one of her wrists. Thankfully, it's a cross-wise cut, or she may have bled out by now. Every time Ilen has tried to enter the home, Carrelin threatens to cut herself again."

"We were called to assist, Ser," one of my people said. She inclined her head toward the other soldiers. "Jen and Valdeson also tried to speak with her, but she won't listen to us either."

I grimaced internally. I couldn't recall her name.

"We didn't want to bother you in the middle of the night," Valdeson added, "but we don't know what else to do."

"You did the right thing," I assured them. "Go back to your posts—I'll try to reason with her."

The trio saluted again, then were gone. I drew a breath and turned to face Ilen. Her expression was pained as I moved past her and into the threshold of Carrelin's quarters.

Carrelin was curled in the center of the room, a knife gripped in her right hand. Tears streaked her face, and her clothing was torn. Blood soaked the left sleeve of her tunic, presumably where she'd sliced her wrist. Dark droplets spattered the floor around her and more marred her gray and green scales. When her gaze met mine, fresh tears spilled from her eyes.

"Carrelin, I'm here. We can talk," I said in as soothing a tone as I could muster. I'd learned weeks ago that a calm demeanor prevailed when she entered her darkest moods.

"What more is there to say, Owen?" She sniffled and renewed her grip on the knife. "I seek release. Aeon will welcome me when I arrive at his gates."

"You're young. You have much to live for. Don't do this."

"You're wrong," she hissed. "I have *nothing!* My manor house was razed when Daesan was overrun, my betrothed was killed in the streets, my brother and father were cut down as they defended our home. I believed we'd weather the remainder of the war with the Murkor, and they *betrayed* us. We're monsters!"

Her words dissolved into a wordless howl of anguish while she coiled her body tighter. She'd spoken the same words nearly every time I was summoned to her home, and each time, they pierced my heart more deeply than a knife ever could. It was why I'd sent the other Serpentus away; she'd unwittingly reopen their wounds with her grief-stricken tongue, and I'd be forced to restart the healing process with them anew.

"We aren't monsters, Carrelin. A monster is defined by their actions, by their intent to harm others. We don't fit that description." I inched toward her. "No, we are survivors."

"I don't want this life," she snarled, then aimed the point of her knife at her throat. "I want an *end*."

I lifted my hands to placate her. "Carrelin, you don't want death either. I've watched you smile as you wander the marketplace, and I've seen you at peace when you visit the temple. There are things to live for, and we can rebuild. In fact, we *are*."

"Do you know why I visit the temple?" she asked in a quavering tone.

"No. Our conversations with the gods are private, and it's not my business to pry."

"I visit to seek answers," she replied. "The gods never speak to me. We are beneath their notice, Owen. We are forsaken."

I'd harbored the same sentiment on occasion, but I knew it would be unwise to commiserate on that point. It would only fuel her determination to take her own life, and I refused to allow that to happen.

"We aren't forsaken." I inched forward again. "The gods listen, though they are often slow to react."

She dropped her right hand to her side and peered at me with an expression of profound longing. "Do you truly believe that?" she whispered as a spark of hope bloomed in her eyes.

"I do."

Her face crumpled as a sob escaped her throat. The knife fell from her grip to clatter on the stone floor, and I darted forward to retrieve it. I swept it behind me with the end of my tail and sent it spinning across the room toward Ilen's location at the door.

I gathered her into my arms and allowed her to sob into my shoulder. A glance behind me showed Ilen had collected the knife. She nodded once, then backed outside and closed the door softly behind her.

"The gods have heard you," I assured her. "They'll help us in time."

"Do you promise?" Her words were muffled by my shoulder and warped by her sobs, but I understood.

"Yes, I promise."

I held her for an interminable length of time. We didn't speak, and she didn't need me to offer her any further assurances this night. I doubted I'd be able to follow through on my promise—no one could predict the actions of the gods—but I'd given her hope enough to carry on once more.

Finally, she pushed away and wiped her eyes with her right hand. "My wrist hurts." She held her left arm toward me and shuddered.

I inspected it gingerly. "The cut is deep. We should go to the apothecary."

She nodded and allowed me to escort her outside. "Why do you insist on helping me?"

"It's the right thing to do." I gestured down the torchlit corridor toward the marketplace. "You need a bandage, and perhaps a few stitches. Let's visit Nirak."

She brightened at the mention of the young apothecary I'd taken her to visit once previously. Like all of the Scorpion Men, Nirak was muscular from years spent training at arms, but his passion had always been in the healing arts. I suspected Carrelin held more than a passing interest in him, and since their return to the Stronghold, it seemed the Scorpion Men had abandoned their mandate regarding cross-species partnerships. Perhaps with the right prompting, she'd find *him* reason enough to continue living.

That was a matter I'd require Tessamir's help with, but she'd be thrilled at the prospect. She'd already arranged several matches between lonely Serpentus while working in the tavern.

Carrelin cradled her left arm as I led her to the apothecary's door. His personal quarters were behind the storefront, and I knew he'd be within. I rapped loudly to announce our presence while she adjusted her tunic and ran her right hand through her hair. Yes, she was definitely attracted to him.

Nirak opened the door several moments later. Despite being awakened in the dark hours of the morning, he appeared alert and was dressed sharply. He wore a clean apron over a dark tunic, and offered Carrelin a tentative smile as he held the door open for us.

"That's a nasty cut," he said once we were inside and Carrelin was seated beside the small table he used as a workbench. "I'll need to sew it up. Ah, Carrelin, what did you do?"

She blushed and stared at her exposed wrist on the tabletop. "It was a bad night."

"Hmm." He glanced at me, eyebrows lifted in question.

"She's better now," I replied. "I believe the danger has passed."

He nodded and pulled several items from the shelf behind the table. "I'll cleanse the wound with a special draught, then sew it up and bandage it after. You don't have to be injured to visit me, you know." He flashed her a brief grin.

"You'd let me stop by?" she asked, her eyes wide.

"Of course. You knew half my herb collection on your first visit. It's rare that I can talk to anyone about my work, and I rather enjoyed our last conversation." He was focused on threading a needle and didn't see her beam in response.

I took their interaction as a sign that my work for the night was complete. "Carrelin, are you well enough to make your way home when he's finished?"

"I'll escort her," Nirak promised with another grin. "Don't worry—she's in good hands."

I exited his shop and chuckled to myself as I made my way home. If Carrelin's bouts of darkness hadn't deterred Nirak yet, there was hope for her. And it appeared I wouldn't need Tessamir's matchmaking skills after all.

Tessamir was sleeping soundly when I returned, but when I wriggled beneath the blankets, she stirred. "Owen?"

"I'm home."

"Good. You need to rest. Zaria invited us to her home to celebrate the conclave tomorrow." She rolled over to face me. "Or is it today?"

I chuckled. "It's today, and I'm more than happy to sleep."

She snickered and snuggled into my arms. "You always are. Was it Carrelin?"

I nodded. "She's a bit enamored with Nirak. The apothecary," I added when she shot me a confused glance. "If I'm not mistaken, he feels the same."

"Owen Greenwaters, you continue to surprise me."

I laughed. "What do you mean?"

"You remembered his name, *and* you picked up on their amorous cues."

"Perhaps you're having an effect on me." I wrapped my arms around her and pulled her closer.

"Of course I am. Kiss me you damned fool, then get some sleep. We can talk more when it's daylight."

I grinned and did as she ordered. I'd never grow tired of her amorous demands, and I certainly couldn't imagine my life without her in it. As she'd told me before, we were partners. In life, in love, in crime… Whatever label I wished to apply.

31

THE PATRON OF FORTUNE

I rose before Tessamir awakened and made my way to the kitchen, disturbed by the vestiges of my last dream. In it, Carrelin had driven the knife into her throat instead of releasing it when I approached. It wasn't the first time I'd experienced nightmares after a tense night spent de-escalating her threats of self-harm, but this one had been more graphic than most.

I rubbed the sleep from my eyes and began to rummage in the larder. Tessamir brought a few items from the marketplace on her way home from the tavern each evening, but it seemed we'd used most of her latest purchase for supper. An onion, a square of cheese, and several eggs peered back at me from within. I groaned and closed the lid.

A moment later, I heard Tessamir rise, and rapid movement issued from our sleeping quarters. The sound of her retching followed seconds later.

Alarmed, I darted toward the room. "Tess?"

The end of her tail snaked out of the tiny alcove that contained the opening in the floor that led to the dank abyss of the waste caverns below. She retched again and groaned.

"Tess?" I asked again.

"I'll be fine. It was only a matter of time."

Confused, I moved closer to her location. "I don't understand."

She chuckled briefly before another bout of retching overcame her. She'd been expecting this sickness, but what did it mean? It certainly didn't mean she was *fine.*

After another minute, she exited the alcove and offered me a grin. I gaped at her, unable to comprehend why she was in an ebullient mood when she'd just vomited repeatedly.

"Come with me. I'll make breakfast."

I stared after her as she disappeared from the room. What in Aeon's hells was going on?

By the time I emerged from our sleeping quarters, she had removed the contents of the larder and was stoking the fire in the tiny hearth nearby, seemingly unfazed by her bout of illness.

"Fucking gods, Tess, what has gotten into you?"

She smirked over her shoulder. "In a word, *you.*"

"What?"

Satisfied with the hearth's flame for a time, she turned to face me. "Do you recall I had news to share with you?"

I lifted my eyebrows. "Yes, but nothing you've said this morning makes sense."

She grinned. "Then allow me to enlighten you. You're going to be a father, and the little one has decided it's amusing to upset my stomach."

I stared at her, uncomprehending. "What?"

She tipped her head back and laughed. "I'm pregnant, Owen. By my estimate, it likely happened the first night after you were healed, the first time we coupled. I visited one of the midwives yesterday to confirm my suspicions, and she warned me about the morning sickness. It should pass in a few weeks."

"We're going to have a family?" I asked, still dumbfounded. My mind refused to process all that she'd said, but excitement at the prospect suffused me.

"Yes." She flashed another grin, then reached for a bowl. As she began to crack eggs into it, she said, "I visited with Emra yesterday as well. I needed to be certain the child was well, and she was once a wizard. We made a short trip into the desert. She can't access her magic here."

"You had an eventful day." I crossed my arms. "Why didn't you tell me sooner?"

"I wanted to be certain." She smiled as she began to stir the eggs with a wooden spoon. "Emra sensed nothing wrong with the child, but it's like us. It's Serpentus."

I chuckled and moved forward to encircle her with my arms from behind. "What else would it be?"

She leaned back and planted a kiss on my jaw. "A part of me feared something would be wrong with it. After the transformation, I couldn't be certain, but Emra has allayed my fears. It's healthy."

I nuzzled her neck. "There was a time not so long ago when I didn't believe I'd ever settle down, let alone start a family."

She laughed. "Now that you have, your growing *family* requires breakfast." She pointed her spoon at the bowl of eggs. "I'm eating for two, and you're between us and the hearth."

I chuckled and moved aside to watch her work. She was a far better cook than I was, and I'd only be in her way if I attempted to help. I'd lost count of the number of times she'd chased me from the kitchen while she prepared our meals, and after my first failed attempt to impress her with my paltry culinary skills, she hadn't allowed me to try again.

"Do you still plan to go with me to Zaria's?" I asked as she dumped the eggs into a pan.

She shrugged. "If I can keep my breakfast down, yes. If not, I'll remain here. She'll understand."

"She was the midwife you visited," I said.

"Yes. The Scorpion Men claim she's the best, and since our peoples are similar, I believed she could help. None of us know what to expect." She paused to flip the omelet in the pan. "I wasn't the first to approach her, you know."

"Rosalin?" I asked.

"It's likely. She and Leorisin were coupling before you were fully healed from the battle. I'd be shocked if she wasn't the first to approach Zaria for advice." She snickered. "She hasn't been to the tavern as she promised either. It's another sign."

I studied her as we ate, marveling anew that she'd chosen *me*. I'd fallen for her in the caverns a lifetime ago, and despite the Soulless' best efforts to derail our lives, we'd endured. We were stronger for it, and I knew without a doubt she'd be the best mother any Serpentus child could ask for. I hoped I'd prove half as capable as I believed she would be.

She finished half of her omelet before darting toward the alcove in the other room. I stared after her guiltily; the sickness was my doing, after all. Gods, I hoped for her sake it would pass quickly.

When she emerged several minutes later, she pushed her half-eaten eggs toward me. "I've had enough for one morning."

"Tess, I—"

She cut me off with a laugh. "This is normal. Relax."

I frowned, skeptical. "You'll tell me if something *is* wrong?"

"Of course. And I believe I'll remain here while you celebrate Vardak's nomination for Warleader. Please give him my regards and tell Zaria she was right."

Three hours later, I found myself in the corridor leading to Zaria's home as a trio of young humans arrived alongside two familiar faces. Coreyaless and Danness walked with them, and Danness nodded a greeting as I neared. To my surprise, Coreyaless moved forward and pulled me into a fierce hug.

"It's good to see one of my most stubborn patients is well," she said as she stepped back. "You must be here for Vardak as well."

I smiled. "I am. His mother was kind enough to invite me."

"She invited all of us," Danness replied. "The boys too. Rostin idolizes Vardak, and where he goes, the others are never far behind."

One of the boys rapped on Zaria's door, and moments later, it opened to reveal Zaria's kindly face. She smiled at them and beckoned us inside, then leaned toward me as she closed the door.

"Is Tess well?"

I was unable to stop the grin from spreading across my face. "She was ill but said I shouldn't worry."

She chuckled. "Yet you do. It's normal, but it will pass. Congratulations, Owen." She gestured toward a table laden with a variety of food. "Please, eat. There's plenty."

I scanned the room. Vardak was seated on one side with the orange-furred feline—Maryn—who I'd since learned was one of his greatest friends. Coreyaless and Danness stood in one corner with Emra and Zaria's eldest son, Patak, while the trio of boys I'd encountered in the hall swarmed the table. Vardak's middle brother, Travin, was seated across the room with his wife and their young son.

I nodded a greeting to Travin. We'd spoken on occasion since my people arrived in the Stronghold, and he'd remembered our conversation with Aj'ana in the caverns. I hadn't realized until recently that Travin was Vardak's brother, though I'd spent time with both. Like Zaria, Travin sported dark hair and brown eyes, while Vardak and Patak were blond.

Though I'd eaten breakfast—and half of Tesssamir's—not long ago, I wouldn't refuse Zaria's hospitality. I moved to the table and filled a plate, then glanced around the room. Maryn had moved away from Vardak in favor of poking fun at Patak, leaving the warrior alone. I decided it was an opportunity to offer my congratulations.

"Vardak, I—"

He held up one hand and shook his head, amused. "I know what you wish to talk about, but it's premature. The conclave is evaluating four of us."

I chuckled and seated myself at his side. "And of the four, you've already done much for...my people. Not all of us are handling the transition as well as we'd hoped. I spent half the night talking Carrelin out of taking her own life."

"I'm sorry." A pained expression crossed his face, and he looked down. "*If* I'm elected, I'll do everything I can to ensure the Serpentus thrive. If I'm not, I will continue to support you by any means possible. Your people deserve the chance to make something of themselves."

I shrugged, still troubled by my encounter with Carrelin the previous evening, despite Tessamir's much happier news. "Many of us were civilians, captured by the Murkor. I understand their former commander asked to take us prisoners in order to spare our lives. The Soulless wanted us dead, but he had a good heart. It's a shame his attempt to save us ended with us trapped in these gods-damned bodies." I sighed. "I suppose your ancestors felt the same."

"By all accounts, they did." Vardak set the plate aside to focus on me. "What was done is nothing short of abhorrent, but you can't give up."

"He's right," Zaria interjected from across the room. "The Scorpion Men struggled for many years in the wake of our own unwanted transformation, yet we persevered. The world must be reminded of the wrongs that were committed against us—and you. If the Serpentus give in to despair and falter, there will be nothing but a written record that will one day be chalked up to little more than legend. Your people deserve better, Owen Greenwaters, if for nothing more than to remind this world that even though Karmada dealt you a sour hand, you overcame it. The Nameless god may be no more, but your people and ours remain as a testament to *why* he needed to die. Without that reminder, people will forget the events of this war in a few generations, and where would we be then?"

She had a valid set of points, ones I'd do well to remember when I next paid Carrelin a visit. I doubted the previous night would be my last, but I prayed I was wrong.

I nodded to Zaria. "Perhaps I've been thinking of this matter selfishly, but it's difficult to plan for the future when we're not even certain what it may look like."

She smiled knowingly but didn't share my secret. It would be Tessamir's decision to share our news when she was ready.

"No one can foresee the future," Zaria said, "except perhaps Minora. Make the most of your life, Owen. Tell the others to do the same. Our world is poorer without the Serpentus in it."

I lingered in Zaria's home with the others well after Vardak was summoned to the conclave. Travin accompanied him on his errand, but the rest of us remained. I hoped he'd be named Warleader, despite his age—he'd proven himself time and again during the war, and I'd grown to respect him immensely. I also considered him a friend.

"How long will it be before we learn of the conclave's decision?" one of the human boys asked. The trio were still seated around the table and had eaten their fill twice over.

"Not long," Zaria assured him. "Our people don't mince words. I'm certain the elders will be finished delivering their judgment soon."

As if on cue, the door to her quarters opened. Travin entered alone, a troubled expression on his face.

His wife stood and moved toward him. "Trav, what happened?"

"Vardak wasn't named Warleader, but he was appointed to a new post." Travin flicked a glance at me. "He's to act as our liaison to the Serpentus people."

"But that's good news," Zaria said. "Where is he?"

Travin grimaced and scratched at the back of his neck. "Flariel called him away. She said her business wouldn't take long, but time is irrelevant to the gods."

"Shit," Patak muttered. "Not again."

The room fell silent as we waited for the door to open a second time. I was pleased with the news of Vardak's new role, but uneasy with Flariel's untimely interference. I understood he had a history with the fire goddess, though he'd never shared the details with me. It was several minutes before the door swung inward again.

Vardak wore a smile and accepted the congratulations of his family and closer friends. I remained seated and awaited my turn, but he surprised me by disentangling himself from the others to speak with me.

"Owen, we need to talk in private."

I lifted my eyebrows in surprise, but nodded. "Of course. Travin mentioned your new role, and I'll admit, I'm pleased they've chosen you."

"Thank you, but that's not why we need to talk. There is…something else."

I narrowed my eyes. "Very well."

Vardak turned to his mother. "Owen and I have urgent business to discuss. I'll return as soon as I'm able." He motioned to me, and I followed him into the corridor.

"How quickly can you summon your people to the temple?" he asked as soon as we were alone.

I shrugged. "I don't know. Why?"

"Karmada has asked to speak with you alone, then she hopes to speak with the others as a group." Vardak frowned. "If you go ahead to the temple, I can summon the others."

I nodded. "Tess can help if you need. And Aren is a great runner."

"Good. I'll meet you there. Don't keep her waiting."

My stomach roiled as I darted through the corridors of the Stronghold toward its exit. I'd cursed the gods, blamed them for our plight, but faced with the prospect of speaking to Karmada, I was filled with dread. I'd sought her aid and raged at her in turns. Had she overheard my furious musings while I'd been a puppet of the Soulless? Was she now here to mete out a divine form of punishment? The mere notion caused my blood to run cold.

Several Serpentus were stationed at the Stronghold's entrance, and I paused to relay the news. "Gather as many of our people as you can as swiftly as you're able, then go to the temple. We've been summoned."

They saluted and dispersed while I continued outside. The temple was only a short distance from the Stronghold—it was Blademon's domain, but it seemed Karmada was utilizing her brother's resources in order to speak with us.

Between the Stronghold and the temple was an expanse of white desert, broken only by the occasional cactus or bleached stone. Heat shimmer rose from the ground in rippling waves as the afternoon sun beat down on the parched landscape. Within moments, I began to sweat, but thankfully, the scales of my lower half protected my body from the burning sands as I sped toward the temple. It was spring—I wasn't looking forward to the intensity of the summer.

A priest clad in white met me in the temple's broad foyer. In my haste, I failed to appreciate the grandeur of the structure; columns supported the vaulted roof, each carved with a different scene of battle. Finely crafted weapons adorned the walls at intervals, while metal sconces illuminated the interior.

The priest bowed, and I noted with mild interest that the stinger at the end of his scorpion's tail had been painted a brilliant shade of crimson. Priests were creatures of ceremony and ritual, no matter their species.

"The goddess of fortune awaits you in the temple's heart," he said. "Come."

I was led through a set of massive stone doors to a room large enough to seat thousands. A ramp led down to a dark, reflective surface in the center, while a series of concentric tiers ringed the space. The room's design reminded me of the jousting arenas I'd once frequented and competed in.

The priest paused as we reached the edge of the mirrored floor. "Wait here. Karmada asked that I inform her of your arrival and that I give you a warning. She is changed."

I frowned in confusion. "What do you mean?"

He tilted his head and shrugged. "You will see."

He skittered across the dark floor to another set of doors and disappeared within.

I raked my hand through my hair. "Fucking gods, what have I landed myself in *now?*" I growled aloud, though no one was present to hear.

A moment later, the doors opened. I looked up at the sound, then gaped as I took in Karmada's towering figure. I recognized her face from illustrations, and again from the recent battle, but her form was drastically different. Where she'd once sported legs, her body was now serpentine. Gray and emerald scales akin to my own decorated her lower half. She'd become Serpentus.

My people had a patron god. We'd been recognized, our desperate prayers heard.

She slithered forward and stopped in the center of the mirrored floor, where she placed her hands on her scaly hips. "I have chosen to become the advocate for your people. Misfortune placed you in the Nameless god's sights, but fortune has brought you to the Stronghold. My siblings believed it fitting that I receive this role." She leaned toward me and smiled. "What do you think of my new form, Owen? You are the first of your people to glimpse it."

"It… It suits you," I stammered.

She laughed, a musical sound. "Your voice has often plagued my thoughts, you know. I'm used to being cursed, but it's rare when a mortal pleads for my aid. Most fear the consequences of an errant prayer bearing my name."

"You aren't the first to claim my actions are atypical." I crossed my arms, more confident as my initial shock dissipated. "A good friend once told me I was an unorthodox knight."

"Yes, Petric Stonewarden. You still grieve his loss."

I looked down. "I suspect I always will."

"The Nameless god has stolen much from all of your people, but you will prevail. I will see to it." She reached down to trace the side of my jaw in a gentle caress. "Already, you have found a place with the Scorpion Men, and the next generation blossoms in the wombs of a few."

I returned her gaze, startled. "You know of Tess?"

She laughed and withdrew her hand. "I know of Tess and several others. What sort of patron would I be if I did not?"

I nodded uneasily as I considered her words. "It's common knowledge that you always require payment for your services. What will you demand from us in return for this?"

Her gaze was compassionate. "Owen, your people have paid thrice over already. We were unable to stop the Nameless god's Soulless from repeating her past crime, and I will *never* seek payment for becoming your patron. You are my people now, and I will favor you above all others from this moment forward." She pointed toward the door I'd entered with the priest. "The others are arriving. Will you do me the honor of a proper introduction?"

I nodded. Who was I to deny her request after her previous declaration? "Of course."

"Good. Once your people are seated, you may begin."

I began to move away, but was stopped when she grasped my shoulder in a firm, yet unyielding grip. "No. They'll react better to my presence if you remain at my side."

I drew a breath and complied, then watched as the other Serpentus began to file into the room. Most fell silent when they noticed Karmada. Some gaped, some bowed, others began to weep. When Tessamir entered, her eyes widened, but she managed a swift bow before moving down the ramp to take her place in the nearly empty bottom tier.

It was Carrelin's reaction that will remain forever ingrained in my memory. She burst into tears when she entered, then darted along the ramp to launch herself into my arms.

"You weren't lying. Oh gods, Owen, you've kept your promise."

When she pushed herself away to sit beside Tessamir, Karmada leaned forward to touch Carrelin's face. "You would make for a good priestess in the temple we must build, Carrelin Valtis."

Carrelin's eyes overflowed with tears—but she beamed at the goddess. "You would allow me to serve you?"

"I would." Karmada rose to her full height, then motioned to me. "Owen, it is time."

I drew a breath and scanned the room, taking in the hundreds of faces of the survivors who had gathered. Hope emanated from them, palpable in its intensity. We'd endured the unthinkable, yet remained standing to face our future together, no matter what it held. We were the Serpentus, and our legacy was about to unfold.

I lifted my hands to gain their attention, but the gesture wasn't required. Every head was turned toward me as I began to speak.

"We've been summoned here today by our new benefactor. Karmada has elected to become our patron. We've been through hell, but we've survived—and with the goddess of fortune on our side, our future has never been brighter."

THANK YOU FOR READING SERPENTUS!

If you enjoyed this book, please consider leaving a review. Likewise, if you haven't read the related series, *The Relics of War*, please consider checking it out! You'll see more of characters like Vardak, Emra, and Jal'den there.

Information about forthcoming novels and release dates will be posted on my website (www.ajcalvin.net), as well as shared via my newsletter. If interested, you can subscribe by visiting my website and clicking on the "Subscribe" tab.

ACKNOWLEDGMENTS

I'm grateful to everyone who takes the time to read my books, and I appreciate each one of you. *You* are the reason I continue to publish my stories.

I'd like to thank a few others personally for their contributions to this final piece.

First, my husband, for his understanding and seemingly endless patience. Serpentus was a concept that would not leave me alone until it was finished, and my husband endured my virtual absence for a couple months while I worked on this novel outside my full-time job. Owen Greenwaters was a demanding character…

I'd also like to thank Sheena Sampsel for lending her editing skills to yet another book of mine, and Jamie Noble for working through another cover project with me. This book cover happens to be one of my favorites that he's illustrated so far, and I think he captured the overall mood—and the book's main character—very well.

ABOUT THE AUTHOR

A.J. Calvin is a science fiction/fantasy novelist hailing from Loveland, Colorado. By day, she works as a microbiologist, but in her free time she writes. She lives with her husband, their cat, Magic, and a fairly large salt water aquarium.

When she is not working or writing, she enjoys scuba diving, hiking, and playing video games.

For more information on the author and news about her writing, please visit her website at www.ajcalvin.net.

www.ingramcontent.com/pod-product-compliance
Lightning Source LLC
Chambersburg PA
CBHW020609310726
48979CB00008B/1408/J

* 9 7 9 8 9 8 8 3 1 9 3 7 5 *